The Way of a Man with a Maid

The Way of a Man with a Maid

Anonymous

MINT EDITIONS

The Way of a Man with a Maid was first published in 1908.

This edition published by Mint Editions 2021.

ISBN 9781513290911 | E-ISBN 9781513293769

Published by Mint Editions®

MINT
EDITIONS

minteditionbooks.com

Publishing Director: Jennifer Newens
Design & Production: Rachel Lopez Metzger
Project Manager: Micaela Clark
Typesetting: Westchester Publishing Services

Contents

VOLUME I
THE TRAGEDY

Chapter 1

I, the man, will not take up the time of my readers by detailing the circumstances under which Alice, the maid, roused in me the desire for vengeance which resulted in the way I adopted and which I am about to relate. Suffice it then to say that Alice cruelly and unjustifiably jilted me! In my bitterness of spirit, I swore that if I ever had an opportunity of getting hold of her, I would make her voluptuous person recompense me for my disappointment and that I would snatch from her by force the bridegroom's privileges that I so ardently coveted. But I had to dissemble! Alice and I had many mutual friends to whom this rupture was unknown; we were therefore constantly meeting each other, and if I gave her the slightest hint of my intentions towards her, it would be fatal to the very doubtful chances of success that I had! And so successfully did I conceal my real feelings under a cloak of generous acceptance of her action that she had not the faintest idea (as she afterwards admitted to me) that I was playing a part.

But, as the proverb says, everything comes to the man who can wait. For some considerable time, it seemed as if it would be wise on my part to abandon my desire for vengeance, as the circumstances of our daily lives were such as did not promise the remotest chance of my getting possession of Alice under conditions of either place or time suitable for the accomplishment of my purpose. Nevertheless, I controlled my patience and hoped for the best, enduring as well as I could the torture of unsatisfied desire and increasing lust.

It then happened that I had occasion to change my residence, and in my search for fresh quarters, I came across a modest suite of a sitting-room and two bedrooms which would by themselves have suited me excellently; but with them, the landlord desired to let what he termed a box or lumber-room. I demurred to this addition, but as he remained firm, I asked to see the room. It was most peculiar both as regards access and appearance. The former was by a short passage from the landing, furnished with remarkably well-fitting doors at each end. The room was nearly square, of a good size and lofty, but the walls were unbroken, save by the one entrance, light and air being derived from a skylight, or rather lantern, which occupied the greater part of the roof and was supported by four strong and stout wooden pillars. Further, the walls were thickly padded, while iron rings were let into them at regular distances all round in two rows, one close to the floor and the other about a height of eight feet; from the roof beams dangled rope pulleys in pairs between the pillars, while the two recesses on the entrance side, caused by the projection of the passage into the room, looked as if they had at one time been separated from the rest of the room by bars, almost as if they were cells. So strange indeed was the appearance of the whole room that I asked its history, and was informed that the house had been built as a private lunatic asylum at the time when the now unfashionable square in which it stood was one of the centres of fashion, and that this was the old "mad-room" in which violent patients were confined, the bolts, rings and pulleys being used to restrain them when very violent, while the padding and the double doors made the room absolutely soundproof and prevented the ravings of the inmates from annoying the neighbours. The landlord added that the soundproof quality was no fiction as the room had frequently been tested by incredulous visitors.

Like lightning the thought flashed through my brain. Was not this room the very place for the consummation of my scheme of revenge? If I succeeded in luring Alice into it, she would be completely at my mercy, for her screams for help would not be heard and would only increase my pleasure, while the bolts, rings, pulleys, etc., supplemented with a little suitable furniture, would enable me to secure her in any way I wished and to hold her fixed while I amused myself with her. Delighted with the idea, I agreed to include the room in my suite. Quietly, but with deep forethought and planning, I got certain furniture made which, while in outward appearance most innocent, as well as most comfortable, was in truth full of hidden mechanisms planned for the special discomfiture of any woman or girl that I might wish to hold in physical control. I had the floor covered with thick Persian carpets and rugs, and the two alcoves converted into nominal photographic laboratories, but in a way that made them suitable for lavatories and dressing-rooms. When completed, the "Snuggery" (as I christened it) was in appearance a distinctly pretty and comfortable room, while in reality it was nothing more or less than a disguised torture chamber!

And now came the difficult part of my scheme.

How to entrap Alice? Unfortunately she was not residing in London but a little way out. She lived with a married sister, and never seemed to come to town except in her sister's company. My difficulty was therefore how to get Alice by herself for a sufficiently long time to accomplish my designs, and sorely I cudgelled my brains over this problem!

The sisters frequently visited town at irregular intervals as dictated by the contingencies of social duties or shopping. True to my policy of l'entente cordiale, I had welcomed them to my rooms for rest and refreshment and had encouraged them to use my quarters; and partly because of the propinquity of the rooms to Regent Street, partly because of the very dainty meals I invariably placed before them, but mainly because of the soothing restfulness induced by the absolute quiet of the Snuggery after the roar and turmoil of the streets, it soon became their regular practice to honour me with their company for luncheon or tea whenever they came to town and had no special engagement. I need hardly add that secretly I hoped these visits might bring me an opportunity of executing my revenge, but for some months I seemed doomed to disappointment. I used to suffer the tortures of Tantalus when I saw Alice unsuspectingly braving me in the very room I had prepared for her violation, within actual reach of me and of hidden machinery that would place her at my disposal, did I set it working, were it not for her sister's presence! In fact, so keenly did I feel the position that I began to plan the capture of both sisters together, to include Marion in the punishment designed for Alice, and the idea in itself was not unpleasing, as Marion was a fine specimen of female flesh and blood of a larger and more stately type than Alice (who was "petite"), and one could do much worse than have her at one's disposal for an hour or two to feel and fuck! So seriously did I entertain this project, that I got an armchair made in such a way that the releasing of a secret catch would set free mechanisms that would be actuated by the weight of the occupant and would cause the arms to fold inwards and firmly imprison the sitter. Furnished with luxurious upholstery and the catch fixed, it made the most inviting of chairs, and from its first appearance, Alice took possession of it, in happy ignorance that it was intended to hold her firmly imprisoned while I tackled and secured Marion!

Before, however, I resorted to this desperate measure, my patience was rewarded! And this is how it happened.

One evening, the familiar note came to say the sisters were coming to town on the next day and would come for lunch. A little before the appointed hour Alice, to my surprise, appeared alone! She said that, after the note had been posted, Marion became ill and had been very poorly all night and so could not come to town, though better. The shopping engagement was one of considerable importance to Alice, and therefore she had come up alone; she had called to explain matters to me, but would not stop to lunch, she would get a cup of tea and a bun somewhere.

Against this desertion of me, I vigorously protested, but I doubt if I would have induced her to stay had not a smart shower of rain come on. This made her hesitate about going out into it with the dress she was wearing, as it would be ruined, and finally she consented to have lunch and leave immediately afterwards.

While she was away in the spare bedroom used by the sisters on their visits, I was in a veritable turmoil of excitement! Alice in my rooms by herself! It seemed too good to be true! But I remembered I yet had to get her into the Snuggery; she was absolutely safe from my designs everywhere but there! But it was imperative that she should be in no way alarmed, and so, with a strong effort, I controlled my panting excitement, and by the time Alice rejoined me in the dining-room I was my usual self.

Lunch was quickly served. At first, Alice seemed a little nervous and constrained, but by tactful conversation, I soon set her at ease and she then chatted away naturally and merrily. I had craftily placed her with her back to the window so that she should not note signs that a bad storm was brewing: and soon, with satisfaction, I saw that the weather was getting worse and worse! But it might at any moment begin to clear away, and so the sooner I could get her into my Snuggery, the better for me—and the worse for her! So, by every means in my power, I hurried on the procedure of lunch.

Alice was leisurely finishing her coffee when a rattle of rain against the window panes, followed by an ominous growl of thunder, made her start from her chair and go to the casement. "Oh! Just look at the rain!" she exclaimed in dismay, "how very unfortunate!"

I joined her at the window: "By Jove, it is bad!" I replied, then added, "and it looks like lasting. I hope that you have no important engagement for the afternoon that will keep you much in the open?" As I spoke, there came a vivid flash of lightning closely followed by a peal of thunder, which sent Alice staggering backwards with a scared face.

"Oh!" she exclaimed, evidently frightened; then, after a pause, "I am a horrid little coward about thunderstorms: they just terrify me!"

"Won't you then take refuge in the Snuggery?" I asked with a host's look of concern. "I don't think you will see the lightning there and you certainly won't hear the thunder, as the room is soundproof. Shall we go there?" and I opened the door invitingly.

Alice hesitated. Was her guardian angel trying to give her a premonitory hint of what her fate would be if she accepted my seemingly innocent suggestion? But at that moment came another flash of lightning, blinding in its intensity, and almost simultaneously a roar of thunder. This settled the question in my favour! "Yes, yes!" she exclaimed, then ran out. I closely following her, my heart beating exultingly! Quickly she passed through the double doors into the Snuggery, the trap I had so carefully set for her! Noiselessly I bolted the outer door, then closed the inner one. Alice was now mine! mine!! At last I had entrapped her! Now my vengeance was about to be consummated! Now her chaste virgin self was to be submitted to my lust and compelled to satisfy my erotic desires! She was utterly at my mercy, and promptly I proceeded to work my cruel will on her!

Chapter 2

The soothing stillness of the room after the roar of the storm seemed most agreeable to Alice. She drew a deep breath of relief and turning to me she exclaimed: "What a wonderful room it really is, Jack! Just look how the rain is pelting down on the skylight, and yet we do not hear a sound!"

"Yes! there is no doubt about it." I replied, "it is absolutely soundproof. I do not suppose that there is a better room in London for my special purpose!"

"What might that be, Jack?" she asked interestedly.

"Your violation, my dear!" I replied quietly, looking her straight in the face, "the surrender to me of your maidenhead!"

She started as if she had been struck. She coloured hotly. She stared at me as if she doubted her hearing. I stood still and calmly watched her. Then indignation and the sense of outraged modesty seized her.

"You must be mad to speak like that!" she said in a voice that trembled with concentrated anger. "You forget yourself. Be good enough to consider our friendship as suspended till you have recovered your senses and have suitably apologised for this intolerable insult. Meanwhile I will trouble you only to call a cab so that I may remove myself from your hateful presence!" And her eyes flashed in her wrathful indignation.

I quietly laughed aloud: "Do you really think I should have taken this step without calculating the consequences, Alice?" I rejoined coolly. "Do you really think I have lost my senses? Is there not a little account to be settled between us for what you did to me not very long ago? The day of reckoning has come, my dear; you have had your innings at my cost, now I am going to have mine at yours! You amused yourself with my heart, I am going to amuse myself with your body."

Alice stared at me, silent with surprise and horror! My quiet determined manner staggered her. She paled when I referred to the past, and she flushed painfully as I indicated what her immediate future would be. After a slight pause I spoke again.

"I have deliberately planned this revenge! I took these rooms solely because they would lend themselves so admirably to this end. I have prepared them for every contingency, even to having to subjugate you by force! Look!" And I proceeded to reveal to her astonished eyes the mechanism concealed in the furniture, etc. "You know you cannot get out of this room till I choose to let you go; you know that your screams and cries for help will not be heard. You now must decide what you will do. I give you two alternatives, and two only, and you must choose one of them. Will you submit yourself quietly to me, or do you prefer to be forced?"

Alice stamped her little foot in her rage: "How dare you speak to me in this way?" she demanded furiously. "Do you think I am a child? Let me go at once!" and she moved in her most stately manner to the door.

"You are no child." I replied with a cruel smile, "you are a lusciously lovely girl possessing everything that I desire and able to satisfy my desires. But I am not going to let you waste time. The whole afternoon will hardly be long enough for the satisfaction of my whims, caprices and lust. Once more, will you submit or will you be forced? Understand that if by the time the clock strikes the half-hour, you do not consent to submit, I shall without further delay proceed to take by force what I want from you! Now make the most of the three minutes you have left." And turning my back on her, I proceeded to get the room ready, as if I anticipated that I would have to use force.

Overcome by her feelings and emotions, Alice sank into an armchair burying her face in her trembling hands. She evidently recognised her dreadful position! How could she yield herself up to me? And yet if she did not, she knew she would have to undergo violation! And possibly horrible indignities as well! I left her absolutely alone, and when I had finished my preparations, I quietly seated myself and watched her. Presently the clock chimed the half-hour. Immediately I rose. Alice quickly sprang to her feet and rushed to the far side of the large divan-couch on which I hoped before long to see her extended naked! It was evident that she was going to resist and fight me, and I welcomed her decision, as now she would give me ample justification for the fullest exercising of my lascivious desires!

"Well, Alice, what is it to be? Will you submit quietly?"

A sudden passion seemed to possess her. She looked me squarely in the eyes for the first time, hers blazing with rage and indignation: "No! no!" she exclaimed vehemently, "I defy you! Do your worst. Do you think you will frighten me into satisfying your lust? Once and for all I give you my answer: No! No! No! Oh! you cowardly brute and beast!" And she laughed shrilly as she turned herself away contemptuously.

"As you please." I replied quietly and calmly, "let those laugh that win! I venture to say that within half an hour, you will not only be offering yourself to me absolutely and unconditionally, but will also be begging me to accept your surrender! Let us see!"

Alice laughed incredulously and defiantly: "Yes, let us see! Let us see!" she retorted contemptuously.

Forthwith I sprang towards her to seize her, but quick as thought she darted away, I in hot pursuit. For a short time she succeeded in eluding me, dodging in and out of the furniture, like a butterfly, but soon I manoeuvred her into a corner and pouncing on her gripped her firmly, then half dragged and half carried her to where a pair of electrically worked rope-pulleys hung between two of the pillars, she struggling desperately and screaming for help. In spite of her determined resistance, I soon made the ropes fast to her wrists, then touched the button; the ropes tightened, and slowly but irresistibly, Alice's arms were drawn upwards till her hands were well above her head and she was forced to stand erect by the tension on her arms. She was now utterly helpless and unable to defend her person from the hands that were itching to invade and explore the sweet mysteries of her garments; but what with her exertions and the violence of her emotions she was in such a state of agitation that I deemed it wise to leave her to herself for a brief space, till she became more mistress of herself, then she would be better able to appreciate the indignities which she would now be compelled to suffer!

Here, I think, I had better explain the mechanical means I had at my disposal for the discomfiture and subjugation of Alice.

Between each two of the pillars that supported the lantern-skylight hung a pair of strong rope-pulleys working on a roller mechanism concealed in the beams and actuated by electricity. Should I want Alice upright, I had simply to attach the ropes to her wrists, and her arms would be pulled straight up and well over her head, thus forcing her to stand erect, and at the same time rendering her body defenceless and at my mercy. The pillars themselves could be utilized as whipping posts, being provided with rings to which Alice could be fastened in such a way that she could not move!

Close by the pillars was a huge divan-couch upholstered in dark green satin admirably to enhance the pearly loveliness of a naked girl. It stood on eight massive legs (four on each long side), behind each of which lay, coiled for use, a stout leather strap worked by rollers hidden in the upholstery and actuated by electricity. On it were piled a lot of cushions of various sorts and consistencies, with which Alice and Marion used to make nests for themselves, little dreaming that the real object of the "Turkish Divan" (as they had christened it) was to be the altar on which Alice's virginity would be sacrificed to the Goddess of Love, the mission of the straps being to hold her in position while being violated, should she not surrender herself quietly to her fate!

By the keyboard of the grand piano stood a duet-stool upholstered in leather and with the usual mechanical power of adjustment for height, only to a much greater extent than usual. But the feature of the stool was its unusual length, a full six feet, and I one day had to satisfy Alice's curiosity by telling her that this was for the purpose of providing a comfortable seat to anyone who might be turning over for the pianist! The real reason was that the stool was, for all practical purposes, a rack actuated by hidden machinery and fitted with a most ingenious arrangement of straps, the efficacy of which I looked forward to testing on Alice's tender self.

The treacherous armchair I have already explained. My readers can now perhaps understand that I could fix Alice in practically any position or attitude and keep her so fixed while I worked my sweet will on her helpless self.

All the ropes and straps were fitted with swivel snap-hooks. To attach them to Alice's limbs, I used an endless band of the strongest and softest silk rope that I could get made. It was an easy matter to slip the band (doubled) round her wrist or ankle, pass one end through the other and draw tight, then snap the free end into the swivel hook. No amount of plunging or struggling would loosen this attachment, and the softness of the silk prevented Alice's delicate flesh from being rubbed or even marked.

Chapter 3

During the ten minutes grace that I mentally allowed Alice in which to recover from the violence of her struggles, I quietly studied her as she stood helpless, almost supporting herself by resting her weight on her wrists. She was to me an exhilarating spectacle, her bosom fluttering, rising and falling as she caught her breath, her cheeks still flushing, her large hat somewhat disarranged, while her dainty well-fitting dress displayed her neat comely figure to its fullest advantage.

She regained command of herself wonderfully quickly, and then it was evident that she was stealthily watching me in horrible apprehension. I did not leave her long in suspense, but after going slowly round her and inspecting her, I placed a chair right in front of her, so close to her its edge almost touched her knees, then slipped myself into it, keeping my legs apart, so that she stood between them, the front of her dress pressing against the fly of my trousers. Her head was now above mine, so that I could peer directly into her downcast face.

As I took up this position, Alice trembled nervously and tried to draw herself away from me, but found herself compelled to stand as I had placed her. Noticing the action, I drew my legs closer to each other so as loosely to hold her between them, smiling cruelly at the uncontrollable shudder that passed through her when she felt the pressure of my knees against hers! Then I extended my arms, clasped her gently round the waist, and drew her against me, at the same time tightening the clutch of my legs, till soon she was fairly in my embrace, my face pressing against her throbbing bosom. For a moment she struggled wildly, then resigned herself to the unavoidable as she recognised her helplessness.

Except when dancing with her, I had never held Alice in my arms, and the embrace permitted by the waltz was nothing to the comprehensive clasping between arms and legs in which she now found herself. She trembled fearfully, her tremors giving me exquisite pleasure as I felt them shoot through her, and murmured beseechingly: "Please don't, Jack!"

I looked up into her flushed face, as I amorously pressed my cheek against the swell of her bosom: "Don't you like it, Alice?" I said maliciously, as I squeezed her still more closely against me. "I think you're just delicious, dear, and I am trying to imagine what it will feel like, when your clothes have been taken off you!"

"No! No! Jack!" she moaned agonisedly, twisting herself in her distress, "let me go, Jack; don't. . . don't. . ." and her voice failed her.

For answer, I maintained her against me with my left arm round her waist, then with my right hand, I began to stroke and press her hips and bottom.

"Oh! . . . don't Jack! don't!" Alice shrieked, squirming in distress and futilely endeavouring to avoid my marauding hand. I paid no attention to her pleadings and cries, but continued my strokings and caressings over her full posteriors and thighs down to her knees, then back to her buttocks and haunches, she, all the while, quivering in a delicious way. Then I freed my left hand, and holding her tightly imprisoned between my legs, I proceeded with both hands to study over her clothes the configuration of her backside and hips and thighs, handling her buttocks with a freedom that seemed to stagger her, as she pressed the front of her person against me, in her efforts to escape from the liberties that my hands were takings with her posterior charms.

After toying delightfully with her in this way for some little time, I ceased and withdrew my hands from her hips, but only to pass them up and down over her incurving sides; thence I passed to her bosom which I began lovingly to stroke and caress to her dismay. Her colour rose as she swayed uneasily on her legs. But her stays prevented any direct attack on her bosom, so I decided to open her clothes sufficiently to obtain a peep at her virgin breasts, and set to work to unbutton her blouse.

"Jack, no! no!!" shrieked Alice, struggling vainly to get loose. But I only smiled and continued to undo her blouse till I got it completely open and threw it back on to her shoulders, only to be baulked as a fairly high bodice covered her bosom. I set to work to open this, my fingers revelling in the touch of Alice's dainty linen. Soon it also was open and thrown back—and then, right before my eager eyes, lay the snowy expanse of Alice's bosom, her breasts being visible nearly as far as their nipples!

"Oh! . . . oh! . . ." she moaned in her distress, flushing painfully at this cruel exposure. But I was too excited to take any notice; my eyes were riveted on the provokingly lovely swell of her breasts, exhibiting the valley between the twin globes, now heaving and fluttering under her agitated emotions. Unable to restrain myself, I threw my arms round Alice's waist drew her closely to me and pressed my lips on her palpitating flesh which I kissed furiously.

"Don't, Jack!" cried Alice, as she tugged frantically at her fastenings in her wild endeavours to escape from my passionate lips; but instead of stopping, my mouth wandered all over her heaving bosom and to her delicious breasts, punctuating its progress with hot kisses which seemed to drive her mad to such a pitch that I through it best to desist.

"Oh! my God!" she moaned as I relaxed my clasp and leant back in my chair to enjoy the sight of her shamefaced distress. There was not the least doubt that she felt most keenly my indecent assault, and so I determined to worry her with lascivious liberties a little longer.

When she had become calmer, I passed my arms round her waist and again began to play with her posteriors, then, stooping down, I got my hands under her clothes and commenced to pull them up. Flushing violently, Alice shrieked to me to desist, but in vain; in a trice, I turned her petticoats up, held them thus with my left hand and with my right I proceeded to attack her bottom now protected only by her dainty thin drawers!

The sensation was delirious! My hand delightedly roved over the fat plump cheeks of her arse, stroking, caressing and pinching them, revelling in the firmness and elasticity of her flesh under its thin covering, Alice all the time, wriggling and squirming in horrible shame, imploring me almost incoherently to desist and finally getting so semi-hysterical, that I was compelled to suspend my exquisite game. To her relief, I dropped her skirts, pushed my chair back and rose.

I had in the room a large plate-glass mirror nearly eight feet high which reflected one at full length. While Alice was recovering from her last ordeal, I pushed this mirror close in front of her, placing it so that she could see herself in its centre. She started uneasily as she caught sight of herself, for I had left her bosom uncovered, and the reflection of herself in such shameful dishabille in conjunction with her large hat (which she still retained) seemed vividly to impress on her the horror of her position!

Having arranged the mirror to my satisfaction, I picked up the chair and placed it just behind Alice, sat down on it, and worked myself forward on it till Alice again stood between my legs, but this time with her back to me. The mirror faithfully reflected my movements and her feminine intuition warned her that the front of her person was now about to become the object of my indecent assault.

But I did not give her time to think. Quickly I encircled her waist again with my arms, drew her to me till her bottom pressed against my chest, then, while my left arm held her firmly, my right hand began to wander over the junction of her stomach and legs, pressing inquisitively her groin and thighs, and intently watching her in the mirror.

Her colour rose, her breath came unevenly, she quivered and trembled on her legs as she pressed her thighs closely together. She was horribly perturbed, but I do not think she anticipated what then happened.

Quietly dropping my hands, I slipped them under her clothes, caught hold of her ankles, then proceeded to climb up her legs over her stockings.

"No! no! for God's sake, don't Jack!" Alice yelled, now scarlet with shame and wild with alarm at this invasion of her most secret parts. Frantically she dragged at her fastenings, her hands clenched, her head thrown back, her eyes dilated with horror. Throwing the whole of her weight on her wrists, she strove to free her legs from my attacking hands by kicking out desperately, but to no avail. The sight in the mirror of her struggles only stimulated me into a refinement of cruelty, for with one hand, I raised her clothes waist high, exposing her in her dainty drawers and black silk stockings, while with the other, I vigorously attacked her thighs over her drawers, forcing a way between them and finally working up so close to her mount of Venus that Alice practically collapsed in an agony of apprehension and would have fallen had it not been for the sustaining ropes which alone supported her as she hung in a semi-hysterical faint.

Quickly rising and dropping her clothes, I placed an armchair behind her, and loosened the pulleys, till she rested comfortably in it, then left her to recover herself, feeling pretty confident that she was now not far from surrendering herself to me, rather than continue a resistance which she could not but see was utterly useless. This was what I wanted to effect. I did not propose to let her off any single one of the indignities I had in store for her, but I wanted to make her suffering the more keen through the feeling that she was, to some extent, a consenting party to actions that inexpressibly shocked and revolted her. The first of these I intended to be the removal of her clothes, and, as soon as Alice became more mistress of herself, I set the pulleys working and soon had her again standing erect with up-stretched arms.

She glanced fearfully at me as if trying to learn what was now going to happen to her. I deemed it as well to tell her, and to afford her an opportunity of yielding herself to me, if she should be willing to do so. I also wanted to save her clothes from being damaged, as she was really beautifully dressed, and I was not at all confident that I could get her garments off her without using scissors to some of them.

"I see you want to know what is now going to happen to you, Alice." I said. "I'll tell you. You are to be stripped naked, utterly and absolutely naked: not a stitch of any sort is to be left on you!"

A flood of crimson swept over her face, invading both neck and bosom (which remained bare); her head fell forward as she moaned: "No! . . . No! . . . oh! Jack. . . Jack. . . how can you. . ." and she swayed uneasily on her feet.

"That is to be the next item in the programme, my dear!" I said, enjoying her distress. "There is only one detail that remains to be settled first, and that is, will you undress yourself quietly if I set you loose, or must I drag your clothes off you? I don't wish to influence your decision, and I know what queer ideas girls have about taking off their clothes in the presence of a man; I will leave the decision to you, only to say that I do not see what you gain by further resistance, and some of your garments may be ruined—which would be a pity! Now, which is it to be?"

She looked at me imploringly for a moment, trembling in every limb, then averted her eyes, but remained silent, evidently torn by conflicting emotions.

"Come, Alice." I said presently, "I must have your decision, or I shall proceed to take your clothes off you as best as I can."

Alice was now in a terrible state of distress! Her eyes wandered all over the room without seeming to see anything, incoherent murmurs escaped from her lips, as if she was trying to speak but could not, her breath went and came, her bosom rose and fell agitatedly. She was endeavouring to form some decision evidently, but unable to do so.

I remained still for a brief space as if awaiting her answer; then, as she did not speak, I quietly went to a drawer, took out a pair of scissors and went back to her. At the sight of the scissors, she shivered, then with an effort, said, in a voice broken with emotion: "Don't. . . undress me Jack! . . . if you must. . . have me, let it be as I am. . . I will. . . submit quietly. . . oh! my God!!" she wailed.

"That won't do, dear." I replied, not unkindly, but still firmly, "you must be naked, Alice; now, will you or will you not undress yourself?"

Alice shuddered, cast another imploring glance at me, but seeing no answering gleam of pity in my eyes but stern determination instead, she stammered out: "Oh! Jack! I can't!! have some pity on me, Jack, and. . . have me as I am! I promise I'll be. . . quiet!"

I shook my head. I saw there was only one thing for me to do, namely, to undress her without any further delay; and I set to work to do so, Alice crying piteously: "Don't Jack, don't! . . . don't!"

I had left behind her the armchair in which I had allowed her to rest, and her blouse and bodice were still hanging open and thrown back on her shoulders. So I got on the chair and worked them along her arms and over her clenched hands on to the ropes; then gripping her wrists in turn one at a time, I released the noose, slipped the garments down and off and refastened the noose. And as I had been quick to notice that Alice's chemise and vest had shoulder-strap fastenings and had merely to be unhooked, the anticipated difficulty of undressing her forcibly was now at an end! The rest of her garments would drop off her, as each became released, and therefore it was in my power to reduce her to absolute nudity! My heart thrilled with fierce exultation, and without further pause, I went on with the delicious work of undressing her.

Alice quickly divined her helplessness and in an agony of apprehension and shame cried to me for mercy! But I was deaf to her pitiful pleadings! I was wild to see her naked!

Quickly I unhooked her dress and petticoats and pulled them down to her feet, thus exhibiting her in stays, drawers and stockings, a bewitching sight! Her cheeks were suffused with shamefaced blushes, she huddled herself together as much as she could, seemingly supported entirely by her arms; her eyes were downcast and she seemed dazed both by the rapidity of my motions and their horrible success!

Alice now had on only a dainty Parisian corset which allowed the laces of her chemise to be visible, just hiding the nipples of her maiden breasts, and a pair of exquisitely provoking drawers, cut wide especially at her knees and trimmed with a sea of frilly lace, from below which emerged her shapely legs encased in black silk stockings and terminating in neat little shoes. She was the daintiest sight a man could well imagine, and, to me, the daintiness was enhanced by her shamefaced consciousness, for she could see herself reflected in the mirror in all her dreadful dishabille!

After a minute of gloating admiration, I proceeded to untie the tapes of her drawers so as to take them off her. At this she seemed to wake to the full sense of the humiliation in store for her; wild at the idea of being deprived of this most intimate of garments to a girl, she screamed in her distress, tugging frantically at her fastenings in her desperation! But the knot gave way, and her drawers, being now unsupported, slipped down to below her knees, where they hung for a brief moment, maintained only by the despairing pressure of her legs against each other. A tug or two from me, and they lay in snowy loads round her ankles and rested on her shoes!

O that I had the pen of a ready writer with which to describe Alice at this stage of the terrible ordeal of being forcibly undressed, her mental and physical anguish, her frantic cries and impassioned pleadings, her frenzied struggles, the agony in her face as garment after garment was removed from her and she was being hurried nearer and nearer to the appalling goal of absolute nudity! The accidental but unavoidable contact of my hands with her person, as I undressed her, seemed to upset her so terribly that I wondered how she would endure my handling and playing with the most secret and sensitive parts of herself when she was naked! But acute as was her distress while being deprived of her upper garments, it was nothing to her shame and anguish when she felt her drawers forced down her legs and the last defence to her cunt thus removed! Straining wildly at the ropes with cheeks aflame, eyes dilated with terror, and convulsively heaving bosom, she uttered inarticulate cries, half choked by her emotions and panting under her exertions.

I gloated over her sufferings and would have liked to have watched them—but I was now mad with desire for her naked charms and also feared that a prolongation of her agony might result in a faint, when I would lose the anticipated pleasure of witnessing Alice's misery when her last garment was removed and she was forced to stand naked in front of me. So unheeding her imploring cries, I undid her corset and took it off her, dragged off her shoes and stockings and with them her fallen drawers (during which process I intently watched her struggles in the hope of getting a glimpse of her holy of holies, but vainly), then slipped behind her; unbuttoning the shoulder-fastenings of her chemise and vest, I held these up for a moment, then watching Alice closely in the mirror, I let go! Down they slid with a rush, right to her feet! I saw Alice flash one rapid stolen half-reluctant glance at the mirror, as she felt the cold air on her now naked skin. I saw her reflection stark naked, a lovely gleaming pearly vision; then instinctively she squeezed her legs together, as closely as she could, huddled herself coweringly as much as the ropes permitted—her head fell back in the first intensity of her shame, then fell forward suffused with blushes that extended right down to her breasts, her eyes closed as she moaned in heartbroken accents: "Oh! oh!! oh!!!" She was naked!

Half delirious with excitement and the joy of conquest, I watched Alice's naked reflection in the mirror. Rapidly and tumultuously, my eager eyes roved over her shrinking trembling form, gleaming white, save for her blushing face and the dark triangular mossy-looking patch at the junction of her belly and thighs. But I felt that, in this moment of triumph, I was not sufficiently master of myself fully to enjoy the spectacle of her naked maiden charms now so fully exposed, besides which, her chemise and vest still lay on her feet. So I knelt down behind her, forced her feet up one at a time and removed these garments, noting as I did so the glorious curves of her bottom and hips. Throwing these garments on to the rest of her clothes, I pushed the armchair in front of her, and then settled myself down to a systematic and critical inspection of Alice's naked self!

As I did so, Alice coloured deeply over face and bosom and moved herself uneasily. The bitterness of death (so to speak) was past, her clothes had been forced off her and she was naked; but she was evidently conscious that much indignity and humiliation was yet in store for her, and she was horribly aware that my eyes were now taking in every detail of her naked self! Forced to stand erect by the tension of the ropes on her arms, she could do nothing to conceal any part of herself, and, in an agony of shame, she endured the awful ordeal of having her naked person closely inspected and examined!

I had always greatly admired her trim little figure, and in the happy days before our rupture, I used to note with proud satisfaction how Alice held her own, whether at garden parties, at afternoon teas or in the theatre or ballroom. And after she had jilted me and I was sore in spirit, the sight of her invariably added fuel to the flames of my desire, and I often caught myself wondering how she looked in her bath! One evening, she wore at dinner a low-cut evening dress and she nearly upset my self-control by leaning forward over the card table by which I was standing, and unconsciously revealing to me the greater portion of her breasts! But my imagination never pictured anything as glorious as the reality now being so reluctantly exhibited to me!

Alice was simply a beautiful girl and her lines deliciously voluptuous! No statue, no model, but glorious flesh and blood allied to superb femininity! Her well-shaped head was set on a beautifully modelled neck and bosom, from which sprang a pair of exquisitely lovely breasts (if anything too full), firm, upstanding, saucy and inviting. She had fine rounded arms with small well-shaped hands, a dainty but not too small waist, swelling grandly downwards and outwards and melting into magnificent curves over her hips and haunches. Her thighs were plump and round, and tapered to the neatest of calves and ankles and tiny feet, her legs being the least trifle too short for her, but adding by this very defect to the indescribable fascination of her figure. She had a graciously swelling belly with a deep navel, and, framed by the lines of her groin, was her mount of Venus, full, fat, fleshy, prominent, covered by a wealth of fine silky dark curly hairs, through which I could just make out the lips of her cunt. Such was Alice as she stood naked before me, horribly conscious of my devouring eyes, quivering and trembling with suppressed emotion, tingling with shame, flushing red and white, knowing full well her own loveliness and what its effect on me must be; and in dumb silence I gazed and gazed again at her glorious naked self, till my lust began to run riot and insist on the gratification of senses other than that of sight!

I did not however consider that Alice was ready properly to appreciate the mortification of being felt. She seemed to be still absorbed in the horrible consciousness of one all-pervading fact, viz. that she was utterly naked, that her chaste body was the prey of my lascivious eyes, that she could do nothing to hide or even screen any part of herself, even her cunt, from me! Every now and then, her downcast eyes would glance at the reflection of herself in the faithful mirror, only to be hastily withdrawn with an access of colour to her already shame-suffused cheeks at these fresh reminders of the spectacle she was offering to me!

Therefore, with a strong effort, I succeeded in overcoming the temptation to feel and handle Alice's luscious body there and then, and being desirous of first studying her naked self from all points of view, I rose and took her in strict profile, noting with delight the arch of her bosom, the proudly projecting breasts, the glorious curve of her belly, the conspicuous way in which the hairs on the mount of Venus stood out, indicating that her cunt would be found both fat and fleshy, the magnificent swell of her bottom! Then I went behind her, and for a minute or two revelled in silent admiration of the swelling lines of her hips and haunches, her quivering buttocks, her well-shaped legs!

Without moving, I could command the most perfect exhibition of her naked loveliness, for I had her back view in full sight while her front was reflected in the mirror!

Presently I completed my circuit, then standing close to her, I had a good look at her palpitating breasts, noting their delicious fullness and ripeness, their ivory skin, and the tiny virgin nipples pointing outwards so prettily, Alice colouring and flushing and swaying herself uneasily under my close inspection. Then I peered into the round cleft of her navel while she became more uneasy than ever, seeing the downward trend of my inspection. Then I dropped on my knees in front of her, and from this point of vantage, I commenced to investigate with eager eyes the mysterious region of her cunt, so deliciously covered with a wealth of close curling hairs, clustering so thickly round and over the coral lips as almost to render them invisible! As I did so, Alice desperately squeezed her thighs together as closely as she could, at the same time drawing in her stomach in the vain hope of defeating my purpose and of preventing me from inspecting the citadel wherein reposed her virginity!

As a matter of fact, she did to a certain extent thwart me, but as I intended before long to put her on her back and tie her down with her legs wide apart, I did not grudge her partial success, but brought my face close to her belly. "Don't! oh don't!" she cried, as if she could feel my eyes as they searched this most secret part of herself; but disregarding her pleadings, I closely scanned the seat of my approaching pleasure, noting delightedly that her mount of Venus was exquisitely plump and fleshy and would afford my itching fingers the most delicious pleasure when I allowed them to wander over its delicate contours and hide themselves in the forest of hairs that so sweetly covered it!

At last I rose. Without a word, I slipped behind the mirror and quickly divested myself of my clothes, retaining only my shoes and socks. Then, suddenly, I emerged and stood right in front of Alice. "Oh!" she exclaimed, horribly shocked by the unexpected apparition of my naked self, turning rosy red and hastily averting her eyes—but not before they had caught sight of my prick in glorious erection! I watched her closely. The sight seemed to fascinate her in spite of her alarmed modesty, she flashed rapid glances at me through half-closed eyes, her colour coming and going. She seemed forced, in spite of herself, to regard the instrument of her approaching violation, as if to assess its size and her capacity!

"Won't you have a good look at me, Alice?" I presently remarked maliciously, "I believe I can claim to possess a good specimen of what is so dear to the heart of a girl!" (She quivered painfully.) After a moment I continued: "Must I then assume by your apparent indifference that you have in your time seen so many naked men that the sight no longer appeals to you?" She coloured deeply, but kept her eyes averted.

"Are you not even curious to estimate whether my prick will fit your cunt?" I added, determined, if I possibly could, to break down the barrier of silence she was endeavouring to protect herself with.

I succeeded! Alice tugged frantically at the ropes which kept her upright, then broke into a piteous cry: "No, no. . . my God, no!" she supplicated, throwing her head back but still keeping her eyes shut as if to exclude the sight she dreaded, "Oh! . . . you don't really mean to. . . to. . ." she broke down, utterly unable to clothe in words the overwhelming fear that she was now to be violated!

I stepped up to her, passed my left arm round her waist and drew her trembling figure to me, thrilling at the exquisite sensation caused by the touch of our naked bodies against each other. We were now both facing the mirror, both reflected in it.

"Don't, oh! don't touch me!" she shrieked as she felt my arm encircle her, but holding her closely against me with my left arm, I gently placed my right forefinger on her navel, to force her to open her eyes and watch my movements in the mirror, which meant that she would also have to look at my naked self, and gently I tickled her.

She screamed in terror, opening her eyes, squirming deliciously: "Don't! oh don't!" she cried agitatedly.

"Then use your chaste eyes properly and have a good look at the reflection of the pair of us in the mirror." I said somewhat sternly; "look me over slowly and thoroughly from head to foot, then answer the questions I shall presently put to you. May I call your attention to that whip hanging on that wall and to the inviting defencelessness of your bottom? Understand that I shall not hesitate to apply one to the other if you don't do as you are told! Now have a good look at me!"

Alice shuddered, then reluctantly raised her eyes and shamefacedly regarded my reflection in the mirror, her colour coming and going. I watched her intently (she being also reflected, my arm was still round her waist holding her against me) and I noted with cruel satisfaction how she trembled with shame and fright when her eyes dwelt on my prick, now stiff and erect!

"We make a fine pair, Alice, eh?" I whispered maliciously. She coloured furiously, but remained silent.

"Now answer my questions: I want to know something about you before going further. How old are you?"

"Twenty-five." she whispered.

"In your prime then! Good! Now, are you a virgin?"

Alice flushed hotly and painfully, then whispered again: "Yes!"

Oh! my exultation! I was not too late! The prize of her maidenhead was to be mine! My prick showed my joy! I continued my catechism.

"Absolutely virgin?" I asked, "a pure virgin? Has no hand ever wandered over those lovely charms, has no eye but mine seen them?"

Alice shook her head, blushing rosy red at the idea suggested by my words. I looked rather doubtingly at her.

"I include female eyes and hands as well in my query, Alice." I continued; "you know that you have a most attractive lot of girl and woman friends and that you are constantly with them. Am I to understand that you and they have never compared your charms, have never, when occupying the same bed. . ." but she broke in with a cry of distress. "No, no, not I, not I, oh! how can you talk to me like this, Jack!"

"My dear, I only wanted to find out how much you already knew so that I might know what to teach you now! Well, shall we begin your lessons?"

And I drew her against me, more closely than ever, and again began to tickle her navel.

"Jack, don't!" she screamed, "oh don't touch me! I can't stand it! really I can't!"

"Let me see if that is really so!" I replied, as I removed my arm from her waist and slipped behind her, taking up a position from which I could command the reflection of our naked figures in the mirror, and thus watch her carefully and note the effect on her of my tender mercy.

Chapter 4

I commenced to feel Alice by placing my hands one on each side of her waist, noting with cruel satisfaction the shiver that ran through her at their contact with her naked skin. After a few caresses, I passed them gently but inquisitively over her full hips, which I stroked, pressed and patted lovingly, then bringing my hands downwards behind her I roved over her plump bottom, the fleshy cheeks of which I gripped and squeezed to my heart's content, Alice the while arching herself outwards in a vain attempt to escape my hands. Then I descended to the underneath portion of her soft round thighs, and finally worked my way back to her waist, running my hands up and down over loins and finally arriving at her armpits.

Here I paused, and to try the effect on Alice, I gently tickled these sensitive spots of herself. "Don't!" she exclaimed wriggling and twisting herself uneasily, "don't, I am dreadfully ticklish, I can't stand it at all!" At once I ceased, but my blood went on fire, as through my brain flashed the idea of the licentiously lovely spectacle Alice would afford if she was tied down with her legs fastened widely apart, and a pointed feather-tip cleverly applied to the most sensitive part of herself—her cunt—sufficient slack being allowed in her fastenings to permit of her wriggling and writhing freely while being thus tickled, and I promised to give myself presently this treat together with the pleasure of trying on her this interesting experiment.

After a short pause, I again placed my hands on her waist, played for a moment over her swelling hips, then slipped them on to her stomach, my right hand taking the region below her waist, while my left devoted itself to her bosom, carefully avoiding for the moment her breasts.

Oh! what pleasure I tasted in thus touching her pure sweet flesh, so smooth, so warm, so essentially female! My delighted hands wandered all over her body, while the poor girl stood quivering and trembling, unable to guess whether her breasts or cunt were next to be attacked.

I did not keep her long in suspense. After a few circlings over her rounded belly, my right hand paused on her navel again, and while my forefinger gently tickled her, my left hand slid quietly on to her right breast which it then gently seized.

She gave a great cry of dismay! Meanwhile my right hand had in turn slipped up to her left breast, and another involuntary shriek from

Alice announced that both of her virgin bubbies had become the prey of my cruel hands!

Oh! how she begged me to release them, the while tossing herself from side to side in almost uncontrollable agitation as my fingers played with her delicious breasts, now squeezing, now stroking, now pressing them against each other, now rolling them upwards and downwards, now gently irritating and exciting their tiny nipples! Such delicious morsels of flesh I had never handled, so firm and yet so springing, so ripe and yet so maidenly, palpitating under the hitherto unknown sensations communicated by the touch of masculine hands on their virgin surfaces. Meanwhile Alice's tell-tale face reflected in the mirror clearly indicated to me the mental shame and anguish she was feeling at this terrible outrage; her flushed cheeks, dilated nostrils, half-closed eyes, her panting heaving bosom all revealing her agony under this desecration of her maiden self! In rapture, I continued toying with her virgin globes, all the while gloating on Alice's image in the mirror, twisting and contorting itself in the most lasciviously ravishing way under her varying emotions.

At last I tore my hands away from Alice's breasts. I slipped my left arm round her waist, drew her tightly against me, then while I held her firmly, my right hand passed gently over her stomach and slowly approached her cunt! Alice instantly guessed my intention! She threw her weight on one leg, then quickly placed the other across her groin to foil my attack, crying: "No no, Jack! . . . not there. . . not there!" at the same time endeavouring frantically to turn herself away from my hand. But the close grip of my left arm defeated her, and disregarding her cries, my hand crept on and on till it reached her hairs! These I gently pulled, twining them round my fingers as I revelled in their curling silkiness. Then amorously, I began to feel and press her gloriously swelling mount of Venus, a finger on each side of its slit. Alice now simply shrieked in her shame and distress, jerking herself convulsively backwards and twisting herself frenziedly. As she was forced to stand on both legs in order to maintain her balance, her cunt was absolutely defenceless, and my eager fingers roved all over it, touching, pressing, tickling, pulling her hairs at their sweet will. Then I began to attack her virgin orifice and tickle her slit, passing my forefinger lightly up and down it, all the time watching her intently in the mirror. Alice quivered violently, her head fell backwards in her agony as she shrieked: "Jack, don't! . . . for God's sake don't!! . . . stop! . . . stop!" But I could feel her cunt opening under my lascivious attentions, and so could she! Her distress became almost uncontrollable. "Oh, my God!" she screamed in her desperation as my finger found its way to her clitoris and lovingly titillated it; spasmodically she squeezed her thighs together in her vain attempts to defend herself. Unheeding her agonised pleadings, I continued to tickle her clitoris for a few delicious moments, then I gently passed my finger along her cunt and between its now half-opened lips till I arrived at her maiden orifice, up which it tenderly forced its way, burying itself in Alice's cunt till it could penetrate no further into her! Alice's agitation now became uncontrollable; she struggled so violently that I could hardly hold her still, especially when she felt the interior of her cunt invaded and my finger investigate the mysteries of its virgin recesses.

Oh! my voluptuous sensations at that moment! Alice's naked quivering body clutched tightly against mine! My finger, half buried in her maiden cunt, enveloped in her soft warm throbbing flesh and gently exploring its luscious interior!! In my excitement I must have pushed my inquisitiveness too far, for Alice suddenly screamed: "Oh! . . . oh! you're hurting me! . . . stop! stop!" her head falling forward on her bosom as she did so! Delighted at this unexpected proof of her virginity and fearful of exciting her sexual passions beyond her powers of control, I gently withdrew my finger and soothed her by passing it lovingly and caressingly over her cunt; then releasing her from my encircling arm, I left her to recover herself. But, though visibly relieved at being at last left alone, Alice, trembled so violently that I hastily pushed her favourite armchair (the treacherous one) behind her, deftly released the pulley-ropes and let her drop into the chair to rest and recover herself, for I knew that her distress was only temporary and would soon pass away and leave her in a fit condition to be again fastened and subjected to some other torture, for so it undoubtedly was to her.

Chapter 5

On this occasion, I did not set free the catch which permitted the arms of the chair to imprison the occupant. Alice was so upset by her experiences that I felt sure she would not give me any trouble worth mentioning when it became time for her torturing to recommence, provided of course that I did not allow her too long a respite, and this, from my own point of view, I did not propose to do as I was wildly longing to play again with her naked charms!

I therefore let her coil herself up in the chair with her face buried in her hands, and greedily gloated over the voluptuous curves of her haunches and bottom which she was unconsciously exhibiting, the while trying to make up my mind as to what I should next do to her. This I soon decided. My hands were itching to handle again her virgin flesh, and so I determined to tie Alice upright to one of the pillars and while comfortably seated close in front of her, to amuse myself by playing with her breasts and cunt again.

She was now lying quietly and breathing normally and regularly, the tremblings and quiverings that had been running intermittently through her having by now ceased. I did not feel quite sure if she had recovered herself yet, but as I watched her, I noticed an attempt on her part to try and slip her wrists out of the silken nooses that attached the ropes to them. This settled the point, and, before she could effect her object and free her hands, I set the ropes working, remarking as I did so: "Well Alice, shall we resume?"

She glanced at me affrightedly, then averted her eyes as she exclaimed hurriedly: "Oh no, Jack! not again, not again!" and shuddered at the recollection of her recent ordeal.

"Yes, my dear!" I replied, "the same thing, though not quite in the same way; you'll be more comfy this time! Now Alice, come along, stand up again!"

"No!" she cried, fighting vainly the now fast tightening ropes which were inexorably raising her to her feet! "Oh, Jack! no! . . . no!!" she pitifully pleaded while opposing the upward pull with all her might but to no avail! I simply smiled cruelly at her as I picked up a leather strap and awaited the favourable moment to force her against the nearest pillar. Presently she was dragged off the chair and now was my time. I pounced on her and rushed her backwards to the pillar, quickly slipping the strap round it and her waist and buckling it, and thus securing her. Then I loosened the pulleys and lowering her arms, I forced them behind her and round the pillar, till I got her wrists together and made them fast to a ring set in the pillar. Alice was now helpless; the whole of the front of her person was at my disposal! She was securely fastened, but, with a refinement of cruelty, I lashed her ankles together and bound them to the pillar! Then I unbuckled the strap round her waist and threw it away, it being no longer needed, placed the armchair in front of her, and sitting down in it, I drew it so close to her that she stood between my parted legs and within easy touch, just as she did when she was being indecently assaulted before she was undressed, only then we both were fully clothed, while now we both were stark naked! She could not throw her head back because of the pillar, and if she let it droop, as she naturally wanted to do, the first thing that her innocent eyes would rest upon would be my excited prick in glorious erection, its blushing head pointing directly towards her cunt as if striving to make the acquaintance of its destined bride.

Confused, shamefaced and in horrible dread, Alice stood trembling in front of me, her eyes tightly closed as if to avoid the sight of my naked self, her bosom agitatedly palpitating till her breasts seemed almost to be dancing! I leant back in my chair luxuriously as I gloated over the voluptuously charming spectacle, allowing her a little time in which to recover herself somewhat before I set to work to feel her again.

Before long, the agitations of her bosom died away; Alice's breathing became quieter. She was evidently now ready for another turn, and I did not keep her waiting, but gently placed my hands on her breasts.

"No, Jack, don't!" she pleaded piteously, moving herself uneasily. My only response was to stroke lovingly her delicious twin globes. As her shoulders were of necessity drawn well back by the pull of her arms, her bust was thrown well forward, thus causing her breasts to stand out saucily and provokingly; and I took the fullest advantage of this. Her flesh was delicious to the touch, so smooth and soft and warm, so springy and elastic. My fingers simply revelled in their contact with her skin! Taking her tempting bubbies between my fingers and thumbs, I amorously pressed and squeezed them, pulled them this way and that way, rubbed them against each other, finally taking each delicate nipple in turn in my mouth and sucking it while my hands made as if they were trying to milk her! Alice, all the while, involuntarily shifted herself nervously, as if endeavouring to escape from my audaciously inquisitive fingers, her face scarlet with shame.

After a delicious five minutes of lascivious toying with her maiden breasts, I reluctantly quitted them, first imprinting on each of her little nipples a passionate kiss which seemed to thrill through her. As I sank back into my chair she took a long breath of relief, at which I smiled, for I had only deserted her breasts for her cunt.

Alice's legs were a trifle short, and her cunt therefore lay a little too low for effective attack from me in a sitting position. I therefore pushed the chair back and knelt in front of her. My intentions were now too obviously plain to her, and she shrieked in her dismay, squirming deliciously.

For some little time, I did not touch her, but indulged in a good look at close quarters at the sweet citadel of her chastity.

My readers will remember that, immediately after I had stripped Alice naked, I had closely inspected her cunt from a similar point of view. But then it was unsullied, untouched; now it had experienced the adoring touch of a male finger, and her sensitive body was still all of a quiver from the lustful handling her dainty breasts had just endured! Did her cunt share in the sexual excitement that my fingers had undoubtedly aroused in her?

It seemed to me that it did! The hair seemed to stand out as if ruffled, the mount of Venus certainly looked fuller, while the coral lips of the cunt itself were distinctly more apart! I could not see her clitoris, but I concluded that it participated in the undoubted excitement that was prevailing in this sweet portion of Alice's body, and of which she evidently was painfully aware by her shrinking quivering movements!

I soon settled the point by gently placing my right forefinger on her slit and lovingly stroking it! An electric shock seemed to thrill through Alice, her limbs contracted, her head fell forward as she screamed: "Don't Jack! . . . oh my God! how can you treat me so?" while she struggled frantically to break the ropes which lashed her legs to the pillar to which she was fastened.

"Don't you like it, dear?" I asked softly with a cruel smile, as I continued gently to play with her cunt.

"No, no." she shrieked, "oh stop! . . . I can't stand it!" And she squirmed horribly. The crack of her cunt now began to open visibly.

I slipped my finger in between the parted lips: another despairing shriek from Alice, whose face now was scarlet! Again I found my progress barred by the membrane that proved her virgin condition! Revelling in the warm moistness of her throbbing flesh, I slowly agitated my finger in its delicious envelope, as if frigging her: "Jack! don't!!" Alice yelled, now mad with distress and shame, but I could not for the life of me stop, and with my left forefinger, I gently attacked her virgin clitoris.

Alice went off into a paroxysm of hysterical shrieks, straining at her fastenings, squirming, wriggling, writhing like one possessed. She was a lovely sight in herself, and the knowledge that the struggling shrieking girl I was torturing was Alice herself and none but Alice added zest to my occupation.

Disregarding her cries, I went on slowly frigging her but carefully refrained from carrying her sexual excitement to the spending point; till I had pushed her powers of self-control to their utmost I did not want her to spend, this crowning humiliation I intended to effect with my tongue. Presently, what I wished was to make Alice endure the most outrageously indecent indignities I could inflict on her virgin person, to play on her sexual sensitiveness, to provoke her nearly into spending, and then deny her the blessed relief; so, exercising every care, and utilising to the utmost the peculiarly subtle power of touch I possessed, I continued to play with her cunt with both my hands, till I drove her nearly frantic with the sexual cravings and excitement I was provoking.

Just then I noticed certain spasmodic contortions of her hips and buttocks, certain involuntary thrusting out of her belly, as if she were begging for closer contact with my busy fingers; I knew this meant that her control over her sexual organs was giving out and that she would be driven into spending if I did not take care; so, most reluctantly, I stopped torturing her for the moment, and leaning back in my chair, I gloatingly watched Alice as little by little she regained her composure, my eyes dwelling delightedly on her trembling and quivering naked body so gloriously displayed.

She breathed a long sigh of heartfelt relief as she presently saw me rise and leave her. She did not however know that my object in doing so was to prepare another and perhaps more terrible ordeal for her virgin cunt!

From a drawer, I took out a long glove-box, then returned and resumed my seat in front of her with the box in my hand. She watched me with painful intensity, her feminine intuition telling her that something horrible was in store for her, and she was not wrong!

Holding the box in such a way that she could see the contents, I opened it. Inside were about a dozen long and finely pointed feathers. Alice at once guessed her fate, viz, that her cunt was to be tickled; her head jerked in her terror as she shrieked: "Oh, my God! not that, Jack! . . . not that!! . . . you'll kill me! I can't stand it!!" I laughed cruelly at her and proceeded to pick out a feather, whereupon she frantically tugged at her fastenings, screaming frenziedly for mercy!

"Steady, dear! steady now, Alice!" I said soothingly, as if addressing a restive mare, then touched her palpitating breasts with the feather's point. "Jack, don't!" she yelled, pressing herself wildly back against the pillar in a impotent effort to escape from the torture caused by the maddeningly gentle titillation, her face crimson. For response, I proceeded to pass the tip of the feather along the lower portion of her glorious bubbies, touching the skin ever so lightly here and there, then tickling her maiden nipples! With redoubled cries, Alice began to squirm convulsively as much as her fastenings would permit, while the effect of the fiendishly subtle torture on her became manifest by the sudden stiffening of her breasts, which now began to stand out tense and full! Noting this, I thought it as well to allow her a little respite, so dropped my hand, but at the same time leant forward till my face touched her breasts, which I then proceeded to kiss lovingly in turn, finally sucking them amorously till they again became soft and yielding. I then made as if I would repeat the torture, but after a touch or two (which produced piteous cries and contortions) I pretended to be moved by her distress, and again dropping my hand, leant back in the chair till she became less agitated.

But as soon as the regular rise and fall of her lovely bosom indicated the regaining of composure, I proceeded to try the ardently longed for experiment, viz. the effect of a feather when applied to a girl's cunt! And no one could have desired a more lovely subject on which to test this much debated question than was being offered by the naked helpless girl now standing terrified between my legs!

Pushing my chair back as much as was desirable, I leant forward, then slowly extended my right arm in the direction of Alice's cunt. A great cry of despair broke from her as she noted the movement, and she flattened her bottom against the pillar in a vain attempt to draw herself back out of reach. But the only effect of her desperate movement was to force forward her mount of Venus, and thereby render her cunt more open to the attack of the feather than it previously was!

Carefully regulating my motions, I gently brought the tip of the feather against the lowest point of Alice's cunt hole, then very softly and gently began to play up and down on and between its delicate coral lips! Alice's head had dropped on to her breast the better, I fancy, to watch my movements; but as soon as the feather touched her cunt, she threw her head backwards, as if in agony, shrieking at the top of her voice, her whole body twisting and contorting wildly. Not heeding her agonised appeals, I proceeded to work along her slit towards her clitoris, putting into play the most subtle titillation I was capable of, sometimes passing the feather all along the slit from one end to the other, sometimes tickling the orifice itself, not only outside but inside; then, ascending towards her clitoris, I would pass the tip of the feather all round it, irritating it without so much as touching it. The effect of my manipulation soon became evident. First the lips of Alice's cunt began to pout, then to gape a little, then a little more as if inviting the feather to pass into it—which it did! Then Alice's clitoris commenced to assert itself and to become stiff and rigid, throbbing excitedly; then her whole cunt seemed as if possessed by an irresistible flood of sexual lust and almost to demand mutely the immediate satisfaction of its cravings! Meanwhile Alice, firmly attached to the pillar, went into a paroxysm of contortions and convulsions, wriggling, squirming, writhing, tugging frantically at her fastenings, shrieking, praying, uttering incoherent exclamations and exclamations, her eyes starting out of her head, her quivering lips, her heaving bosom with its wildly palpitating breasts all revealing the agony of body and mind that she was enduring! Fascinated by the spectacle, I continued to torture her by tickling her cunt more and more scientifically and cruelly, noting carefully the spots at which the tickling seemed most felt and returning to those ultra-sensitive parts of her cunt, avoiding only her clitoris—as I felt sure that were this touched, Alice would spend—till her strength became exhausted under the double strain. With a strangled shriek Alice collapsed just as I had forced the feather up her cunt and was beginning to tickle the sensitive interior. Her head fell forward on her bosom, her figure lost its self-supporting rigidity, she hung flaccidly, prevented from falling only by her wrists being shackled together round the pillar! There was nothing to be gained by prolonging the torture, so quickly

ANONYMOUS

I unfastened her, loosed her wrists and ankles from their shackles, and carried her to the large divan-couch, where I gently laid her, knowing that she would soon recover herself and guessing that she now would not need to be kept tied and that she had realised the futility of resistance.

Chapter 6

The couch on which I had placed Alice was one of the cunning pieces of furniture that I had designed for use, should I succeed in capturing her. It was unusually long, nearly eight feet by about three and a half feet wide, upholstered in dark green satin and stuffed in such a way as to be delightfully soft and springy and yet not to allow one's person to sink into it. In appearance it resembled a divan, but in stern reality it was a rack, for at each end there was a concealed mechanism that worked stout leather straps, its object in life being to extend Alice at full length, either on her back or her front (as I might wish), and to maintain her fixed thus while I amused myself with her or worked my cruel will on her! From about halfway down the sides, there issued a pair of supplementary straps also worked by a mechanism, by means of which Alice's legs could be pulled widely apart and held so, should I want to devote myself to her cunt or fuck her against her will.

I did not wish to fatigue her with another useless struggle, so before she recovered the use of her faculties, I attached the corner straps to her wrists and ankles, leaving them quite loose and slack, so that she could move herself freely. Hardly had I effected this when Alice began to come to herself; immediately I quitted her and went to a part of the room where my back would be turned to her, but from which I could nevertheless watch her by means of a mirror.

I saw her draw a deep breath, then slowly open her eyes and look about her as if puzzled. Then, almost mechanically, one of her hands stole to her breasts and the other to her cunt, and she gently soothed these tortured parts by stroking them softly, as if to relieve them of the terrible tickling they had been subjected to! Presently she raised herself to a sitting position, then tried to free herself from the straps on her wrists and ankles.

I now considered that she must have fully recovered, so I returned to her and without a word, I touched the spring and set the mechanism working noiselessly. Immediately the straps began to tighten. As soon as she observed this, Alice started up in fright, at once detecting that she would be spread-eagled on her back if she did not break loose! "No, no, no!" she cried, terrified at the prospect; then she desperately endeavoured to slip out of her fastenings, but the straps were tightening quickly and in the struggle she lost her balance and fell backwards on the couch, and before she could recover herself, she was drawn into a position in which resistance was impossible! With cruel satisfaction, I watched her, disregarding her frenzied appeals for mercy! Inch by inch, she was pulled flatter and flatter, till she rested on her back; then, inch by inch, her dainty legs were drawn asunder, till her heels rested on the edges of the couch! Then I stopped the machinery. Alice was now utterly helpless! In speechless delight, I stood gazing at her lovely body as she lay on her back, panting after her exertions, her bosom heaving and fluttering with her emotions, her face rosy red with shame, her lovely breasts and virgin cunt conspicuously exposed, stark naked, a living Maltese cross!

When I had sufficiently gratified my senses of sight and she had become a little calmer, I quietly seated myself by her waist, facing her feet, then bending over her, I began delightedly to inspect the delicious abode of Alice's maidenhead, her virgin cunt, now so fully exhibited! With sparkling eyes, I noted her full, fleshy mount of Venus, the delicately tinted coral lips quivering under sensations hitherto alien to them, the wealth of close clustering curly hair; with intense delight, I saw that, for a girl of her height and build, Alice had a large cunt, and that her clitoris was well developed and prominent, that the lips were full and her slit easy to open! Intently I scanned its every feature— the sweet junction of her belly and thighs, her smooth plump thighs themselves, the lines of her groin—while Alice lay trembling in an agony of shame and fright, horribly conscious of the close investigation her cunt was undergoing and in terrible dread of the sequel!

Shakespeare sings (in Venus and Adonis):

> *Who sees his true-love in her naked bed,*
> *Teaching the sheets a whiter hue than white,*
> *But, when his glutton eye so full hath fed,*
> *His other agents aim at like delight?*

So it was with me! My hands were tingling to explore the mysteries of Alice's cunt, to wander unchecked over her luscious belly and thighs. My prick was in a horrible state of erection. I could hardly restrain myself from falling on her and ravishing her as she lay there so temptingly helpless. But with a strong effort, I did suppress my rioting lustful desires and tore myself away from Alice's secret charms for a brief spell.

I turned round so as to face her, still seated by her waist, and placed my hands on her lovely breasts. As I lovingly squeezed them, I lowered my face till I almost touched hers, then whispered: "You delicious beauty, kiss me!" at the same time placing my lips on hers. Alice flushed hotly, but did not comply. I had never yet either kissed her or received a kiss from her and was mad for one! "Alice kiss me!" I repeated somewhat sternly, looking threateningly at her and replacing my lips on her mouth. Reluctantly she complied, I felt her lips open as she softly kissed me! It was delicious! "Give me another!" I demanded, putting my right cheek in position to receive it. She complied. "Yet another!" I commanded, tendering my left cheek. Again she complied. "Now give me two more, nice ones, mouth to mouth!" Again came the sweet salute, so maddeningly exciting that, hastily quitting her breasts, I threw my arms round her neck, drew her face to mine, then showered burning kisses on her mouth, eyes and cheeks till she gasped for breath, blushing rosy red. Reluctantly I let her go; then to her dismay, I again turned round and bent over her cunt, and after a long look at it, expressive of the deepest admiration, I gently placed my hands on her belly and, after softly stroking it, began to follow the converging lines of her groin. Alice shrieked in sudden alarm, "No, no—Oh! my God, no, no. . . don't touch me there! . . . Oh! no! not there!" and struggled desperately to break loose. But I disregarded her cries and continued my invasion; soon my itching fingers reached the forest of hairs that covered her mount, she squirming deliciously, then rested on her cunt itself. An agonised shriek of "Oh! . . . Oh!!!" from Alice, as she writhed helplessly with quivering hips, proclaimed my victory and her shame!

Shall I ever forget the sensations of that moment? At last, after weary longings and waitings, Alice's cunt was at my mercy. I not only had it in the fullest possible view, but was actually touching it! My fingers, ranged on either side of the delicate pinky slit, were busy amorously pressing and feeling it, now playing with its silky curly hairs and gently pulling them, now tenderly stroking its sweet lips, now gently opening them so as to expose its coral orifice and its throbbingly agitated clitoris. Resting as I was on Alice's belly, I could feel every quiver and tremor as it passed through her, every involuntary contortion induced by the play of my fingers on this most delicate and susceptible part of her anatomy, the fluttering of her palpitating and heaving bosom. I could hear the involuntary exclamations, the "ohs!"

and the "ahs!" that broke from her in her shame and mental anguish at thus having to endure this handling and fingering of her maiden cunt and the strange half-terrifying sensations thereby provoked!

Half mad with delight, I continued to toy sweetly with Alice's cunt, till sudden unmistakeable wriggles of her bottom and hips and her incoherent exclamations warned me that I was trying her too much, if not goading her into spending, and as I had determined that Alice's first sacrifice to Venus should be induced by the action of my tongue on her cunt, I reluctantly desisted from my delightful occupation, to her intense relief.

Turning round, I again clasped her in my arms, rained hot kisses on her unresisting lips and cheeks, murmuring brokenly: "O Alice! . . . O Alice! . . ." Then pressing my cheek against hers, I rested with her clasped in my arms, her breasts quivering against my chest, till we both grew calmer and her tremblings ceased.

For about five minutes there was dead silence, broken only by Alice's agitated breathing. Soon this ceased, and she seemed to have recovered command of herself again. Then softly I whispered to her "Will you not surrender yourself to me now, Alice dear! surely it is plain to you that you cannot help yourself?"

She drew her face away from me, and murmured: "No, no, I can't, I can't. . . let you. . . have me! O let me go! . . . let me go!!!"

"No." I replied sternly, releasing my clasp of her and resuming my sitting attitude by her waist, "no, my dear! you shan't go till you've been well punished and well fucked! But as I said before, I think you will change you mind presently!"

She looked questioningly at me, fear in her eyes. I rose. Her eyes followed me, and when she saw me select another fine-pointed feather and turn back to her, she instantly divined my intentions and frantically endeavoured to break the ropes that kept her thighs apart, shrieking: "Oh no, no, my God no, I can't stand it! . . . you'll kill me!"

"Oh no, I won't!" I replied quietly, seating myself by her knees, so as to command both her cunt and a view of her struggles which I knew would prove most excitingly delicious! Then without another word, I gently directed the point of the feather against the lowest part of her cunt's virgin orifice, and commenced to tickle her.

Chapter 7

A fearful scream broke from Alice, a violent quivering spasm shook her from head to foot. Her muscles contracted, as she vainly strove to break free. Arching her back she endeavoured to turn herself first on one side and then the other, tugging frantically at the straps, anything as long as she could dodge the feather. But she could do nothing. The more she shrieked and wriggled, the greater was the pleasure she was affording me; so, deaf to her cries and incoherent pleadings, I continued to tickle her cunt, sometimes up and down the slit, sometimes just inside, noting with cruel delight how its lips began to gape open under the sexual excitement now being aroused and how her throbbing clitoris began to erect itself. Alice presented a most voluptuous spectacle: clenched hands, half-closed eyes, heaving breasts, palpitating bosom, plunging hips, tossing bottom, jerking thighs—wriggling and squirming frantically, uttering broken and incoherent exclamations, she shrieked and prayed.

I thought it wise to give her a pause for rest and partial recovery. I withdrew the feather from between the lips of her cunt, then gently stroked them caressingly. "Ah! . . . Ah! . . ." she murmured half unconsciously, closing her eyes. I let her lie still, but closely watched her.

Presently, her eyes opened half dreamily, she heaved a deep breath. I made as if to resume the tickling. "No, no." she murmured faintly, "it's no use! . . . I can't stand it! . . . don't tickle me any more!"

"Well, will you yield yourself to me?" I asked. Alice lay silent for a moment, then with an evident effort said, "Yes!"

Letting the feather fall between her parted legs, I leant forward and took her in my arms: "There must not be any mistake, Alice." I said softly. "Are you willing to let me do to you anything and everything that I may wish?"

Half opening her eyes she nodded her head in assent. "And do you promise to do everything and anything that I may wish you to do?"

She hesitated: "What will you want me to do?" she murmured.

"I don't know." I replied, "but whatever it may be you must do it. Do you promise?"

"Yes!" she murmured, reluctantly.

"Then kiss me, kiss me properly in token of peace!" I whispered in her ear, placing my lips on hers; and deliciously she kissed me, receiving

ANONYMOUS

at the same time my ardent reciprocations. Then I unclasped her and began to play with her breasts.

"Mayn't I get up now?" she murmured, moving herself uneasily as she felt her breasts being squeezed.

"Not just yet, dear." I replied. "I've excited you so terribly that it is only fair to you that I should give you relief, and as I know that in spite of your promise you will not behave as you should do, simply from inexperience, I will keep you as you are till I have solaced you!"

"Oh, what are you going to do to me?" she asked in alarm, in evident fear that she was about to be violated.

"Restore you to ease, dear, by kissing you all over; now lie still and you will enjoy the greatest pleasure a girl can taste and yet remain virgin!"

With heightened colour she resigned herself to her fate. I took her again in my arms, and sweetly kissed her on her eyes, her cheeks, her hair. Then releasing her, I applied my lips to her delicious breasts, and showered burning kisses all over them, revelling in their sweet softness and their exquisite elasticity. Taking each breast in turn, I held it between finger and thumb, then enveloping the dainty little nipple between my lips, I alternately played on it with my tongue and sucked it, all the while squeezing and toying with the breast, causing Alice to experience the most lascivious sensations she had yet known, except perhaps when her cunt was being felt. "Stop! Oh, for God's sake stop!" she exclaimed in her confusion and half fright as to what might happen. "For heaven's sake, stop!" she screamed as I abandoned one breast only to attack the other. But the game was too delightful: to feel her glorious throbbing ripe bubbies in my mouth and quivering under my tongue, while Alice squirmed in her distress, was a treat for a god; so, disregarding her impassioned pleadings, I continued to suck and tongue-tickle them till their sudden stiffening warned me that Alice's sexual instincts were being roused and the result might be a premature explosion when she felt the grand assault on her cunt.

So I desisted reluctantly. Again I encircled her neck with my arms, kissed her pleading mouth and imploring eyes as she lay helpless; then with my tongue I touched her navel. She cried, "No, no, oh! don't." struggling desperately to get free, for it began to dawn on her innocent mind what her real torture was to be. I did not keep her in suspense. Thrusting my hands under her and gripping the cheeks of her bottom so as to steady her plungings, I ran my tongue down lightly over the lines of her abdomen and began tenderly to kiss her cunt. She shrieked in her terror as she felt my lips on those of her cunt, and with frantic wrigglings endeavoured to escape my pursuing mouth. At this critical moment, I lightly ran my tongue along Alice's slit. The effect was astounding! For a moment she seemed to swoon under the subtle titillation, but on my tongue again caressing her cunt, only this time darting deeper between its lips, she went off into a paroxysm of shrieks and cries, wriggling and squirming in a most wonderful way considering how strongly I had fastened her down; her eyes seemed to start out of her head under the awful tickling that she was experiencing; she plunged so frantically that although I was tightly gripping her buttocks she almost dislodged my mouth, the rigid muscles of her lovely thighs testifying to the desperate effort she was making to get loose. But the subtle titillation had aroused her sexual desires, without her recognising the fact in her distress. Her cunt began to open of its own accord, soon the clitoris was revealed turgid and stiff, quivering in sexual excitement, then her orifice began to yawn and show the way to paradise; deeper and deeper plunged my tongue into its satiny recess, Alice mechanically and unconsciously thrusting herself upwards as if to meet my tongue's downward dartings and strokes. Her head rolled from side to side, as, with half-closed eyes, she struggled with a fast increasing feeling that she must surrender herself to the imperious call of her sexual nature, yet endeavouring desperately not to do so under so long established notions of chastity. Her breath came in snatches, her breasts heaved and panted, half-broken exclamations escaped from her quivering lips. The time had arrived for the sacrifice and the victim was ready. Thrusting my tongue as deeply into her cunt as I could force it, I gave her one final and supreme tickling, then taking her clitoris between my lips, I sucked hard at it, the while tickling it with my tongue. . . It was too much for Alice "Stop. . . stop. . . it's coming! . . . it's coming!" she gasped. An irresistible wave of lust swept away the last barriers of chastity, and with a despairing wail: "Oh. . . Oh. . . I. . . can't. . . help. . . it. . . Oh. . . Oh. . . Oh!!!" she spent frantically!

Feeling her go, I sprang to my feet to watch Alice as she spent. It was a wonderful sight! There she lay on her back, completely naked, forced to expose her most secret charm, utterly absorbed in the sensations of the moment, her body pulsating and thrilling with each sexual spasm, her closed eyes, half-open lips and stiff breasts indicating the intensity of the emotions that possessed her. And so she remained for a minute or two, as if in a semi-swoon.

Presently I noticed a relaxing of her muscles; then she drew a long breath and dreamily opened her eyes. For a moment she seemed dazed and almost puzzled to know where she was; then her eyes fell on me, and in flash she remembered everything. A wave of colour surged furiously over her face and bosom at the thought that I had witnessed her unconscious transports and raptures as she yielded herself to her sexual passions in spite of herself; stirring uneasily, she averted her eyes, flushing hotly again. I stooped down and kissed her passionately; then, without a word, I unfastened her, raised her from the settee and supported her to the large armchair, where she promptly curled herself up, burying her blushing face in her hands.

I thought it wisest to leave her undisturbed for a brief space, so busied myself quietly in pouring out two glasses of wine, and knowing what severe calls were going to be made on Alice's innate sexual powers I took the opportunity to fortify these by dropping into her glass the least possible dose of cantharides.

Chapter 8

My readers will naturally wonder what my condition of mind and body was after both had been subjected to such intense inflammation as was inevitable from my close association with Alice dressed and Alice naked.

Naturally I had been in a state of considerable erotic excitation from the moment that Alice's naked charms were revealed, especially when my hands were playing with her breasts and toying with her cunt. But I had managed to control myself. The events recorded in the last chapter however proved too much for me. The contact of my lips and tongue with Alice's maiden lips, breasts and cunt and the sight of her as she spent were more than I could stand, and I was nearly mad with lust and an overwhelming desire that she should somehow provide me with relief.

But how could it be arranged? I wanted to keep her virgin as long as I possibly could, for I had not nearly completed my carefully prepared programme of fondlings and quasi torturings that impart double spice and salaciousness when perpetrated on a virgin. To fuck her therefore was out of the question. Of course there was her mouth, and my blood boiled at the idea of being sucked by Alice; but it was patent that she was too innocent and inexperienced to give me this pleasure. There were her breasts: one could have a delicious time no doubt by using them to form a tunnel and to work my prick between them, but this was a game better played later on. There were her hands, and sweetly could Alice frig me, if she devoted one dainty hand to my prick, while the other played with my testicles, but nothing would be easier than for her to score off me heavily, by giving the latter an innocent wrench which would throw me out of action entirely. The only possible remaining method was her bottom, and while I was feverishly debating its advisability, an innocent movement of hers and the consequent change of attitude suddenly displayed the superb curves and general lusciousness of her posteriors. In spite of my impatience, I involuntarily paused to admire their glorious opulence! Yes! I would bottom-fuck Alice, I would deprive her of one of her maidenheads!

But would she let me do so? True, she had just sworn to submit herself to my caprices whatever they might be, but such a caprice would no doubt never have entered into her innocent mind, and unless she did submit herself quietly, I might be baffled and in the excitement of the struggle and the contact with her warm naked flesh, might spend and "waste my sweetness on the desert air!" Suddenly a cruelly brilliant idea struck me, and at once I proceeded to act on it.

She was still lying curled up in the armchair. I touched her on her shoulder; she looked up hurriedly.

"I think you have rested long enough, Alice." I said. "Now get up, I want you to put me right!" And I pointed to my prick now in a state of terrible erection! "See!" I continued, "you must do something to put it out of its torment, just as I have already so sweetly allayed your lustful cravings!" She flushed painfully! "You can do it either with your mouth or by means of your bottom—now say quick—for I am just bursting with lust for you!"

She hid her face in her hands! "No, no." she exclaimed. "No, oh no! I couldn't, really I couldn't!"

"You must!" I replied somewhat sternly, for I was getting mad with unsatisfied lust. "Remember the promises you have just made! Come now, no nonsense! Say which you'll do!"

She threw herself at my feet. "No, no." she cried, "I can't!"

Bending over her, I gripped her shoulders: "You have just sworn that you would let me do to you anything I pleased, and that you would do anything I might tell you to do; in other words, that you would both actively and passively minister to my pleasures. I have given you your choice! If you prefer to be active, I will lie on my back and you can suck and excite me into spending; if you would rather be passive, you can lie on your face and I will bottom-fuck you! Now which shall it be?"

"No, no, no!" she moaned in her distress, "I can't do either! really I can't!"

Exasperated by her non-compliance, I determined to get by force what I wanted, and before she could guess my intentions, I had gripped her firmly round her body, then half carried and half dragged her to the piano duet stool which also contained a hidden mechanism. On to it I forced her, face downwards, and in spite of her resistance, I soon fixed the straps to her wrists and ankles; then I set the mechanism working, sitting on her to keep her in the proper position, as she desperately fought to get loose. Cleverly managing the straps, I soon got Alice into the desired position, flat on her face and astride the stool, her wrists and ankles being secured to the longitudinal wooden bars that maintained the rigidity of the couch.

Alice was now fixed in such a way that she could not raise her shoulders or bosom, but by straightening her legs, she could heave her bottom upwards a little. Her position was perfect for my purpose, and lustfully I gloated over the spectacle of her magnificent buttocks, her widely parted thighs affording me a view of both of her virgin orifices, both now at my disposal!

I passed my hands amorously over the glorious backside now at my mercy, pinching, patting, caressing and stroking the luscious flesh; my hands wandered along her plump thighs, revelling in their smoothness and softness, Alice squirming and wriggling deliciously! Needless to say her cunt was not neglected, my fingers tenderly and lovingly playing with it and causing her the most exquisitely irritating titillation.

After enjoying myself in this way for a few minutes and having thoroughly felt her bottom, I left her to herself for a moment while I went to a cupboard, Alice watching my movements intently. After rummaging about, I found what I sought, a riding whip of some curious soft substance, very springy and elastic, calculated to sting but not to mark the flesh. I was getting tired of having to use force on Alice to get what I wanted and considered it would be useful policy to make her learn the result of not fulfilling her promises; and there is no better way of bringing a girl to her senses than by whipping her soundly, naked if possible! And here was Alice, naked, fixed in the best possible position for a whipping!

As I turned towards her, whip in hand, she instantly guessed her fate and shrieked for mercy, struggling frantically to get loose. Deaf to her pitiful pleadings, I placed myself in position to command her backside, raised the whip, and gave her a cut right across the fleshiest part.

A fearful shriek broke from her! Without losing time, I administered another, and another, and another, Alice simply now yelling with the pain, and wriggling in a marvellous way considering how tightly she was tied down. I had never before whipped a girl, although I had often read and been told of the delights of the operation to the operator, but the reality far surpassed my most vivid expectations! And the naked girl I was whipping was Alice, the object of my lust, the girl who had jilted me, the girl I was about to ravish! Mad with exultation, I disregarded her agonised shrieks and cries. With cruel deliberation, I selected the tenderest parts of her bottom for my cuts, aiming sometimes at one luscious cheek, then the other, then across both, visiting the tender inside of her widely parted thighs! Her cries were music to my ears in my lustful frenzy, while her wriggles and squirms and the agitated plungings of her hips and buttocks enthralled my eyes. But soon, too soon, her strength began to fail her, her shrieks degenerated into inarticulate exclamations. There was now little pleasure in continuing her punishment, so most reluctantly I ceased.

Soothingly I passed my right hand over Alice's quivering bottom and stroked it caressingly, alleviating in a wonderfully short time the pain. In spite of the severity of the whipping she had received, she was not marked at all! Her flesh was like that of a baby, slightly pinker perhaps, but clean and fresh. As I tenderly restored her to ease, her tremblings died away, her breath began to come more freely and normally, and soon she was herself again.

"Well, has the nonsense been whipped out of you, Alice?" I asked mockingly. She quivered, but did not answer.

"What, not yet?" I exclaimed, pretending to misunderstand her. "Must I give you another turn?" and I raised the whip as if to commence again.

"No, no!" she cried in genuine terror, "I'll be good!"

"Then lie still and behave yourself." I replied, throwing the whip away into a corner of the room.

From a drawer I took a pot of cold cream. Alice who was fearsomely watching every movement of mine, cried in alarm: "Jack, what are you going to do to me? . . . oh tell me!" My only response was to commence to lubricate her arsehole, during which operation she squirmed delightfully; then placing myself full in her sight, I set to work to anoint my rampant prick. "Guess, dear!" I said.

She guessed accurately. For a moment she was struck absolutely dumb with horror, then struggling desperately to get free, she cried: "Oh! my God! . . . no Jack! . . . no! . . . you'll kill me!"

"Don't be alarmed." I said quietly, as I caressed her quivering buttocks; "think a moment—larger things have come out than what is now going in! Lie still, Alice, or I shall have to whip you." Then placing myself in position behind her, I leant forward till the head of my prick rested against her arsehole.

"My God!—no! no!" she shrieked, frantically wriggling her buttocks in an attempt to thwart me. But the contact of my prick with Alice's flesh maddened me; thrusting fiercely forward, I, with very little difficulty, shoved my prick halfway up Alice's bottom with apparently little or no pain to her; then falling on her, I clasped her in my arms and rammed myself well into her, till I felt my balls against her and the cheeks of her bottom against my stomach.

My God! it was like heaven to me! Alice's naked quivering body was closely pressed to mine!—my prick was buried to its hairs in her bottom, revelling in the warmth of her interior! I shall never forget it! Prolonging my rapturous ecstasy, I rested motionless on her, my hands gripping and squeezing her palpitating breasts so conveniently placed for my delectation, my cheek against her averted face, listening to the inarticulate murmurs wrung unconsciously from her by the violence of her emotions and the unaccountably strange pleasure she was experiencing, and which she confessed to by meeting my suppressed shoves with spasmodic upward heavings of her bottom—oh! it was paradise!

Inspired by a sudden thought, I slipped my right hand down to Alice's cunt and gently tickled it with it with my forefinger, but without penetrating. The effect was marvellous! Alice plunged wildly under me with tumultuous quiverings, her bosom palpitating and fluttering: "Ah! . . . Ah! . . ." she exclaimed, evidently a prey to uncontrollable sexual cravings! Provoked beyond endurance I let myself go! For a few moments there was a perfect cyclone of frenzied upheavings from her, mixed with fierce down-thrustings from me, then blissful ecstasy as I spent madly into Alice, flooding her interior with my boiling tribute! "Ah! . . . ah! . . ." she gasped, as she felt herself inundated by my hot discharge! Her cunt distractedly sought my finger, a violent spasm shook her, and with a scarcely articulate cry indicative of the intensest rapture, Alice spent on my finger with quivering vibrations, her head falling forward as she half swooned in her ecstasy!! She had lost the maidenhead of her bottom!!!

For some seconds we both lay silent and motionless, save for an occasional tremor, I utterly absorbed in the indescribable pleasure of spending into Alice as she lay tightly clasped in my arms! She was the first to stir (possibly incommoded by my superincumbent weight), gently turning her face towards me, colouring furiously as our eyes met! I pressed my cheek against hers, she did not flinch but seemed to respond. Tenderly I kissed her, she turned her face fully towards me and of her own accord she returned my kiss! Was it that I had tamed her? Or had she secretly tasted certain pleasure during the violation of her bottom? Clasping her closely to me I whispered: "You have been a good girl this time, Alice! a very good girl!!" She softly rubbed her cheek against mine! "Did I hurt you?" I asked.

She whispered back: "Very little at first, but not afterwards!"

"Did you like it?" I enquired maliciously. For answer she hid her face in the leather seat, blushing hotly. But I could feel her thrill!!

A moment's silence, then she raised her head again, moved uneasily, then murmured: "Oh! let me get up now!"

"Very well." I replied and unclasping my arms from round her, I slowly drew my prick out of her bottom, untied her—then taking her into one of the alcoves I showed her a bidet all ready for her use and left her. Passing into the other, I performed the needful ablutions to myself, then radiant with my victory and with having relieved my overcharged desires, I awaited Alice's reappearance.

Chapter 9

Presently Alice emerged from her screen, looking much freshened up by her ablutions. She further had taken the opportunity to put her hair in order, it having become considerably disarranged and rumpled by her recent strugglings.

Her face had lost the woebegone look, and there was a certain air of almost satisfaction about her which I could not understand, for she smiled as our eyes met, at the same time faintly colouring, and concealing her cunt with her left hand as she approached me.

I offered her a glass of wine, which she drank, then I passed my left arm round her waist and drew her to the armchair, into which I placed myself, making her seat herself on my thighs and pass her right arm round my neck. Then drawing her closely to me, I proceeded to kiss her ripe lips, to which she made no resistance but gave no response.

We sat in silence for a minute or two, I gently stroking her luscious breasts while trying to read in her eyes what her present frame of mind really was, but unsuccessfully. Undoubtedly, during the ravishment of her bottom, she had tasted some pleasure sufficiently delicious to make her condone for its sake her "violation à la derrière" and practically to pardon her violator!—what could it be?

I thought I would try a long shot, so presently whispered in her ear, "Wouldn't you like that last all over again?"

I felt her quiver. She was silent for a moment, then asked softly, "Do you mean as a further punishment?" steadily keeping her eyes averted from me and flushing slightly.

"Oh! no." I replied, "it was so very evident that it was not 'punishment' to you." and I tried to catch her eyes as I pressed her amorously to me. "I meant as a little entr'acte."

Alice blushed furiously! I felt her arm round my neck tighten its embrace, and she nestled herself closer to me! "Not all!" she murmured gently.

"How much then? . . . or which part?" I whispered again.

"Oh! how can I possibly tell you!" she whispered back, dropping her face on to my shoulder and snuggling up to me, then throwing her left arm also round me, thereby uncovering her cunt.

I took the hint! "May I guess?" I whispered.

Without waiting for a reply. I slipped my right hand down from her breasts and over her rounded belly, then began gently to toy with her hairs and caress her slit! Alice instantly kissed me twice passionately! She was evidently hot with lust, inflamed possibly by the dose of cantharides she had unknowingly swallowed!

"Am I right?" I whispered. She kissed me again!

"Then let me arrange you properly." I said. "Come, we'll sit in front of the mirror and look at ourselves!" Alice blushed, not quite approving of the idea, but willing to please me.

So I moved the armchair in front of the mirror and seated myself in it. I then made Alice place herself on my thighs, her bottom being right over my prick, which promptly began to return to life, raising its drooping head until it rested against her posteriors. Passing my left arm round her waist, I held her firmly to me. Then I made her part her legs, placing her left leg between mine while her right leg rested against the arm of the chair, my right thigh in fact separating her thighs.

Alice was now reflected in the mirror in three-quarters profile, but her parted legs allowed the whole of her cunt with its glorious wealth of hair to be fully seen! Her arms hung idly at her sides—I had made her promise not to use them.

We gazed at our reflection for a moment, our eyes meeting in the glass! Alice looked just lovely in her nakedness!

"Are you ready?" I asked with a significant smile. Alice wriggled a little as if to settle herself down more comfortably, then turning her face (now all aflame and rosy red) to me she almost shame-facedly nodded, then kissed me!

"Keep your cheek against mine, and watch yourself in the glass, Alice." I whispered, then I gently placed my right hand on her sweet belly and slowly approached her cunt!

A thrill, evidently of pleasure, quivered through her as she felt my fingers pass through her hairs and settle on her cunt! "Ah!" she murmured, moving deliciously over my prick as I commenced to tenderly frig her, now fingering her slit, now penetrating her still virgin orifice, now tickling her clitoris—causing her all the time the most deliciously lascivious transports, to which she surrendered herself by licentiously oscillating and jogging herself backwards and forwards as if to meet and stimulate my finger!

Presently Alice became still more excited; her breasts stiffened, her nostrils dilated! Noting this, I accelerated the movements of my finger, at the same time clasping her more firmly to me, my eyes riveted on her image in the glass and gloating over the spectacle she presented in her voluptuous raptures! Suddenly she caught her breath! Quickly I tickled her on her clitoris! "Oh! . . . Oh! . . . oh!!!" she exclaimed—then spent in ecstasy, maddening me by the quiverings of her warm buttocks, between which my now rampant prick raged, held down!

I did not remove my finger from Alice's cunt, but kept it in her while she spent, slightly agitating it from time to time, to accentuate her ecstasy. But, as soon as I considered her sexual orgasm had exhausted itself, I began again to frig her. Then an idea flashed through my brain: why should I not share her raptures? Carefully I watched for an opportunity! Soon I worked her again into an awful state of desire; panting with unsatisfied lust and furiously excited (the result of the cantharides!), Alice jerked herself about madly and spasmodically on my thighs! Presently an unusually violent movement of hers released my prick from its sweet confinement under her bottom; promptly it sprang up stark and stiff! Quick as thought, I gripped Alice tightly and rammed myself fiercely into her bottom!! "No! . . . no! . . . no! . . ." she cried and strove to rise and so dislodge me, but I pressed her firmly down on my thighs and compelled her to remain impaled on my prick, creating a diversion by frigging her harder than ever!!

"Kiss me." I gasped, frantic with lust under my sensations in Alice's bottom and the sight of her naked self in the glass, quivering, palpitating, wriggling!! Quickly Alice pressed her lips on mine, our breaths mingled, our tongues met, my left hand caught hold of one of her breasts and squeezed it as her eyes closed. An electric shock ran through her! . . . then Alice spent frantically, plentifully bedewing my finger with her virgin distillation!—at the same moment receiving inside her my boiling essence, as I shot it madly into her, my prick throbbing convulsively under the contractions of her rear sphincter muscles, agitated and activated by her ecstatic transports.

Oh! the sensations of the moment! How Alice spent! How I discharged into her!!

It must have been a full minute before either of us moved, save for the involuntary tremors that, from time to time, ran through us as our sexual excitement died away! Alice, now limp and nerveless, but still impaled on my prick, reposed on me, my finger dwelt motionless in her cunt, luxuriating in its envelope of warm throbbing flesh! And so we rested, exhausted after our lascivious orgy, both half unconscious!

I was the first to come to myself, and as I caught sight of our reflection in the mirror, the licentious tableau we presented sent an involuntary quiver through me which my prick communicated to Alice, thus rousing her! As she dreamily opened her eyes, her glance also fell on the mirror! She started, became suddenly wide-awake, flushed rosy red, then hid her face in her hands, murmuring brokenly: "Oh! . . . how horrible! . . . how horrible! . . . what. . . have you. . . made me do? . . ." half sobbing in her shame now that her sexual delirium had subsided, and horribly conscious that my prick was still lodged in her bottom and impaling her. Foreseeing her action, I brought my right arm to the assistance of my left and held her forcibly down, so preventing her from rising and slipping off me.

"What's the matter, Alice?" I asked soothingly, as she struggled to rid herself of my prick.

"Oh! let me go! let me go!" she begged, still with her face in her hands and in such evident distress that I deemed it best to comply and let her hurry off to her bidet, as she clearly desired.

So I released Alice; she slowly drew her bottom off my prick and rushed behind her screen. Following her example, I repaired to my corner and after the necessary ablutions, I awaited Alice's return.

Chapter 10

Pending Alice's reappearance, I debated with myself the important question, what next should I do to her? There was no doubt that I had succeeded in taming her, that I had now only to state my wishes and she would comply with them! But this very knowledge seemed to destroy the pleasure I had anticipated in having her in such utter subjection; the spice of the proceeding up to now had undoubtedly lain in my forcing her to endure my salacious and licentious caprices, in spite of the most determined and desperate resistance she could make! And once she became a dull and passive surrogate of a proud and voluptuous girl, I should practically be flogging a dead horse were I to continue my programme!

But there was one experience which on no account was to be omitted, forming as it did the culmination of my revenge as well as of my lust, one indignity which she could not and would not passively submit to, one crowning triumph over her which she could never question or deny—and this was. . . her violation!—the ravishing of her maidenhead!!

Alice was now fully educated to appreciate the significance of every detail of the process of transforming a girl into a woman; my fingers and lips had thoroughly taught her maiden cunt its duty, while my prick, when lodged in the throbbing recesses of her bottom, had acquainted her with the phenomenon of the masculine discharge at the crisis of pleasure, of the feminine ecstasy in receiving it, while her transports in my arms, although somewhat restricted by the circumstances, had revealed to her the exquisitely blissful sensations mutually communicated by such close clinging contact of male and female flesh! Yes! I would now devote the rest of the afternoon to fucking her!

Hardly had I arrived at this momentous decision than Alice came out of her alcove after an unusually prolonged absence. She had evidently thoroughly refreshed and revived herself, and she looked simply fetching as she halted hesitatingly on passing through the curtains, shielding her breasts with one hand and her cunt with the other, in charming shame-faced confusion. Obedient to my gesture, she came timidly towards me; she allowed me to pass my arm round her waist and kiss her, and then to lead her to the table where I made her drink a small tumbler of champagne that I had previously poured out for her, and which seemed to be most welcome to her. Then I gently whispered to her that we would lie down together on the couch for a little rest, and soon we were cosily lying at our ease, she pressed and held amorously against me by my encircling arms.

For a minute or two we rested in silence, then the close conjunction of our naked bodies began to have the inevitable result on me—and I think also on her! Clasping her closely against me, I murmured: "Now, Alice darling, I think the time has come for you to surrender to me your maidenhead. . . for you to be my bride!" And I kissed her passionately.

She quivered, moved herself uneasily as if trying to slip out of my encircling arms, trembled exceedingly, but remained silent.

I made as if to place her on her back, whispering: "Open your legs, dear!"

"No! no! Jack!" Alice exclaimed, struggling to defend herself, and successfully resisting my attempt to roll her over on to her back, "let me go, dear Jack! . . . surely you have revenged yourself on me sufficiently!" And she endeavoured to rise.

I held her down firmly and, in spite of her determined resistance, I got her on her back and myself on her. But she kept her legs so obstinately closed that in the position in which I was, I could not get mine between them. I began to get angry. Gripping her to me till her breasts flattened themselves against my chest, I raised my head and looked her sternly in the eyes.

"Now, Alice, no more nonsense." I said brusquely. "I'm going to fuck you! Yield yourself at once to me and do as I tell you or I shall tie you down on this couch and violate you by force in a way you won't like! Now once and for all, are you going to submit or are you not?"

She closed her eyes in an agony of distress.

"Jack! . . . Jack! . . ." she murmured brokenly then stopped as if unable to speak in her emotion.

"I can only take it that you prefer to be ravished by force rather than be treated as a bride! Very well!" I rejoined. And I slipped off her as if to rise and tie her down. But she caught my hand; looked at me so pleadingly and with so piteous an expression in her lovely eyes that I sat down by her side on the couch.

"Upon my word I don't understand you, Alice!" I said, not unkindly. "You have known all along that you were to lose your maidenhead and you have solemnly promised to yield it to me and to conform to all my desires, whatever they might be. Now, when the time has arrived for you to he fucked you seem to forget all your promises!"

"But. . . but. . ." she stammered, "I didn't know. . . then! . . . I thought. . . there. . . was. . . only one way! . . . so. . . I promised! . . . but you. . . have. . . had me twice. . . another way! . . . oh! let me off! . . . do let me off! . . . I can't submit! . . . truly I can't. . . have me again. . . the. . . other way. . . if. . . you must! . . . but not. . . this way! . . . oh! . . . not this way!! . . ."

With my right hand, I stroked her cunt gently, noting how she flinched when it was touched! "I want this virginity, Alice! this virginity of your cunt!—your real maidenhead!—and you must let me have it! Now am I to whip you again into submission? Don't be foolish! you can guess how this whip will hurt when properly applied, as it will be. You know you'll then have to give in! why not do so at once, and spare yourself the pain and indignity of a severe whipping?"

Alice moaned pitifully: "Oh, my God!"—then was silent for a few seconds, her face working painfully in her distress! Then she turned to me: "I must give in!" she murmured brokenly, "I couldn't endure. . . to be whipped. . . naked. . . as I am! . . . so. . . take me. . . and do. . . what you desire! . . . only. . . treat. . . me as kindly. . . as you can! . . . Now. . . I don't know. . . why. . . I ask it. . . but. . . kiss me. . . kiss me. . . let me think. . . I'm. . . your wife. . . and on. . . my wedding night! . . . not. . ."—she stopped, struggling with her emotions, then bravely put up her mouth with a pitiful smile to be kissed.

Promptly I took her lovely naked form lovingly in my arms, and pressing her to me till her breasts flattened against me, I passionately kissed her trembling lips again and again until she gasped for breath. Then stooping, I repeated the caress on each heaving breast and then on her palpitating cunt, kissing the latter over and over again and interspersing my kisses with delicate lingual caresses! Then I succeeded in soothing her natural agitation at thus reaching the critical point of her maiden existence.

Chapter 11

Thus at last Alice and I found ourselves together naked on the Couch of Love!—she, ill at ease and downcast at having thus to yield up her virginity and dreading horribly the process of being initiated by me into the mysteries of sexual love!—I overjoyed at the prospect of soon ravishing Alice and conquering her maidenhead! Side by side on our backs, we lay in silence, my left hand clasping her right, till she had regained her composure a little.

As soon as I saw she had become calmer, I slipped my arms round her, and turning on my side towards her, I drew her tenderly to me, but still keeping her flat on her back; then I kissed her lips again and again ardently, murmuring lovingly between my kisses, "My little wifie! . . . my wee wifie!"—noting delightedly how her downcast face brightened at my adoption of her fantasy, and feeling her respond almost fondly to my kisses.

"May I learn something about my wifie?" I whispered as I placed my right hand on Alice's maiden breasts and began feeling them as if she was indeed my bride! Alice smiled tenderly, yielding herself to my caprice, and quivering anew under the voluptuous sensations communicated to her by my inquisitive fingers. "Oh! what little beauties! oh! what darling bubbies!" I murmured amidst fresh kisses!—Alice now beginning to look quite pleased at my using her own pet name for her treasures and commencing to enter almost heartily into my game. I continued to fondle and squeeze her luscious breasts for a little longer, then carried my hand lower down her, but suddenly arrested it, whispering: "May I?"

At this absurd travesty of a bridegroom's chivalrous respect for his bride Alice fairly laughed (poor girl! her first laugh in that room that day!) then gaily nodded, putting up her lips for more kisses! Overjoyed to see her thus forgetting her woes, I pressed my lips on hers and kept them there, punctuating with kisses the feigningly timid advance of my hand over her belly, till it invaded the precincts of her cunt! "Oh! my darling! . . . oh! my sweetheart! . . . oh! my wifie! . . ." I murmured passionately as my fingers roved wantonly all over Alice's virgin cunt, playing with her hairs, feeling and pressing insidiously but irritatingly its fleshiness, and toying with her slit but not penetrating it! Alice all the while abandoned herself freely to the lascivious sensations induced by my fingerings, jogging her buttocks upwards, waggling her hips, exclaiming "Ah!" and "Oh!" in spite of my lips being glued to hers and nearly suffocating her with kisses!

After a few minutes of this delicious exploitation of the most private part of Alice's body, I stopped my finger on her virgin orifice. "Pardon me, sweet!" I whispered; then gently inserted it into Alice's cunt as far as I could, as whispered; to assure myself as to her virgin condition, all the time smothering her with kisses. Keenly appreciating the comicality of my proceedings, in spite of the serious lover-like air I was assuming, Alice laughed out heartily, unconsciously heaving herself up so as to meet my finger and slightly opening her thighs to allow it freer access to her cunt, my tongue taking advantage of her laughter to dart through her parted lips in search of her tongue, which she then sweetly resigned to my ardent homage! "Oh! wifie! . . . my wifie! . . . my sweet wifie! . . . my virgin wifie! . . ." I murmured, as if enchanted to find her a maid! "Oh! what a delicious cunny you have!—so fat! so soft! so juicy!—wifie!! . . . oh wifie!! . . ." I breathed passionately into her ear, as I agitated my finger inside her cunt, half frigging her and stopping her protests with my kisses, till I saw how I was exciting her! "Little wifie!" I whispered with a grin I could not for the life of me control, "Little wifie! shall I. . . make you come?" In spite of her almost uncontrollable and self-absorbing sexual irritation, Alice laughed out, then nodded, closing her eyes as if in anticipation of her now fast approaching ecstasy! A little more subtle titillation and Alice spent blissfully on my ministering finger, jerking herself about lasciviously and evidently experiencing the most voluptuous raptures and transports!!

I waited till her sexual spasm has ceased: "Wifie!" I whispered, rousing her with my kisses, "little wifie! oh you naughty girl! how you seemed to enjoy it! . . . tell me, wifie! was it then so good?" As she opened her eyes, Alice met mine, brimming with merriment; she blushed rosy red, then clasped me in her soft arms and kissed me passionately, murmuring: "Darling! oh! darling!!" then burst out laughing at our ridiculousness! And so we lay for a few delicious moments, clasped in each other arms.

Presently I murmured: "Now, wifie! you'll like to learn something about me, eh?" Alice laughed merrily at the quaint conceit, then coloured furiously as she remembered that it would mean the introduction of her virgin hands to my virile organs! "Sit up, wifie! dear, and give me your pretty hands." I said.

Alice, now rosy red with suppressed excitement and lust, quickly raised herself to a sitting position at my side. I took her dainty hands in mine, she yielding them rather coyly, turned on my back, opened my legs, and then guided her right hand on to my prick and her left to my testicles, then left her to indulge and satisfy in any manner she saw fit her senses of sight and touch, wondering whether it would occur to her that the fires she was about to excite in me would have to be extinguished in her virgin self when she was being ravished, as before long she would be!

For certainly half a minute, Alice intently inspected my organs of generation, leaning over me and supporting herself by placing her right hand on my stomach and her left on my thigh. I wondered what thoughts passed through her mind as she gazed curiously on what very soon would be the instruments of her violation and the conquerors of her virginity. But she made no sign.

Presently she steadied herself on her left hand, then timidly, with her right hand, she took hold of my prick gently, glancing curiously at me as if to note the effect of the touch of her soft hand on so excitable a part of my person, then smiling wickedly and almost triumphantly as she saw me quiver with pleasure! Oh! the exquisite sensations that accompanied her touch! Growing bolder, she held my prick erect and gently touched my balls with her slender forefinger, as if to test their substance, then took them in her hand, watching me eagerly out of the corner of her eye to note the effect on me! I was simply thrilling with the pleasure! For a few minutes she lovingly played with my organs, generally devoting a hand to each, but sometimes she would hold my prick between one finger and thumb, while with her other hand, she would amuse herself by working the loose folds of skin off and on the knob! At another time, she would place my prick between her soft warm palms and pretend to roll it. Another time she seized a testicle in each hand, oh! so gently! and sweetly caressed them! Had I not taken the edge off my sexual ardour by the two spendings in Alice's bottom, I must have discharged under the tenderly provocative ministration of her fingers! As it was, I had to exercise every ounce of my self-control to prevent an outburst!

Presently I said quietly but significantly: "Little wifie! may I tell you that between husband and wife kissing not only is sanctioned but is considered even laudable!" Alice laughed nervously, glanced quickly at me, then with heightening colour, looked intently at my prick, which she happened at that moment to be grasping tightly in her right hand, its head protruding above her thumb and fingers, while with her left forefinger she was delicately stroking and tickling my balls! After a moment's hesitation, she bent down, squeezed my prick tightly (as if to prevent anything from issuing out of it), then softly kissed its head! Oh! my delicious sensations as her lips touched my prick! Emboldened by the success of her experiment, Alice set to work to kiss my balls sweetly, then passed her lips over the whole of my organs of generation, showering kisses on them, but favouring especially my balls, which had for her a wonderful attraction, burying her lips in my scrotum, and (I really believe!) tonguing them! Such attentions could only end in one way! Inflamed almost beyond endurance by the play of her sweetly irritating lips, my prick became so stiff and stark that Alice in alarm thought she had better cease her ministrations, and with blushing cheeks and a certain amount of trepidation, she lay herself down alongside of me.

By this time I was so mad with lust that I could hardly control myself, and as soon as Alice lay down I seized her in my arms, drew her to me, showered kisses on her lips, then with an abrupt movement, I rolled her over on to her back, slipping on top of her. In an effort to counteract my attack she separated her legs the better to push me back! Quick as thought, I forced myself between them.

Now is she in the very lists of love, Her champion mounted for the hot encounter. SHAKESPEARE, Venus and Adonis

Alice was at my mercy! I could not have her at better advantage! She struggled desperately to dislodge, me, but to no avail!

Gripping her tightly, I got my stiff and excited prick against the lips of her cunt, then pushing steadily, I drove it into Alice, burying its head in her. Despite her fearful struggles and rapid movements of her buttocks and hips, I made another thrust, entering still further into her cunt, then felt myself blocked! Alice screamed agonisedly, "Oh! . . . oh! stop! . . . you're hurting me!" throwing herself wildly about in her pain and despair, for she recognised that she was being violated! Knowing that it was her maiden membrane that was stopping my advance into her, and that this now was the last defence of her virginity, I rammed into her vigorously! Suddenly I felt something give way inside her and my prick glided well up her cunt, and it did not require the despairing shriek that came from Alice to tell me that I had broken through the last barriers and had conquered her virginity!

Oh! my exultation! At last I had ravished Alice, I had captured her maidenhead, and was now actually fucking her in spite of herself! She, poor girl, lay beneath me, tightly clasped in my arms, a prey to the keenest shame, deprived of her maidenhead, transfixed with my prick, her cunt suffering martyrdom from its sudden distension and smarting with the pain of her violation! Pitying her, I lay still for some seconds so as to allow the interior of her cunt to stretch a bit, but I was too wrought up and mad with lust to remain inactive long in such surroundings.

With a final thrust, I sent my prick well home, Alice's hairs and mine interweaving. She shrieked again! Then agitating myself gently on her, I began to fuck her, first with steady strokes of my buttocks, then with more rapid and uneven shoves and thrusts, she quivering under me, overwhelmed by her emotions at thus finding her pure body compelled to become the recipient of my lust and by the strangely delicious pleasure that the movements of my prick inside her cunt were arousing in her! Alice no longer struggled, but lay passive in my arms, unconsciously accommodating herself to my movements on her, and involuntarily working her hips and bottom, instinctively yielding to the promptings of her now fast-increasing sexual cravings by jogging herself up as if to meet my down-thrusts!

Shall I ever forget my sensations at that moment? Alice, the long desired Alice, the girl of all girls, the unconscious object of my concupiscence—Alice lay underneath me, tightly clasped in my arms, naked, quivering, her warm flesh throbbing against mine, my prick lodged in her cunt, her tearful face in full sight, her breasts palpitating and her bosom heaving in her agitation!—gasping, panting in the acutest shame and distress at being violated, yet unconsciously longing to have her sexual desires satisfied while dreading the consummation of her devirginisation! I could no longer control myself. Clasping her yielding figure still more closely against me, I let myself go—thrusting, ramming, shoving and agitating my prick spasmodically in her, I frenziedly set to work to fuck her! A storm of rapid tumultuous jogs, a half strangled "oh! . . . oh!! . . . oh!!! . . ." from Alice and I spent deliriously into her, deluging her with my hot discharge, at the same moment feeling the head of my prick christened by the warm gush that burst from Alice as she also frantically spent, punctuating the pulsations of her discharge by voluptuous upheavings of her wildly agitated bottom.

I remained master of myself notwithstanding my ecstatic delirium, but Alice fainted under the violence of the sexual eruption for the first time legitimately induced within her! My warm kisses on her upturned face however soon revived her. When she came to herself and found herself still lying naked in my arms and harbouring my prick in the freshly opened asylum of her cunt, she begged me to set her free! But she had not yet extinguished the flames of lust and desire which her provocative personality and appetising nakedness had kindled and which she had stimulated to white heat by the tender manipulations and kisses she had bestowed on my testicles and prick! The latter still remained rampant and stiff and burned to riot again within the deliciously warm and moist recesses of Alice's cunt—while I longed to make her expire again in the sweet agonies of satisfied sexual desire, and to witness and share her involuntary transports and wondrous ecstasies as she passed from sexual spasm to spasm while being sweetly fucked!

So I whispered amidst my kisses: "Not yet, Alice! not yet! once more, Alice! you'll enjoy it this time!"—then began gently to fuck her again.

"No! no! . . ." she cried, plunging wildly beneath me in her vain endeavours to dislodge me, "not again! . . . oh! not again! Let me go! . . . stop! . . . oh! please, do stop!" she implored, almost in tears, and in terrible distress at the horrible prospect of being ravished a second time.

I only shook my head negatively, and endeavoured to stifle her cries with my kisses. Seeing that I was determined to enjoy her again, Alice, now in tears, ceased her pleadings and resigned herself to her fate.

In order to control more easily her struggles, I had thrown my arms over hers, thus pinioning them in my grip of herself. Seeing now that she did not intend to resist me, except perhaps passively, I relaxed my embrace, set her arms free, passed mine round her body, then whispered: "Hug me tightly, you'll be more comfy now, Alice!" She did so. "That's much better, isn't it?" I murmured. She tearfully smiled, then nodded affirmatively, putting up her lips to be kissed.

"Now just lie quietly and enjoy yourself." I whispered, then began to fuck her with slow and steady piston-like thrusts of my prick up and down her cunt. At once Alice's bosom and breasts commenced to palpitate under me, fluttering deliciously against my chest. Exercising the fullest control I possibly could bring to bear on my seminal reserves, so as to prolong to the utmost extent my voluptuous occupation, and that Alice should have every opportunity of indulging and satisfying her sexual appetites and cravings and of fully tasting the delights of copulation, I continued to fuck her steadily, watching her blushing upturned face and learning from her tell-tale eyes how she was getting on.

Presently she began to agitate her hips and jog herself upwards, then her breath came and went quickly, her eyes turned upwards and half closed, a spasm convulsed her. . . she spent! I stopped for a moment. After a few seconds, Alice opened her eyes, blushing rosy red as she met mine. I kissed her lips tenderly, whispering "Good?" She nodded and smiled. I resumed. Soon she was again quivering and wriggling under me, as a fresh wave of lust seized her; again her eyes closed and again Alice spent blissfully! I saw that I had now thoroughly roused her sexual desires and that she had surrendered herself to their domination and that they were imperiously demanding satisfaction!

I clasped her closely to me, whispered quickly: "Now, Alice, let yourself go!" And set to work in real earnest, thrusting rapidly and ramming myself well into her! Alice simply abandoned herself to her sensations of the moment! Hugging me to her, she agitated herself wildly under me, plunging madly, heaving herself furiously upwards, tossing her head from side to side—she seemed as if overcome and carried away by a torrent of lust and madly endeavouring to satisfy it. I could hardy hold her still. How many times she spent I do not know, but her eyes were constantly half closing and opening again as spasm after spasm convulsed her. Suddenly she exclaimed frenziedly: "Now! . . . Now! let me have it! . . . let me have it all! . . ." Immediately I responded—a few furious shoves, and I poured my boiling essence into Alice, spending frantically in blissful ecstasy! "Ah! . . . Ah! . . ." she cried, quivering in rapturous transports as she felt herself inundated by my warm discharge!—then a paroxysm swept through her, her head fell back, her eyes closed, her lips opened as she spent convulsively in her turn!

She fainted right away! it had been too much for her! I tried to bring her to herself by kisses and endearments, but did not succeed. So I drew my prick cautiously out of Alice's cunt, all bloodstained, staunched with a handkerchief the blood, etc., that oozed out of Alice and bore unimpeachable evidence of the rape that had been committed on her virginity, and sprinkled her face with water.

When at length she came to, I assisted her to rise, as she seemed half dazed, and supported her as she tottered to her alcove, where she half fell into a low chair. I brought her a glass of wine which she drank gratefully, and which somewhat revived her. Then I saw that she had everything she could want—water, soap, syringe, towels, etc. She asked me to leave her, adding she was now all right. Before doing so, I stooped down to receive the first kiss she would give as a woman, having had her last as a girl. Alice threw her arms round my neck, drew my face to hers, then kissed me passionately over again, quite unable to speak because of her emotion! I returned her kisses with interest, wondering whether she was wishing to make me comprehend that she pardoned me for violating her!

Presently Alice whispered: "May I dress now?" I had intended to have fucked her again, but I saw how overwrought she was; beside that, the afternoon was late and there was just comfortable time left for her to catch her train home. So I replied, "Yes, dear, if you like; shall I bring your clothes here?" She nodded gratefully. I carefully collected her garments and took them to her, then left her to herself to dress; pouring out a bumper of champagne, I celebrated silently but exultingly the successful completion of my vengeance and my victory over Alice's virginity, then retired to my alcove and resumed my garments.

In about a quarter of an hour Alice appeared, fully dressed, hatted and gloved. I threw open the doors and she passed out without a word but cast a long comprehensive glance round the room in which she had passed so memorable an afternoon. I called a hansom, placed her in it and took her to her station in plenty of time for her train; she was very silent during the drive but made no opposition when I took her hand in mine and gently stroked it. As the train started, I raised my hat with the customary salute, to which she responded in quite her usual pleasant way; no one who witnessed our parting would have dreamt that the pretty ladylike girl had just been forcibly ravished by the quiet gentlemanly man, after having first been stripped naked and subjected to shocking indignities! And as I drove home, I wondered what the outcome of that afternoon's work would be.

VOLUME II
THE COMEDY

Chapter 1

I will now tell my readers that four months have elapsed since the events recorded in the previous volume. During this period, Alice and I had frequently met at the houses of mutual friends who were under the impression that by thus bringing us together, they were assisting in making a match between us. Our rapture was known only to our two selves, and Alice had quickly recognized that complete silence as to what had happened to her in my Snuggery was her safest policy. And really, there was some excuse for the incorrect impression under which our friends were laboring, for our mutual embarrassment, when we first met after her violation, and her inability to altogether subdue on subsequent occasions a certain agitation and heightened color when I appeared on the scene, were to be symptoms of the "tender passion" that was supposed to be consuming us both.

But Alice's manner to me insensibly became kinder and kinder as time went on. Unknown to herself, there was in her composition a strain of strong sensuality which had lain dormant under the quiet peacefully virtuous life of an English Miss that she had hitherto led; and it only wanted some fierce sexual stimulant to fan into flame the smoldering fires of her lust. This now had been supplied.

She afterwards confessed to me that, when the sense of humiliation and the bitter regrets for her ravished virginity had died down, she found herself recalling certain moments in which she had tasted the most exquisite pleasure, in spite of the dreadful indignities to which her stark naked self was being submitted, and then unconsciously beginning to long to experience them again till a positive, though unacknowledged, craving sprang up, which she was quite unable to stifle but did not know how to satisfy! When such promising conditions prevail, kind Mother Nature and sweet lady Venus generally come into operation. Soon Alice began to feel towards me the tender regard that every woman seems to cherish towards the fortunate individual who has taken her maidenhead! As I have just stated, she became kinder and kinder, till it was evident to me that she had pardoned my brutality. Instead of almost shrinking from me, she undoubtedly seemed to welcome me and was never averse to finding herself alone with me in quiet corners and nooks for two.

On my side, I was beginning to experience a fierce desire once more to hold her naked in my arms and revel in the delights of her delicious person, to taste her lips as we mutually spent in each other's clasped embrace, in other words, to fuck her! Kind Mother Nature had taken us both into her charge: now sweet lady Venus came on the scene.

One evening, Alice and I met at the house of a lady hostess, who placed us together at the dinner table. I naturally devoted myself to Alice afterwards in the drawing room. When the guests began to depart, our hostess asked me if I would mind seeing Alice home in my taxicab, which, of course, I was delighted to do. Strangely enough, the possibilities of a tête-à-tête did not occur to me, and it was only when Alice returned to the hall cloaked and veiled and our hostess had told her that I had very kindly offered to take her home in my taxi that the opportunity of testing her real feelings was suggested to me by the vivid blush that, for a moment, suffused her face and elicited a sympathetic but significant smile from our hostess, who evidently thought she had done us both a good turn. And so she had, but not in the direction she fondly thought!

The taxi had hardly begun to move when we both seemed to remember that we were alone together for the first time since the afternoon on which Alice had been first tortured scientifically, and then ravished! Overcome by some sudden inspiration, our eyes sought each other. In the dim light, I saw Alice's face working under the rush of her emotion, but she was looking at me with eyes full of love and not of anger. She began to cuddle up against me perhaps unconsciously, at the same time turning her face up as if seeking a kiss. I could not resist the mute invitation. Quickly I slipped my left arm 'round her, drew her to me (she yielding to me without a struggle), pressed my lips on hers and fondly rained kisses on her mouth. "Jack!" she murmured lovingly. I felt her thrill under my kisses, then catch her breath and quiver again! I recognized the symptoms. Promptly I slipped my right hand under her clothes, and before she could offer any resistance (even had she desired to do so, which she evidently did not), my hand had reached the sweet junction of her belly and thighs and my fingers began to attack the folds of her chemise through the opening of her drawers in their feverish impatience to get at her cunt! "Jack! Oh, Jack!" Alice again murmured as she pressed herself against me as closely as she could, while at the same time she began to open her thighs slightly, as if to facilitate the operations of my ardent fingers, which, just at that moment succeeded in displacing the last obstacle and were now resting on her cunt itself.

Alice quivered deliciously at the touch of my hand on her bare flesh as I gently and tenderly stroked her cunt, playing lovingly on its moist palpitating lips and twining her hairs 'round my fingers, but as soon as she felt me tickle her clitoris (time was short and we were fast nearing her rooms, besides which it would have been cruel to have aroused her sexual passions without satisfying them), she threw all restraint to the winds and madly agitated her cunt against my hand, wiggling divinely as I set to work frigging her. Soon came the first blissful ecstasy; a delicious spasm thrilled through her as she spent deliriously on my fingers—then another—and another—and yet another—till, unable to spend any more, she gasped brokenly: "Stop, Jack! . . . I can't go on!" only half-conscious and utterly absorbed in the overpoweringly exquisite sensations of the moment and the delicious satisfying of the longings and cravings which had been tormenting her. It was full time that we stopped, for the taxi was now turning into her street.

Quickly (but reluctantly) I withdrew my hand from Alice's cunt, now moist with her repeated spendings, and I just managed to get her clothes into some sort of order when the cab stopped at her door. I sprang out first and assisted Alice to alight, which she did almost totteringly as she had not yet recovered from her trance of sexual pleasure.

"I'll see you right into your rooms, so that I may be able truly to report that I have faithfully executed the orders," I said laughingly, more for the benefit of the chauffeur than of Alice.

"Thanks very much!" she replied quietly, and, having collected her wraps, I followed her into the house and up the staircase to her apartments on the first floor, carefully closing the door after me.

Alice threw herself into my arms in an ecstasy of delight. I rather think that she expected me to take the opportunity to fuck her—and gladly would I have done so, as I was in a terrible state of lust: but I always hated "snatchfucking" and if I started with her long enough for her to undress and be properly fucked, it might arouse suspicions that would damage her reputation.

So after a passionate embrace, I whispered, "I must not stop here, darling: when will you come to lunch?"

Alice blushed deliciously, instantly comprehending the significance of my invitation. "Tomorrow!" she murmured, hiding her face on my shoulder.

"Thanks, sweetheart—tomorrow then! Now get to bed and have a good night's rest. Good night my darling!" and after a few more passionate kisses, I left her and rejoined my taxi.

Next morning, after ordering a lunch cunningly calculated to excite and stimulate Alice's lascivious instincts, I made the usual tour of inspection 'round my flat, and from sheer force of habit, I began to test the mechanism concealed in the Snuggery furniture, then suddenly remembered that its assistance was now no longer needed; it had done its duty faithfully; with its help I had stripped, tortured, and violated Alice—and today she was coming of her own free will to be fucked.

The reflection that I would now have to dismantle all this exquisite machinery caused me quite a pang—then I found myself wondering whether it would not be as well to let it remain—on the off chance of its being useful on some later occasion.

In my circle of acquaintants, there were many pretty and attractive girls, married and unmarried, and, if I could only lure some of them into the Snuggery, the torturing and ravishing of them would afford me the most delicious of entertainment, although the spice of revenge that pervaded my outraging of Alice would be absent!

But how was I to effect the luring? They were not likely to come to lunch alone with me, and if accompanied by anyone, it would simply mean that I should again experience the irritating disappointments that I suffered when Marion used to accompany Alice, and, by her presence, prevent the accomplishment of my desires. Besides this, many of the girls I lusted after were hardly more than casual acquaintances whom I could not venture to invite to my flat, except in the company of some mutual friend.

Therein came my inspiration—why not try and induce Alice herself to act as decoy and assistant? If I could only instill in her a taste for Sadism and Sadique pleasures and a penchant for her own sex, and let her see how easily she could satisfy such lascivious fancies by cooperating with me, the possibilities were boundless!

A luncheon invitation to her and our selected victim would, in nine cases out of ten, be accepted by the latter; after lunch, the adjournment to the Snuggery would follow as a matter of course at her suggestion—and then her assistance in stripping the girls would be invaluable, after which we could, together, put the girl through a course of sexual torture, painless but distressingly effective, and quench in each other the fires of lust which would spring up as we gloated over our victim's shame and mental agony! Yes! Here was the solution of the difficulty; somehow or other, I must induce Alice to give me her cooperation.

Chapter 2

I will not take up my readers' time by detailing the incidents of Alice's visit.

She was exceedingly nervous and so timid that I saw it was absolutely necessary for me to treat her with the greatest tenderness and delicacy and in no way to offend her susceptibility. She yielded herself to me with pretty bashfulness, blushing divinely when I drew off her last garment and exposed her naked body to my eager eyes; and her transports of delirious pleasure during her first fucking were such that I shall never forget! I had her four delicious times—and when she left, I felt certain that it only wanted a little diplomacy to secure her cooperation!

She, naturally, was more at her ease on her next visit, and I ventured to teach her the art of sucking! When her sweet lips for the first time received my eager prick between them and her warm tongue made its first essays in the subtle art of titillation, I experienced the most heavenly bliss—such as I had never tasted before at the mouth of any woman; and when, after prolonging my exquisite rapture till I could no longer restrain myself, I spent in her mouth in a delirium of pleasure, her pretty confusion was something to be remembered!

I thought I might safely venture to convert her when she paid her third visit, and to this end, I selected from my collection of indecent photographs several that told their tale better than could be expressed by words. Among these was a series known as the "Crucifixion," in which a lovely girl (evidently a nun from her despoiled garments scattered on the floor) was depicted bound naked to a cross, while sometimes the Lady Abbess (in her robes) alone, and sometimes in conjunction with one of the Sisters, indulged their wanton fancies and caprices on the poor girl's breasts and cunt as she hung helpless! One photograph showed the girl fastened naked to a Maltese Cross, the Lady Abbess had inserted her finger into the Nun's cunt while the Sister tickled the Nun's clitoris! In another photograph, a monk was introduced who, kneeling before the Nun (still fastened on a Maltese Cross) sucked her cunt while his uplifted hands, in the attitude of prayer, attacked her helpless breasts! Another series, entitled "La Barrière" depicted various phases in the ravishment of a girl by two ruffians in a solitary part of the Bois de Boulogne.

The rest were mostly scenes of Tribadism and of Lesbian love, and interspersed with them were a few representing flagellation by a girl on a girl, both being stark naked!

I was puzzled how best to lead up to the subject, when Alice herself gave me the desired opening. We had just finished our first fuck and were resting on the broad couch, lying in each other's arms, her gentle hand caressing my prick with a view to its restoration to life. She had been rather more silent than usual, for she generally was full of questions which she used to ask with pretty hesitation and delicious naivety—and I was cudgeling my brains to invent a suitable opening.

Suddenly Alice turned to me and said softly, "Jack, I'd awfully like to know one thing!—when you had me tied up tight on that dreadful afternoon and. . . did all sorts of awful things to me, did it give you any pleasure besides the satisfaction of revenging yourself on me?"

"Will you hate me if I confess, dear, that the sight of your agony, shame, and distress, as you struggled naked, gave me intense pleasure!" I replied as I drew her once more closely against me. "I knew I wasn't hurting you or causing you bodily pain; and the knowledge that your delicious wriggling and writhing, as you struggled naked to get loose, was instigated by your shame at being naked and your distress at finding your sexual passions and instincts aroused in spite of yourself, and irritated till you could no longer control them, and so felt yourself being forced to do what was so horribly repugnant to you, in other words. . . to. . . spend!—and not only to spend, but to spend with me watching you! All this gave me the most extraordinary pleasure! When I stopped to let you have a little rest or else put you into another position, I felt the pleasure arising from vengeance gratified, but when I began again to torture you, especially when I was tickling your cunt with a feather, while you were fastened down on your back with legs tied widely apart, I must confess that the pleasure was the pleasure of cruelty! My God! darling, how you did wriggle then!"

"I thought I would have died!" Alice whispered as she snuggled up against me (apparently not displeased by my confession), yielding herself sweetly to the pressure of my encircling arm. "I wasn't in pain at all, but oh! my sensations! My whole self seemed to be concentrated just. . . where you were tickling me! and I was nearly mad at being forced to endure such indignity; and on top of it all came that awful tickling, tickling, tickling!"

She shuddered at the recollection; I pressed her still more tightly against me and kissed her tenderly, but held my tongue—for I knew not what to say! Presently Alice spoke again. "And so it really gave you pleasure to torture me, Jack?" she asked almost cheerfully, adding before I could reply, "I was very angry with my maid this morning and it would have delighted me to have spanked her severely. Now, would such delight arise from revenge or from being cruel?"

"Undoubtedly from being cruel," I replied, "the infliction of the punishment is what would have given you the pleasure, and behind it would come the feeling that you were revenging yourself. Here's another instance—you women delight in saying nasty, cutting things to each other in the politest of ways. Why? Not from revenge, but from the satisfaction afforded by the shot going home. If you had given your maid a box on the ears this morning, you would have satisfied your revenge without any pleasure whatever; but if I had been there and held your maid down while you spanked her bottom, your pleasure would have arisen from the infliction of the punishment. Do you follow me, dear?"

"Yes, I see it now," Alice replied, then added archly, "I wish you had been there, Jack! It would have done her a lot of good!"

"I sometimes wonder why you keep her on," I said musingly. "She's a pert minx and at times must be very aggravating. Let me see—what's her name?"

"Fanny."

"Yes, of course—a case of 'pretty Fanny's way,' for she certainly is a pretty girl and a well-made one. My dear, if you want to do bottom slapping, you won't easily find a better subject, only I think she will be more than you can manage single-handed, and it may come to her slapping your bottom, my love!"

Alice laughed. "Fanny is a most perfect maid, a real treasure, or I would not keep her on—for as you say, she is too much for me. She's very strong and very high-spirited, but wants taming badly."

"Bring her some afternoon, and we'll tame her between us!" I suggested, seemingly carelessly, but with well-concealed anxiety, for was I not now making a direct attempt to seduce Alice into Sadism?

Alice started, raised herself on her elbows, and regarded me questioningly. I noticed a hard glitter in her eyes, then she caught her breath, colored, and exclaimed softly, "Oh, Jack, how lovely it would be!"

I had succeeded! Alice had succumbed to the sudden temptation!

For the second time, her strain of lascivious sexuality had been conquered.

"Shall we try?" I asked with a smile, secretly delighted at her unconcealed eagerness and noting how her eyes now brimmed over with lust and how her lovely breasts were heaving with excitement.

"Yes! Yes! Jack!" she exclaimed feverishly, "but how can it be managed?"

"That shouldn't be much trouble," I replied. "Take her out with you shopping some afternoon close by here, then say you want to just pop in to see me about something. En route, tell her about this room, how it's sound-proof. It will interest her and she will at the same time learn information that will come in useful later on. Once in here, follow my lead. I suppose you would like to have a hand in torturing her?"

"Oh! Jack! Will you really torture Fanny?" exclaimed Alice, her eyes sparkling with eagerness. "Will you fasten her down as you did me?"

I nodded.

"Yes! Yes! Let me have a turn at her!" she replied vivaciously. Then after a pause she looked queerly at me and added, "And will you. . ." At the same moment she significantly squeezed my prick.

"I think so, unless of course you would rather I didn't, dear," I replied with a laugh. "I suppose you have no idea whether she is a virgin or not?"

"I can't say!" Alice replied, blushing a little. "I've always fancied she was and have treated her as such."

"And what sort of treatment is that?" I queried mischievously, and was proceeding to cross-question Alice when she stopped me by putting her hand over my mouth.

"Well, we'll soon find out when we get her here," I remarked philosophically, much to her amusement. "But, darling, your lessons in the Art of Love are being neglected; let us resume them. There is just time for one—I think you must show me that you haven't forgotten Soixante-neuf!"

Alice blushed prettily, slipped out of my embrace, and soon her cunt was resting on my lips while her gentle hands and mouth busied themselves with my delighted prick and balls! She worked me so deliciously that she made me spend twice in her mouth, by which time I had sucked her completely dry! Then we reluctantly rose to perform the necessary ablutions and resume our clothes.

"When shall I bring Fanny here, Jack?" asked Alice as she was saying goodbye to me.

"Oh! You naughty, lustful, cruel girl!" I exclaimed with a laugh in which she somewhat shamefacedly joined. "When do you think?"

"Will. . . tomorrow afternoon do?" she asked, avoiding my eyes.

"Yes, certainly," I replied, kissing her tenderly. "Let it be tomorrow afternoon!" And so we parted.

This is how it came to pass that Alice's first experiments in Sadique pleasures were to be made on the person of her own maid.

Chapter 3

Next afternoon, after seeing that everything was in working order in the Snuggery, I threw open both doors as if carelessly, and taking off my coat as if not expecting any visitors, I proceeded to putter about the room, keeping a vigilant eye on the stairs. Before long, I heard footsteps on the landing but pretended not to know that any one was there till Alice tapped merrily on the door saying, "May we come in, Jack?"

"Good Heavens! Alice?" I exclaimed in pretended surprise as I struggled hurriedly to get into my coat. "Come in! How do you do? Where have you dropped from?"

"We've been shopping—this is my maid, Jack"—(I bowed and smiled, receiving in return a distinctly pert and not too respectful nod from Fanny)—"and as we were close by, I thought I would take the chance of finding you in and take that enlargement if it is ready."

By this time I had struggled into my coat. "It's quite ready," I replied. "I'll go and get it, and I don't know why those doors should stand so unblushingly open," I added with a laugh.

Having closed them, noiselessly locking them, I disappeared into the alcove I used for myself, and pretended to search for the enlargement—my real object being to give Alice a chance of letting Fanny know the nature of the room. Instinctively she divined my idea, and I heard her say, "This is the room I was telling you about, Fanny—look at the double doors, the padded walls, the rings, the pillars, the hanging pulley straps! Isn't it queer?"

Fanny looked about her with evident interest. "It is a funny room, Miss! And what are those little places for?" she asked, pointing to the two alcoves.

"We do not know, Fanny," Alice replied. "Mr. Jack uses them for his photographic work now."

As she spoke, I emerged with a large print which was to represent the supposed enlargement, and gave it to Alice who at once proceeded to closely examine it.

I saw that Fanny's eyes were wandering all over the room, and I moved over to her. "A strange room Fanny, eh?" I remarked. "Is it not still; no sound from outside can get in, and no noise from inside can get out! That's a fact; we've tested it thoroughly!"

"Lor', Mr. Jack!" she replied in her forward familiar way, turning her eyes on me in a most audacious and bold way, then resuming her survey of the room.

While she was doing so, I hastily inspected her. She was a distinctly pretty girl, tall, slenderly but strongly built, with an exquisitely well-developed figure. A slightly turned-up nose and dark flashing eyes gave her face a saucy look, which her free style of moving accentuated, while her dark hair and rich coloring indicated a warm-blooded and passionate temperament. I easily could understand that Alice, with her gentle ways, was no match for Fanny, and I fancied that I should have my work cut out for me before I got her arms fastened to the pulley ropes.

Alice now moved towards us, print in hand. "Thanks awfully, Jack, it's lovely!" and she began to roll it up. "Now, Fanny, we must be off!"

"Don't bother about the print, I'll send it after you," I said. "And where are you off to now?"

"Nowhere in particular," she replied. "We'll look at the shops and the people.

Good-bye, Jack!"

"One moment," I interposed. "You were talking the other day about some perfection of a lady's maid that you didn't want to lose"— (Fanny smiled complacently)—"but whose tantrums and ill tempers were getting to be more than you could stand." (Fanny here began to look angry.) "Somebody suggested that you should give her a good spanking"—(Fanny assumed a contemptuous air)—"or, if you couldn't manage it yourself, you should get someone to do it for you!" (Fanny here glared at me.) "Is this the young lady?"

Alice nodded, with a curious glance at Fanny, who was now evidently getting into one of her passions.

"Well, as you've nothing to do this afternoon, and she happens to be here, and this room is so eminently suitable for the purpose, shall I take the young woman in hand for you and teach her a lesson?"

Before Alice could reply, Fanny with a startled exclamation darted to the door, evidently bent on escape, but in spite of her vigorous twists of the handle, the door refused to open, for the simple reason that, unnoticed by her, I had locked it. Instantly divining that she was a prisoner, she turned hurriedly 'round to watch our movements, but she was too late! With a quickness learned on the football field, I was onto her and pinned her arms to her sides in a grip that she could not break out of, despite her frantic struggles. "Let me go! Let me go, Mr. Jack!" she screamed. I simply chuckled as I knew I had her safe now! I had to exert all my strength and skill, for she was extraordinarily strong and her furious rage added to her power, but in spite of her desperate resistance, I forced her to the hanging pulleys where Alice was eagerly waiting for us. With astonishing quickness she made fast the ropes to Fanny's wrists and set the machinery going—and in a few seconds the surprised girl found herself standing erect with her arms dragged up taut over her head! "Well done, Jack!" exclaimed Alice, as she delightedly surveyed the still struggling Fanny! The latter was indeed a lovely subject of contemplation, as with heaving bosom, flushed cheeks, and eyes that sparkled with rage, she stood panting, endeavoring to get back her breath, while her agitated fingers vainly strove to get her wrists free from the pulley ropes. We watched her in victorious silence, waiting for the outbursts of wrathful fury that we felt would come as soon she was able to speak!

It soon came! "How dare you, Mr. Jack!" Fanny burst out as she flashed her great piercing eyes at us, her whole body trembling with anger. "How dare you treat me like this? Let me loose at once, or, as sure as I am alive, I'll have the law on you and also on that mealy-mouthed smooth-faced demure hypocrite who calls herself my mistress. Indeed! She who looks on while a poor girl is vilely treated and won't raise a finger to help her! Let me go at once, Mr. Jack! and I'll promise to say and do nothing; but my God!"—(here her voice became shrill with overpowering rage)—"my God! if you don't, I'll make it hot for the pair of you when I get out!" And she glared at us in her impotent fury.

"Your Mistress has asked me to give you a lesson, Fanny," I replied calmly, "and I'm going to do so! The sooner you recognize how helpless you really are, and submit yourself to us, the sooner it will be over; but if you are foolish enough to resist, you'll have a long doing and a bad time! Now, if I let you loose, will you take your clothes off quietly?"

"My God! No!" she cried indignantly, but, in spite of herself she blushed vividly! "Then we'll take them off for you!" was my cool reply. "Come along, Alice, you understand girl's clothes. You undo them and I'll get them off somehow!"

Quickly Alice sprang up, trembling with excitement, and together we approached Fanny, who shrieked defiance and threats at us in her impotent fury as she struggled desperately to get free. But, as soon as she felt Alice's fingers unfastening her garments, her rage changed to horrible apprehension, and as one by one they slipped off her, she began to realize how helpless she was! "Don't, Miss!" she exclaimed pitifully. "My God! Stop her, Sir!" she pleaded, the use of these more respectful terms of address sufficiently proclaiming her changed attitude. But we were obdurate, and soon Fanny stood with nothing but her chemise left on, her shoes and stockings having been dragged off her at the special request of Alice, whose uncontrolled enjoyment of the work of stripping her maid was delicious to witness.

She now took command of operations. Pointing to a chair just in front of Fanny she exclaimed: "Sit there, Jack, and watch Fanny as I take off her last garments."

"For God's sake, Miss, don't strip me naked!" shrieked Fanny, who seemed to expect that she would be left in her chemise and to whom the sudden intimation that she was to be exposed naked came with an appalling shock! "Oh, Sir! For God's sake, stop her!" she cried, appealing to me as she saw me take my seat right in front of her and felt Alice's fingers begin to undo the shoulder-strap fastenings which alone kept her scanty garments on her. "Miss Alice! . . . Miss Alice! don't! . . . for God's sake, don't," she screamed in a fresh outburst of dismay as she felt her vest slip down her body to her feet and knew now her only covering was about to follow. In despair she tugged frantically at the ropes which made her arms so absolutely helpless, her agitated, quivering fingers betraying her mental agony! "Steady, Fanny, steady!" exclaimed Alice to her struggling maid as she proceeded to unfasten the chemise, her eyes gleaming with lustful cruelty.

"Now, Jack!" she said warningly, then let go, stepping back a pace, herself the better to observe the effect! Down swept the chemise, and Fanny stood stark naked!

"Oh! Oh!" she wailed, crimson with shame, her face hidden on her bosom which now was wildly heaving in agitation. It was a wonderful spectacle!—in the foreground Fanny, naked, helpless, in an agony of shame—in the background but close to her was Alice, exquisitely costumed and hatted, gloating over the sight of her maid's absolute nudity, her eyes intently fixed on the gloriously luscious curves of Fanny's hips, haunches, and bottom! I managed to catch her eye and motioned to her to come sit on my knees that we might, in each other's close company, study her maid's naked charms, which were so reluctantly being exhibited to us. With one long, last look she obeyed my summons. As she seated herself on my knees she threw her arms around my neck and kissed me rapturously, whispering, "Jack! Isn't she delicious?" I nodded smiling, then in turn muttered in her ear, "And how do you like the game, dear?"

Alice blushed divinely. A strange languishing voluptuous half-wanton, half-cruel look came into her eyes. Placing her lips carefully on mine, she gave me three long-drawn-out kisses, the significance of which I could not possibly misunderstand, then whispered almost hoarsely, "Jack, let me do all the. . . torturing and be content this time, with. . . fucking Fanny. . . and me, too, darling!"

"She's your maid, and so-to-speak your property, dear," I replied softly, "so arrange matters just as you like. I'll leave it all to you and won't interfere unless you want me to do anything."

She kissed me gratefully, then turned her eyes on Fanny, who during this whispered conference had been standing trembling, her face still hidden from us, her legs pressed closely against each other as if to shield her cunt as much as possible from our sight.

I saw Alice's eyes wander over Fanny's naked body with evident pleasure, dwelling first on her magnificent lines and curves, then on her lovely breasts, and finally on the mass of dark curling moss-like hair that covered her cunt.

She was a most deliciously voluptuous girl, one calculated to excite Alice to the utmost pitch of lust of which she was capable, and while secretly regretting that my share in the process of taming Fanny was to be somewhat restricted, I felt that I would enjoy the rare opportunity of seeing how a girl, hitherto chaste and well-mannered, would yield to her sexual instincts and passions when she had, placed at her absolute disposal, one of her own sex in a state of absolute nakedness!

Presently Alice whispered to me, "Jack, I'm going to feel her!" I smiled and nodded. Fanny must have heard her, for as Alice rose, she for the first time raised her head and cried in fear, "No, Miss, please, Miss, don't touch me!" and again she vainly strained at her fastenings, her face quivering and flushed with shame. But disregarding her maid's piteous entreaties, Alice passed behind her, then kneeling down began to stroke Fanny's bottom, a hand to each cheek!

"Don't, Miss!" yelled Fanny, arching herself outwards and away from Alice, and thereby, unconsciously, throwing the region of her cunt into greater prominence! But with a smile of cruel satisfaction, Alice continued her sweet occupation, sometimes squeezing, sometimes pinching Fanny's glorious halfmoons, now and then extending her excursions over Fanny's round, plump thighs, once, indeed, letting her hands creep up them till I really thought (and so did Fanny from the way she screamed and wriggled) that she was about to feel Fanny's cunt!

Suddenly Alice rose, rushed to me and, kissing me ardently, whispered excitedly, "Oh, Jack! She's just lovely! Such flesh, such a skin! I've never felt a girl before, I've never touched any girl's breasts or. . . cunt. . . except, of course, my own," she added archly, "and I'm wild at the idea of handling Fanny.

Watch me carefully, darling, and if I don't do it properly, tell me!" And back to Fanny she rushed, evidently in a state of intense eroticism! This time Alice didn't kneel, but placed herself close behind Fanny (her dress in fact touching her). Suddenly she threw her arms around Fanny's body and seized her breasts. "Miss Alice. . . don't!" shrieked Fanny, struggling desperately, her flushed face betraying her agitation. "Oh! how lovely! . . . how delicious! . . . how sweet! . . ." cried Alice, wild with delight and sexual excitement as she squeezed and played with Fanny's voluptuous breasts! Her head with its exquisite hat was just visible over Fanny's right shoulder, while her dainty dress showed on each side of the struggling, agitated girl, throwing into bold relief her glorious shape and accentuating in the most piquant way Fanny's stark nakedness! Entranced, I gazed at the voluptuous spectacle, my prick struggling to break through the fly of my trousers! Fanny had now ceased her cries and was enduring in silence, broken only by her involuntary "Ohs," the violation of her breasts by Alice, whose little hands could scarcely grasp the luscious morsels of Fanny's flesh that they were so subtly torturing, but which, nevertheless, succeeded in squeezing and compressing them and generally playing with them till the poor girl gasped in her shame and agony, "Oh! Miss Alice! . . . Miss Alice! . . . stop! . . . stop!" her head falling forward in her extreme agitation.

With a smile of intense satisfaction, Alice suspended her torturing operations and gently stroked and soothed Fanny's breasts till the latter indicated that she had, in a great degree, regained her self-control. Then Alice's expression changed. A cruel hungry light came into her eyes as she smiled wickedly at me. I saw her hands quit Fanny's breasts and glide over Fanny's stomach till they arrived at her maid's cunt! Fanny shrieked as if she had been stung. "Miss Alice. . . Miss Alice! . . . Don't! Don't touch me there! Oh! . . . Oh! My God, Miss Alice. . . oh! Miss Alice! Take your hands away! . . ." at the same time twisting and writhing in a perfectly wonderful way in her frantic endeavors to escape from her mistress's hands, the fingers of which were now hidden in her cunt's mossy covering as they inquisitively traveled all over her Mount Venus and along the lips of the orifice itself. For some little time they contented themselves with feeling and pressing and toying caressingly with Fanny's cunt; then I saw one hand pause while the first finger of the other gently began to work its way between the pink lips, which I could just distinguish, and disappear into the sweet cleft.

"Don't, Miss!" yelled Fanny, her agonized face now scarlet while in her distress she desperately endeavored to defend her cunt by throwing her legs in turn across her groin, to Alice's delight—her telltale face proclaiming the intense pleasure she was tasting in thus making her maid undergo such horrible torture!

Presently I noted an unmistakable look of surprise in her eyes; her lips parted as if in astonishment, while her hand seemed to redouble its attack on Fanny's cunt. She exclaimed, "Why Fanny, what's this?"

"Oh! Don't tell Mr. Jack, Miss!" shrieked Fanny, letting her legs drop as she could no longer endure the whole weight of her struggling body on her slender wrists. "Don't let him know!"

My curiosity was naturally aroused and intently I watched the movements of Alice's hand, which the fall of Fanny's legs brought again into full view. Her forefinger was buried up to the knuckle in her maid's cunt! The mystery was explained; Fanny was not a virgin!

Alice seemed staggered by her discovery. Abruptly she quit Fanny, rushed to me, threw herself on my knees, then, flinging her arms 'round my neck, she whispered excitedly in my ear, "Jack! She's been. . . had by someone. . . my finger went right in!"

"So I noticed, darling!" I replied quietly as I kissed her flushed cheek. "It's rather a pity! But she'll stand more fucking than if she had been a virgin, and you must arrange your program accordingly! I think you'd better let her rest a bit now; her arms will be getting numb from being kept over her head. Let's fasten her to that pillar by passing her arms 'round it and shackling her wrists together. She can then rest a bit and, while she's recovering from her struggles, hadn't you better. . . slip your clothes off also—for your eyes hint that you'll want. . . something before long!"

Alice blushed prettily, then whispered as she kissed me ardently, "I'd like. . . something now, darling!" She ran away to her dressing room.

Left alone with Fanny, I proceeded to transfer her from the pulley to the pillar; it was not a difficult task as her arms were too numb (as I expected) to be of much use to her and she seemed stupefied at our discovery that her maidenhead no longer existed. Soon I had her firmly fastened with her back pressing against the pillar. This new position had two great advantages. She could no longer hide her face from us, and the backwards pull of her arms threw her breasts out. She glanced timidly at me as I stood admiring her luscious nakedness while I waited for Alice's return.

"When did this little slip happen, Fanny?" I asked quietly.

She colored vividly: "When I was seventeen, Sir," she replied softly but brokenly. "I was drugged. . . and didn't know till after it was done! It's never been done again, Mr. Jack," she continued with pathetic earnestness in her voice, "never! I swear it, Sir!" After a short pause she whispered, "Oh! Mr. Jack! Let me go! . . . I'll come to you whenever you wish. . . and let you do what you like but. . . I'm afraid of Miss Alice today. . . she seems so strange! . . . Oh! my God! She's naked!" she screamed in genuine alarm as Alice came out of her toilet room with only her shoes and stockings on, and her large matinee hat, a most coquettishly piquantly indecent object! Poor Fanny went red at the sight of her mistress and didn't know where to look as Alice came dancing along, her eyes noting with evident approval the position into which I had placed her maid.

"Mes compliments, mademoiselle!" I said with a low bow as she came up.

She smiled and blushed, but was too intent on Fanny to joke with me. That's lovely, Jack!" she exclaimed after a careful inspection of her now-trembling maid, "but surely she can get loose!"

"Oh, no!" I replied with a smile, "but if you like, I'll fasten her ankles together!"

"No, no, Sir!" Fanny cried in terror.

"Yes, Jack, do!" exclaimed Alice, her eyes gleaming with lust and delight.

She evidently had thought out some fresh torture for Fanny, and with the closest attention, she watched me as I linked her maid's slender ankles together in spite of the poor girl's entreaties!

"I like that much better, Jack," said Alice, smiling her thanks. Catching me by the elbow, she pushed me towards my alcove saying, "We both will want you presently, Jack!" Looking roguishly at me she continued, "So get ready! But tell me first where are the feathers?"

"Oh, that's your game!" I replied with a laugh. She nodded, coloring slightly, and I told her where she would find them.

I had a peep-hole in my alcove through which I could see all that passed in the room, and being curious to watch the two girls, I placed myself by it as I slowly undressed myself.

Having found the feathers, Alice placed the box near her, then going right up to Fanny, she took hold of her own breasts, raised them till they were level with the trembling girl's. Leaning on Fanny so that their stomachs were in close contact, she directed her breasts against Fanny's, gently rubbing her nipples against her own while she looked intently into Fanny's eyes! It was a most curious sight! The girl's naked bodies were touching from their ankles to their breasts, their cunts were so close to each other that their hairs formed one mass, while their faces were so near to each other that the brim of Alice's matinee hat projected over Fanny's forehead! Not a word was said! For about half a minute Alice continued to rub her breasts gently against Fanny's with her eyes fixed on Fanny's downcast face.

Suddenly I saw both naked bodies quiver, and Fanny raised her head and for the first time responded to Alice's glance, her color coming and going! At the same moment, a languorous voluptuous smile swept over Alice's face, and gently she kissed Fanny, who flushed rosy red, but, as far as I could see, did not respond.

"Won't you. . . love me, Fanny?" I heard Alice say softly but with a curiously strained voice! Immediately I understood the position. Alice was lusting after Fanny! I was delighted! It was clear that Fanny had not yet reciprocated Alice's passion, and I determined that Alice should have every opportunity of satisfying her lust on Fanny's naked helpless body till the latter was converted to Tribadism with Alice as the object.

"Won't you. . . love me, Fanny!" again asked Alice softly, now supplementing the play of her breasts against Fanny's by insinuating significant pressings of her stomach against Fanny's, again kissing the latter sweetly. But Fanny made no response, and Alice's eyes grew hard with a steely cruel glitter that boded badly for Fanny!

Quitting Fanny, Alice went straight to the box of feathers, picked out one, and returned to Fanny, feather in hand. The sight of her moving about thus, her breasts dancing, her hips swaying, her cunt and bottom in full view, her nakedness intensified by her piquant costume of hat, shoes and stockings, was enough to galvanize a corpse. It set my blood boiling with lust and I could hardly refrain from rushing out and compelling her to let me quench my fires in her! I, however, did resist the temptation, and rapidly undressed to my shoes and socks so as to be ready to take advantage of any chance that either of the girls might offer; but I remained in my alcove with my eye to the peephole as I was curious to witness the denouement of this strangely voluptuous scene, which Alice evidently wished to play single-handed.

No sooner did Fanny catch sight of the feather than she screamed. "No! . . . no! Miss Alice! . . . don't tickle me!" at the same time striving frantically to break the straps that linked together her wrists and her ankles. But my tackle was too strong! Alice meanwhile had caught up a cushion which she placed at Fanny's feet and right in front of her, she knelt on it, resting her luscious bottom on her heels and, having settled herself down comfortably, she, with a smile in which cruelty and malice were strangely blended, gloatingly contemplated her maid's naked and agitated body, then slowly and deliberately applied the tip of the feather to Fanny's cunt! "Oh, my God! Miss Alice, don't!" yelled Fanny, writhing in delicious contortions in her desperate endeavors to dodge the feather. "Don't, Miss!" she shrieked, as Alice, keenly enjoying her maid's distress and her vain efforts to avoid the torture, proceeded delightedly to pass the feather lightly along the sensitive lips of Fanny's cunt and finally set to work to tickle Fanny's clitoris, thereby sending her so nearly into hysterical convulsions that I felt it time I interposed.

As I emerged from my alcove, Alice caught sight of me and dropped her hand as she turned towards me, her eyes sparkling with lascivious delight! "Oh, Jack! Did you see her?" she cried excitedly.

"I heard her, dear!" I replied ambiguously, "and began to wonder whether you were killing her, so came out to see."

"Not to worry!" she cried, hugely pleased. "I'm going to give her another turn!" That declaration produced from Fanny the most pitiful pleadings, which seemed, however, only to increase Alice's cruel satisfaction, and she was proceeding to be as good as her word when I stopped her.

"You'd better let me first soothe her irritated senses, dear," I said, and, with one hand, I caressed and played with Fanny's full and voluptuous breasts, which I found tense and firm under her sexual excitement, while with the other, I stroked and felt her cunt, a procedure that evidently afforded her considerable relief although, at another time, it doubtless would have provoked shrieks and cries! She had not spent, though she must have been very close to doing it; and I saw that I must watch Alice very closely indeed during the "turn" she was going to give Fanny for my special delectation, lest the catastrophe I was so desirous of avoiding should occur, for in my mind, I had decided that when Alice had finished tickling Fanny, she should have an opportunity of satisfying her lustful cravings on her, when it would be most desirable that Fanny should be in a condition to show the effect on her of Alice's lascivious exertions.

While feeling Fanny's cunt, I naturally took the opportunity to see if Alice's penetrating finger had met with any difficulty entering and had thus caused Fanny the pain that her shrieks and wriggles had indicated. I found the way in intensely tight, a confirmation of her story and statement that nothing had gone in since the rape was committed on her. Although therefore I could not have the gratification of taking her virginity, I felt positive that I should have a delicious time and that practically, I should be violating her, and I wondered into which of the two delicious cunts now present I would shoot my surging and boiling discharge as it dissolved in Love's sweetest ecstasies! "Now, Alice, I think she is ready for you!" I said when I had stroked and felt Fanny to my complete satisfaction.

"No, no, Miss Alice!" shrieked Fanny in frantic terror, "for God's sake, don't tickle me again!"

Disregarding her cries, Alice, who had with difficulty restrained her impatience, quickly again applied the feather to Fanny's cunt, and a wonderful spectacle followed; Fanny's shrieks, cries, and entreaties filled the room while she wiggled and squirmed and twisted herself about in the most bewitchingly provocative manner, while Alice, with parted lips and eyes that simply glistened with lust, remorselessly tickled her maid's cunt with every refinement of cruelty, every fresh shriek and convulsion bringing a delightful look on her telltale face. Motionless, I watched the pair, till I noticed Fanny's breasts stiffen and become tense. Immediately I covered her cunt with my hand, saying to Alice, "Stop, dear, she's had as much as she can stand!" Reluctantly, she desisted from her absorbing occupation and rose, her naked body quivering with aroused but unsatisfied lust.

Now was the time for me to try and effect what I had in mind: The introduction of both girls to Tribadism! "Let us move Fanny to the large couch and fasten her down before she recovers herself," I hastily whispered to Alice.

Quickly we set her loose, between us we carried her, half-fainting, to the large settee couch where we lay her on her back and made fast her wrists to the two top corners and her ankles to the two lower ones. We now had only to set the machinery going and she would lie in the position I desired, namely spread-eagled!

Alice clutched me excitedly and whispered hurriedly, "Jack, do me before she comes to herself and before she can see us! I'm just mad for it!" And, indeed, with her flushed cheeks, humid eyes, and heaving breasts, this was very evident! But although I was also bursting with lust and eager to fuck either Alice or her maid, it would not have suited my program to do so! I wanted Alice to fuck Fanny! I wanted the first spending of both girls to be mutually provoked by the friction of their excited cunts one against the other! This was why I stopped Alice from tickling her maid into spending, and it was for this reason that I had extended Fanny on her back in such a position that her cunt should be at Alice's disposal! "Hold on, darling, for a bit!" I whispered back. "You'll soon see why! I want it as badly as you do, my sweet, but am fighting it till the proper time comes! Run away now, and take off your hat, for it will now only be in the way," and I smiled significantly as I kissed her.

Alice promptly obeyed. I seated myself on the couch by the side of Fanny, who was still lying with eyes closed but breathing almost normally. Bending over her, I closely inspected her cunt to ascertain whether she had or had not spent under the terrific tickling she had just received! I could find no traces whatever, but to make sure, I gently drew the lips apart and peered into the sweet coral cleft, but again saw no traces. The touch of my fingers on her cunt, however, roused Fanny from her semi-stupor and she dreamily opened her eyes, murmuring, "Oh, Sir, don't!" as she recognized that I was her assailant, then she looked hurriedly 'round as in search of Alice.

"Your mistress will be here immediately," I said with a smile. "She has only gone away to take off her hat!" The look of terror returned to her eyes, and she exclaimed, "Oh, Mr. Jack, do let me go, she'll kill me!"

"Oh, no!" I replied as I laughed at her agitation. "Oh, no, Fanny, on the contrary, she's now going to do to you the sweetest, nicest, and kindest thing one girl can do to another! Here she comes!"

I rose as Alice came up full of pleasurable excitement as to what was now going to happen, and slipped my arm lovingly 'round her waist. She looked eagerly at her now trembling maid, then whispered, "Is she ready for us again, Jack?"

"Yes, dear!" I answered softly. "While you were away taking off your hat, I thought it as well to see in what condition her cunt was after its tickling! I found it very much irritated and badly in want of Nature's soothing essence! You, darling, are also much in the same state, your cunt also wants soothing! So I want you girls to soothe each other! Get onto Fanny, dear, take her in your arms, arrange yourself on her so that your cunt lies on hers and gently rub yours against hers! Soon both of you will be tasting the sweetest ecstasy! In other words, fuck Fanny, dear."

Alice looked at me in wondrous admiration! As she began to comprehend my suggestion, her face broke into delightful smiles, and when I stooped to kiss her, she exclaimed rapturously, "Oh, Jack! how sweet! . . . how delicious!" as she gazed eagerly at Fanny. But the latter seemed horrified at the idea of being submitted thus to her mistress's lustful passion and embraces, and attempted to escape, crying in her dismay: "No, no, Sir!—oh, no, Miss!—I don't want it, please!"

"But I do, Fanny," cried Alice with sparkling eyes as she gently, but firmly, pushed her struggling maid onto her back and held her down forcibly, till I had pulled all four straps tight, so that Fanny lay flat with her arms and legs wide apart in Maltese-Cross fashion, a simply entrancing spectacle! Slipping my hands under her buttocks, I raised her middle till Alice was able to push a hard cushion under her bottom, the effect of which was to make her cunt stand out prominently; then turning to Alice, who had assisted in these preparations with the keenest interest but evident impatience, I said, "Now dear, there she is! Set to work and violate your maid!"

In a flash Alice was on the couch and on her knees between Fanny's widely parted legs. Excitedly she threw herself on her maid, passed her arms 'round her and hugged her closely as she showered kisses on Fanny's still-protesting mouth till the girl had to stop for breath. With a few rapid movements, she arranged herself on her maid so that the two luscious pairs of breasts were pressing against each other, their stomachs in close contact, and their cunts touching! "One moment, Alice!" I exclaimed, just as she was beginning to agitate herself on Fanny. "Let me see that you are properly placed before you start!"

Leaning over her bottom, I gently parted her thighs, till between them I saw the cunts of the mistress and the maid resting on each other, slit to slit, clitoris to clitoris, half hidden by the mass of their closely interwoven hairs, the sweetest of sights! After restoring her thighs to their original position, closely pressed against each other, I gently thrust my right hand between the girl's navels, and worked it along amidst their bellies till it lay between their cunts! "Press down a bit, Alice!" I said, patting her bottom with my disengaged hand.

Promptly she complied with two or three vigorous downward thrusts which forced my palm hard against Fanny's cunt while her own pressed deliciously against the back of my hand. The sensation of thus feeling at the same time these two full, fat, fleshy, warm and throbbing cunts between which my hand lay in sandwich fashion was something exquisite; and it was with the greatest reluctance that I removed it from the sweetest position it is ever likely to find herself in, but Alice's restless and involuntary movements proclaimed that she was fast yielding to her feverish impatience to fuck Fanny and to taste the rapture of spending on the cunt of her maid, the emission provoked by its sweet contact and friction against her own excited organ!

She still held Fanny closely clasped against her and with head slightly thrown back, she kept her eyes fixed on her maid's terrified averted face with a gloating hungry look, murmuring softly, "Fanny, you shall now. . . love me!" Both the girls were quivering, Alice from overwhelming and unsatisfied lust, Fanny from shame and horrible apprehension! Caressing Alice's bottom encouragingly, I whispered, "Go ahead, dear!" In a trice her lips were pressed to Fanny's flushed cheeks on which she rained hot kisses as she slowly began to agitate her cunt against her maid's with voluptuous movements of her beautiful bottom.

"Oh! Miss. . ." gasped Fanny, her eyes betraying the sexual emotion that she felt beginning to overpower her, her color coming and going! Alice's movements became quicker and more agitated; soon she was furiously rubbing her cunt against Fanny's with strenuous downward thrusting strokes of her bottom, continuing her fierce kisses on her maid's cheeks as the latter lay helpless with half-closed eyes, tightly clasped in her mistress's arms!

A hurricane of sexual rage seemed to seize Alice! Her bottom wildly oscillated and gyrated with confused jerks, thrusts, and shoves as she frenziedly pressed her cunt against Fanny's with a rapid jogging motion: suddenly Alice seemed to stiffen and become almost rigid, her arms gripped Fanny more tightly than ever, her head fell forward on Fanny's shoulder as an indescribable spasm thrilled through her, followed by convulsive vibrations and tremors! Almost simultaneously

Fanny's half-closed eyes turned upwards till the whites were showing, her lips parted, she gasped brokenly, "Oh! . . . Miss. . . Alice! . . . Ah. . . ah!" then thrilled convulsively while quiver after quiver shot through her! The blissful crisis had arrived! Mistress and maid were deliriously spending, cunt against cunt, Alice in rapturous ecstasy at having so deliciously satisfied her sexual desires by means of her maid's cunt, while forcing the latter to spend in spite of herself, while Fanny was quivering ecstatically under heavenly sensations hitherto unknown to her (owing to her having been unconscious when she was ravished) and now communicated to her wondering senses by her mistress whom she still felt lying on her and in whose arms she was still clasped!

Intently I watched both girls, curious to learn how they would regard each other when they had recovered from their ecstatic trance. Would the mutual satisfaction of their overwrought sexual cravings wipe out the animosity between them, which had caused the strange events of this afternoon, or would Alice's undoubted lust for her maid be simply raised to a higher pitch by this satisfying of her sexuality on her maid's body, and would Fanny consider that she had been violated by her mistress and therefore bear a deeper grudge than ever against her! It was a pretty problem and I eagerly awaited the situation.

Alice was the first to move. With a long-drawn breath, indicative of intense satisfaction, she raised her head off Fanny's shoulder. The slight movement roused Fanny, who mechanically turned her averted head towards Alice, and as the girls languidly opened their humid eyes, they found themselves looking straight at each other! Fanny colored like a peony and quickly turned her eyes away; Alice, on the contrary, continued to regard the blushing face of her maid. A look of gratification and triumph came into her eyes, then she deliberately placed her lips on Fanny's and kissed her, saying softly but significantly, "Now it's Mr. Jack's turn, my dear!" Raising her head, she, with a malicious smile, watched Fanny to see how she would receive the intimation.

Fanny darted a startled, horrified glance at me, another at her mistress.

Seeing that both our faces only confirmed Alice's announcement, she cried pitifully, "No, no, Mr. Jack! No, no! Miss Alice! Oh, Miss, how can you be so cruel?"

With a malicious smile, Alice again kissed her horrified maid, saying teasingly, "You must tell us afterwards which of us you like best, Fanny, and, if you're very good and let Mr. Jack have as good a fuck as you have just given me, we'll have each other in front of you for your special edification!"

She kissed Fanny once more and rose slowly off her, exposing as she did so her own cunt and that of her maid. I shot a quick glance at both in turn. The girls had evidently spent profusely, their hairs glistened with tiny drops of love-dew, while, here and there, bits were plastered down.

Alice caught my glance and smiled merrily. "I let myself go, Jack!" she laughed. "But there will be plenty when you are ready!" she added wickedly.

"I'll just put myself right, then I'll do lady's maid to Fanny and get her ready for you!" With a saucy look, she whispered, "Haven't I sketched out a fine program!"

"You have indeed!" I replied as I seized and kissed her. I wish only that I was to have you first, dear, while I'm so rampant!"

"No, no," she whispered, kissing me again: "I'm not ready yet! Fuck Fanny well, Jack! It will do her good, and you'll find her a delicious mover!" And she ran off to her alcove.

I sat down on the couch by Fanny's side and began to play with her breasts, watching her closely. She was in a terrible state of agitation, her head rolling from side to side, her eyes closed, her lips slightly apart, while her bosom heaved wildly. As my hands seized her breasts gently she started, opened her eyes, and seeing that it was me she piteously pleaded, "Oh, Mr. Jack! Don't. . .

don't. . ." She could not bring herself to say the dreadful word that expressed her fate.

"Don't. . . what, Fanny?" I asked maliciously. With effort she brought out the word. "Oh! Sir! Don't. . . fuck me!"

"But your mistress has ordered it, Fanny, and she tells me you are very sweet, and so I want it! And it will be like taking your maidenhead, only much nicer for you, as you won't have the pain that girls feel when they are first ravished and you'll be able to taste all the pleasure!"

"No, no, Mr. Jack," she cried. "Don't. . . fuck me."

Just then Alice came up with water, a sponge, and a towel. "What's the matter, Jack?" she asked.

"Your maid says she doesn't want to be fucked, dear; perhaps you can convince her of her foolishness!"

Alice was now sponging Fanny's cunt with sedulous care, and her attentions were making Fanny squirm and wriggle involuntarily in the most lovely fashion, much to her mistress's gratification. When Alice had finished, she turned to me and said, "She's quite ready, Jack! Go ahead!"

"No, no, Sir!" yelled Fanny in genuine terror, but I quickly got between her legs and placed myself on her palpitating stomach, clasped her in my arms and directed my prick against her delicious cleft. I got its head inside without much difficulty. Fanny was now wild with fright and shrieked despairingly as she felt me effect an entrance into her, and as my prick penetrated deeper and deeper, she went off into a paroxysm of frantic plunging in the hope of dislodging me.

I did not experience half the difficulty I had anticipated in getting into Fanny, for her spendings under Alice had lubricated the passage, but she was exceedingly tight and I must have hurt her for her screams were terrible! Soon, however, I was into her till our hairs mingled. I lay still for a little while to allow her to recover a bit, and before long her cries ceased and she lay panting in my arms.

Alice, who was in my full sight and had been watching with the closest attention and the keenest enjoyment this violation of her maid, now bent forward and said softly, "She's all right, Jack! Go on dear!" Promptly I set to work to fuck Fanny, at first with long, slow, piston-like strokes of my prick, then more and more rapid thrusts and shoves, driving myself well up into her.

Suddenly I felt Fanny quiver deliciously under me. . . she had spent! Delightedly I continued to fuck her. . . soon she spent again, then again, and again, quivering with the most exquisite tremors and convulsions as she lay clasped tightly in my arms, uttering almost inarticulate "Ahs" and "Ohs" as the spasm of pleasure thrilled her. Now I began to feel my own ecstasy quickly approaching! Hugging Fanny against me more closely than ever, I let myself go and rammed furiously into her as she lay quivering under me till the rapturous crisis overtook me. Madly I shot her my pent-up torrent of boiling virile balm, inundating her sweetly excited interior and evidently causing her the most exquisite bliss, for her head fell backwards, her eyes closed, her nostrils dilated, her lips parted, as she exclaimed, "Ah! . . . Ah! . . .

Ah! . . ." when feeling each jet of my hot discharge shoot into her. Heavens! How I spent! The thrilling, exciting and provocative events of the afternoon had worked me up into a state of sexual excitement that even the ample discharge I had spent into Fanny did not quench my ardor, and as soon as the delicious thrills and spasms of pleasure had died away, I started fucking her a second time. But Alice intervened. "No, Jack!" she exclaimed softly, adding archly, "you must keep the rest for me! Get off quickly, dear, and let me attend to Fanny!"

Unable to challenge her veto, I reluctantly withdrew my prick from Fanny's cunt after kissing her ardently. I rose and retired to my alcove, while Alice quickly took Fanny into her charge and attended to her with loving care! When I returned, Fanny was still lying on her back, fastened down to the couch, and Alice was sitting by her and talking to her with an amused smile as she gently played with her maid's breasts. As soon as Fanny caught sight of me, she blushed rosy red, while Alice turned and greeted me with a welcoming smile.

"I've been trying to find out from Fanny which fuck she liked best," she said with a merry smile, "but she won't say! Did she give you a good time, Jack?"

"She was simply divine!" I replied as I stopped and kissed the still-blushing girl! "Then we'll give her the reward we promised," replied Alice, looking sweetly at Fanny. "She shan't be tied up any more and she'll see you fuck me presently! Set her free, Jack," she added, and soon Fanny rose confusedly from the couch on which she had tasted the probably unique experience of being fucked in rapid succession first by a girl and then by a man!" She was very shamefaced and her limbs were very stiff from having been retained so long in one position, but we supported her to the sofa where we placed her between us. We gently chafed and massaged her limbs till they regained their powers and soothed her with our kisses and caresses, while our hands wandered all over her naked and still trembling body, and soon she was herself again.

"Now!" exclaimed Alice, who was evidently in heat again, "are you ready?"

"Look, dear!" I replied, holding up my limp prick for her inspection, adding with a smile: "Time, my Christian friend!"

She laughed, took my prick gently in her hands and began to fondle it, but as it did not show the signs of returning life she so desired to see, she caught hold of Fanny's hand and made it assist hers, much to Fanny's bashful confusion.

But her touch had the desired effect, and soon I was stiff and rampant again! "Thanks, Fanny!" I said as I lovingly kissed her blushing face. "Now, Alice, if you will!"

Quickly Alice was on her back with parted legs. Promptly I got onto her and drove my prick home up her cunt. Clasping each other closely, we set to work and fucked each other deliciously till we both spent in delirious transports of pleasure which heightened Fanny's blushes, as with humid eyes she watched us in wondering astonishment and secret delight! After exchanging ardent kisses, we rose. "Come, Fanny, we must dress and be off I didn't know it was so late!" exclaimed Alice. Off the girls went together to Alice's alcove while I retired to mine. I was delighted that their departure should be thus hurried as it would bypass the possible awkwardness of a more formal leave-taking. Soon we all were dressed. I called a taxi and put the girls into it, their faces discreetly veiled, and as they drove off, I felt that the afternoon had not been wasted!

Chapter 4

Two days after this memorable afternoon, I received the following letter from Alice:

My darling Jack,

I must write and tell you the sequel to yesterday's lovely afternoon at the Snuggery.

Fanny didn't say a word on the way home, but was evidently deeply thinking and getting more and more angry. She went straight to her room and I to mine. I did not expect she would resume her duties, in fact I rather anticipated she would come in to say she was going away at once! But in about ten minutes she came in as if nothing had happened, only she wouldn't speak unless it was absolutely necessary.

At eight o'clock she brought me the dinner menu as usual for my orders. I told her I felt too tired to dress and go down, so would dine in my own room and that she must dine with me, as she was looking so tired and upset generally. She looked surprised, and I think she hesitated about accepting my invitation, but did so.

At dinner, of course, she had to talk. I saw she had refreshing and appetizing food and she made a good dinner. I also induced her to drink a little Burgundy, which seemed to do her a lot of good, and she gradually became less sulky.

When the table was cleared, she was going away, but I asked her to stay and rest comfortably if she had done her work for the day. To my surprise she seemed glad to do so. I installed her in a comfortable chair and made her chat with me about things in general, carefully avoiding anything that might recall the events of the afternoon!

After some little time so passed, she rose and stood before me in a most respectful attitude and said, "Miss Alice, you've always been a very kind mistress to me. You've treated me with every consideration, you've paid me well, you've given me light work. Would you mind telling me why you were so awfully cruel to me this afternoon?"

I was very surprised, but fortunately ideas came! "Certainly I will, Fanny," I replied. "I think you are entitled to know. Come and sit by me and we can talk it over nicely."

I was then on the little sofa with padded back and ends, and which you know just holds two nicely. Fanny hesitated for a moment and then sat down.

"I've tried to be a good mistress to you, Fanny," I said gravely, "because you have been a very good maid to me. But, of late, there has been something wrong with you; your temper has been so queer that, though you have never disobeyed me, you have made your obedience very unpleasant, and I found myself wondering whether I had not better send you away. But I very much didn't want to lose you—(here she half moved toward me)—and so I thought I'd talk the case over with Mr. Jack, who is one of my best friends and always helps me in all troublesome matters. He said something must be wrong with you, and there undoubtedly is—and you must presently tell me what it is—and advised that he should give you a good shock, which he has done!"

"My God, yes, Miss Alice!" Fanny replied almost tearfully.

"But there is a second reason, Fanny," I continued, "which will explain to you why you were forced to submit yourself to me and to Mr. Jack. Am I wrong in guessing that your queer temper has been caused by your not being able to satisfy certain sexual cravings and desires? Tell me frankly!"

"Yes!" she whispered bashfully.

"We felt sure of it!" I continued. "Mr. Jack said to me, 'Look here, Alice, isn't it absurd that you two girls should be living in such close relations as mistress and maid, and yet should go on suffering from stifled natural sexual functions when you could and should so easily soothe each other?' Then he explained to me how!"

I gently took her hand; she yielded it to me without hesitation "Now, Fanny, do you understand? Shall we not agree to help each other, to make life pleasanter and more healthy for us both? We tried each other this afternoon, Fanny! Do you like me sufficiently?"

She blushed deeply, then glanced shyly but lovingly at me. I took the hint. I slipped my arm 'round her and she yielded to my pleasure. I drew her to me and kissed her fondly, whispering, "Shall we be sweethearts, Fanny?"

She sank into my arms murmuring, "Oh, Miss Alice!" her eyes shining with love! Our lips met; we sealed our pact with kisses! Just then ten o'clock struck. "Now we'll have a nightcap and go to bed," I said to her. "Will you get the whiskey and siphon, dear, and mix my allowance and also one for yourself, as it will do you good?"

Fanny rose and served me with the "grog" as I call it, and when we had finished, we turned out the lights and went to my bedroom.

After she had done my hair and prepared me for bed as usual, I said to her softly, "Now go and undress dear, and come back," and significantly kissed her. She blushed sweetly and withdrew. I undressed.

Presently there was a timid tap on the door, and Fanny came in shyly in her "nightie." "Take it off, dear, please," I said softly. "I want to see you. I was too excited to do so this afternoon!" Bashfully and with pretty blushes she complied. I made her lie on my bed naked and had a good look at her all over, back, front, everywhere! Jack, she is a little beauty! When I kissed her after I had thoroughly examined her, she put her arms around my neck and whispered, "May I look at you, Miss?" So in turn I lay down naked and she looked me all over and played with me, kissed me here and there till the touch of her lips and hands set my blood on fire. "Come, darling!" I whispered.

In a moment she was on the bed by me with parted legs. I got between them and on her, and in each other's arms we lay spending, she sometimes on me, I oftener on her, till we fell asleep still clasped against each other! Oh, Jack, you don't know what a good turn you did us yesterday afternoon! Today Fanny is another person, so sweet and gentle and loving! An indescribable thrill comes over me when I think that I have this delicious girl at my command whenever I feel like I'd like to be—naughty! You must come and see us soon, and have some tea, and my maid and me!

Your loving sweetheart,
Alice

P.S.—I cross-questioned Fanny last night as to her experiences of that afternoon. I must tell you some day how she described what she went through; it will thrill you! But one thing I must tell you now! She says that she never felt anything so delicious as her sensations when in your arms, after you had got into her! I asked her if she would go to you some afternoon if you wanted a change from me. She blushed sweetly and whispered, "Yes, Miss, if you didn't mind!"

Chapter 5

Among our friends was a very pretty lady, Connie Blunt, a young widow whose husband died within a few weeks of the marriage. She had been left comfortably off and had no children.

She was a lovely golden-haired girl of about twenty-two years, slight, tall, and beautifully formed, a blue-eyed beauty with a dazzling skin and pure complexion.

She and Alice were great friends and she was Alice's pet chaperone. The two were constantly together, Alice generally passing the night at Mrs. Blunt's flat when they were going to a ball or any late entertainment, and I suppose that the sweet familiarity that exists between girl friends enabled Alice to see a good deal of her friend's physical charms, with the result that she fell in love with her. But hint as delicately and as diplomatically as she dared of the pleasures tasted by girl sweethearts, Mrs. Blunt never by word or deed or look gave Alice any encouragement. In fact, she seemed ignorant that such a state of affection could or did exist.

I used to tease Alice about her ill-success and she took my chaff very goodnaturedly, but I could see that she was secretly suffering from the "pangs of ill-requited love," and had it not been for the genuine affection that existed between her and her maid Fanny, which enabled Alice to satisfy with the help of Fanny's cunt the desires provoked by Mrs. Blunt, things might have fared badly with Alice.

Among ardent girls, an unrequited passion of this sort is apt to become tinged with cruel desire against the beloved one, and one day, when Alice was consoling herself with me, I saw that this was getting to be the case with her passion for Mrs. Blunt, and my fertile imagination suggested to me means by which she might attain to the desired end.

We were discussing Mrs. Blunt. "I am getting hungry for Connie, Jack!" Alice had said mournfully. "Very hungry!"

"Dear, I'd like to help you, and I believe I can," I remarked sympathetically, "but I shall want a lot of help from you. Could you bring yourself to torture her?"

"Oh, yes!" replied Alice briskly, "and I'd dearly like to do it!" And into her eyes came the Sadique glint I knew so well! "But it would never do, Jack! She'd never have anything to do with me again. I thought of this, but it won't do!"

"I'm not so sure!" I said reflectively. "Let me give you my ideas as clearly as I can, and you can tell me if you think them workable."

"Wait a moment, Jack!" she exclaimed, now keenly interested. "Let me get on you, it's better for both of us," she added archly, and soon she was lying flat on me, her breasts resting on my chest and my prick snugly lodged up her cunt while my arms retained her in position.

"Now are you ready to discuss matters seriously?" I asked with a mischievous smile.

She nodded merrily. "Go ahead, you dear old Jack, my most faithful friend," she added with sudden tenderness as she kissed me with unusual affection.

"Then listen carefully, dear. The gist of my plan is that you must pretend to be what Mrs. Blunt thinks you are, but which is precisely what you are not: an innocent and unsophisticated virgin!"

"Oh, you beast!" hissed Alice in pretended indignation but with laughing eyes. "And who's responsible for that, Sir?"

"I'm delighted to say that I am, dear!" I replied with a tender smile to which Alice responded by kissing me affectionately. "Anyhow, you've got to pretend to be what you're not! You must get Mrs. Blunt to chaperone you here to lunch. When we all are here afterwards, we'll manage to make her sit down in the Chair of Treachery"—(Alice's eyes lit up)—"which of course will at once pin her. Immediately I'll collar you and fasten you to one pair of pulleys—I'll have two pairs working that day—and I'll fasten Mrs. Blunt to the other pair, so that you will face each other." (Alice's face was now a study in rapt attention.) "You both will then be stripped naked in full sight of each other"—(Alice blushed prettily)—"and you both will also be tortured in front of each other! You must agree to be tortured dear, to keep up the swindle!"

"I shan't mind, Jack!" Alice whispered, kissing me.

"But there will be this great difference to your former experience, both when you were done by yourself and when we did Fanny together, the girl that is being tortured is to be first blindfolded." (Alice's eyes opened widely with surprise.) "I shall keep Mrs. Blunt fastened in the usual way, but for you, I shall use a new and most ingenious set of straps which can be put on and taken off in a jiffy by anyone knowing the trick. So when I have fastened Mrs. Blunt for, say, cunt tickling, I'll blindfold her, then I'll silently let you loose and let you tickle her. . ."

"Oh Jack! How lovely!" exclaimed Alice delightedly, again kissing me.

". . . and tie you up quickly when you're finished, then I'll take off the bandage.

She is sure to think it was me." Alice laughed merrily. "I must blindfold you, dear, when it's your turn, for your eyes may give you away while your mouth will be quite safe!" Alice nodded her head approvingly.

"I don't, however, propose to give you girls much torture. After you both have had a turn, I'll tie Mrs. Blunt to this couch just as we did Fanny. Then I'll threaten you with a whip, and you must pretend to be terrorized and consent to do everything I tell you. I'll first set you free and blindfold Mrs. Blunt, then order you to feel her, then to suck her and then to fuck her!"

"Jack, you're a genius!" exclaimed Alice admiringly.

"After you've fucked Mrs. Blunt, I'll have her while you look on!" Alice blushed. "Then it will be your turn. I'll terrorize Mrs. Blunt in reality and make her operate on you, and I'll have you in front of her!" Alice here kissed me with sparkling eyes, then, in her delight, began to agitate herself on my prick.

"Steady, dear!" I exclaimed, slipping my hands down to her heaving bottom to keep her still. "I can't think and talk and fuck at the same time! Let me do the first two now and the third afterwards if you don't mind!"

"I'm very sorry, Jack!" Alice replied demurely but with eyes full of merriment. "I'll try and lie still on you, but your magnificent plan is exciting me most awfully! The very idea of having Connie, oh, Jack!" and again she kissed me excitedly.

"Where were we?—oh, yes," I continued. "I'll compel Mrs. Blunt to perform on you and then I'll have you in her presence. Under the threat of the whip, I'll make you both swear that you'll never let out what has been happening and send you home! You must choose some day when you are staying with her, dear, for then you'll go back together and pass the evening together, and if you don't establish a sexual relation with her, I'm afraid I can't help you! Now, what do you honestly and frankly think of my plan, dear?"

"Just splendid, and lovely, Jack!" she replied enthusiastically, and in a different tone of voice she whispered hastily, "Jack, I really must, now. . ." and began to work herself up and down on me. I saw she was too erotically excited to think seriously and so let her have her way. She fucked me most deliciously, quivering voluptuously when she spent and when she felt my warm discharge shoot into her. After the necessary ablutions, we dressed, as Alice had to leave early to keep a dinner engagement.

"Think it over carefully, dear," I said as I put her in a taxi. "Let me have your opinion from the point of view of a girl." And so we parted.

Next day, as I was about to commence my solitary lunch, who should appear but Alice and Fanny. I greeted them warmly, especially Fanny, whom I had not seen since the never-to-be-forgotten afternoon when Alice and I converted her. She blushed prettily as we shook hands.

"Have you had lunch?" was my natural inquiry.

"No," replied Alice, "but we didn't come for that. I wanted to discuss with you certain points about Connie."

"Lunch first and Connie afterwards!" I said laughing. "Sit down, Alice, sit down, Fanny, and make yourselves at home."

We had a merry lunch. I noticed with great approval that Fanny did not in any way presume, but was natural and respectful, also that she worshipped Alice! In due course we adjourned to the Snuggery where we settled ourselves down comfortably.

"Now, Alice, let's get down to business. Have you found some holes in my plan, or have you brought some new ideas?"

"Well, neither," she said smiling, "but there are one or two things I thought I ought to tell you. I hope, Jack, dear, you won't mind my having told Fanny—she is as gone on Connie as I am and so is keen on helping me in any way she can!"

Fanny blushed.

"Two heads are always supposed to be better than one, dear," I said with a smile, "and in a matter like this I am sure that two cunts should be better than one!"

Alice playfully shook her fist at me. "Well, Jack, Fanny says that she talked to Connie's maid and that her mistress is a virgin! Will this matter?"

I looked inquiringly at Fanny. "She was with Mrs. Blunt before her marriage and has never left her, Sir," said Fanny respectfully, "and she told me she was certain that marriage had never been. . . I forget the word, Miss!" she added, looking at her mistress.

"Consummated, Jack!" said Alice. "Do you know that I believe it must be so; it explains certain things!"

"What things, dear?" I asked innocently.

"Things that you're not to know, Sir!" she retorted, coloring slightly, while Fanny laughed amusedly. It was delightful to me to note the excellent terms on which the two girls were and to think of my share in bringing about this "entente cordiale!"

"I don't see how it can matter!" I said reflectively. "It will certainly make the show more piquant, a virgin widow is a rarity, and if I am able to carry out my program as planned, it will fall to you, dear, to show her how her cunt works!"

Both girls laughed delightedly. "It will be very interesting!" I added.

"This brings me to the second point nicely, Jack," said Alice. "Fanny would like awfully to be present. Can it be worked, Jack?"

"It shall be worked if it is possible," I said as I smiled at Fanny's eager expression. "I consider I am in debt to her for the delicious time she gave me when last here!" Fanny colored vividly while her mistress laughed merrily.

"Let me think!"

It was a bit of a poser, but my fertile imagination was equal to the occasion.

"By Jove!" I exclaimed as a sudden idea struck me, "I think it can be done! Listen you two." The girls leaned forward in pretty eagerness.

"You and Mrs. Blunt must come here together, Alice! That's inevitable. You'll be here by one o'clock, for we must have an early lunch and a long afternoon." Alice nodded significantly.

"Let Fanny follow you in half an hour's time, lunching at home, as I don't see how I can give her lunch here. She must not be seen by Mrs. Blunt, or the latter will be suspicious! When you arrive, Fanny, come straight into this room and hide yourself in my alcove! There's a peep-hole there, from which you will be able to see all that passes. If Mrs. Blunt's curiosity should lead her to wish to see my alcove, I will choke her off by saying it is my photographic dark room and there is something there which would spoil if light is admitted now. So you'll be certain to see the fun, Fanny." She smiled gratefully, as did also Alice. "When you see that I have worked my plan successfully and your mistress and Mrs. Blunt are fastened to the pulleys, take off your clothes noiselessly, even your shoes, and when I have blindfolded Mrs. Blunt, you can slip out and share with your mistress in the pleasure of torturing her! You mustn't speak and you must move noiselessly, for her senses will be very acute. What do you say to this, Alice?"

"Jack! It will be just lovely!" exclaimed Alice, while Fanny, too respectful to speak, looked her satisfaction and gratitude. "What a time Connie will have between the three of us!" she added, laughing more wickedly.

"Now, what's the next point?" I asked. Alice looked towards Fanny, then replied, "There is nothing more, is there, Fanny?"

"No, Miss!" she answered.

"Then we'll be off! Thanks awfully, Jack, I'm really very grateful to you for arranging about Fanny. Come, Fanny!" and they rose.

"Where to now?" I asked. "You are a pair of gadabouts!"

Alice laughed. "My dentist's, worse luck!"

"Poor fun!" I said. "For you or Fanny?"

"Me, unfortunately. Fanny will have to sit in the waiting room."

I glanced at her maid, and a sudden desire to have her again seized me.

"Look here, Alice," I said, "I'm going to ask you a favor! Will you allow me to have the company of your maid this afternoon?"

Fanny blushed rosy red over cheeks and brow. Alice laughed merrily as she regarded her blushing maid and caught her shy glances.

"Certainly, Jack, as far as I am concerned!" she replied. "What do you say, Fanny? Will you stay and take care of Mr. Jack?"

Fanny glanced shyly at us both. "Yes, Miss, if you don't mind!" And vivid blushes covered her face as she caught Alice's amused and half-quizzing look.

"Then I'll be off!" Alice exclaimed. "Don't trouble to come down, Jack. Byebye, Fanny, for the present."

But of course I wasn't going to let Alice leave unescorted, so I accompanied her downstairs and saw her into a taxi, under a shower of good-natured chaff from her. Then, two steps at a time, I hurried back to the Snuggery, where I found Fanny standing where we had left her, evidently very nervous at being alone with me.

I took her gently in my arms and kissed her blushing upturned face tenderly, sat down and drew her onto my knees.

"It is sweet of you to be so kind, dear," I said, looking lovingly at her. She blushed, then raising her eyes to mine she said softly, "I couldn't refuse, Sir, after you had been so very kind to me about Mrs. Blunt."

I laughed. "Not for my own sake then?"

"Oh, I didn't mean that, Sir!" she exclaimed hastily in pretty confusion.

"Then it is for my own sake, dear?" I asked with a smile.

"Yes, Sir!" she whispered bashfully as she looked into my eyes timidly but lovingly. I drew her to me and kissed her lips passionately. I gently began to unbutton her blouse.

"Do you wish me to. . . undress, Sir?" she murmured nervously.

"Yes, please, dear!" I whispered back. "Use your mistress's room; does your mistress. . . have you naked, Fanny?" I asked softly.

"Yes, Sir," she nodded blushing.

"Then I'll do the same!" I replied with a smile as I freed her and led her to Alice's alcove, then undressed myself in mine.

Presently Fanny emerged, stark naked, a delicious object, her face covered with blushes, one hand shielding her breasts and the other over her cunt! I sprang to meet her and led her to the couch and made her sit on my knee, thrilling at the touch of her warm, firm, soft flesh.

"What shall we do, Fanny?" I asked mischievously as I slipped my hand down to her cunt and lovingly played with it. My caress seemed to set her on fire; she lost her restraint, suddenly threw her arms around my neck and kissing me passionately murmured, "Do anything you like to me, Sir!"

"May I suggest a little sucking first, and then some sweet fucking?" I said softly. Her eyes beamed assent.

I laid her flat on her back, opened her legs widely, and after feasting my eyes on her lovely cunt, I applied my lips to it and tongued her till she quivered and wriggled with delight. Alice had evidently taught her this delicious pleasure. I got on her and thrust my prick well up her; she clasped me delightedly in her arms, and letting herself go, passed from one spending to another, wriggling voluptuously, till she had extracted from me all I could give her, and which I shot into her excited interior with rapturous ecstasy—and between fucking and sucking we passed a delicious afternoon! In the enforced intervals for rest and recovery, I learned from her all about her sexual relationship with her mistress. She described the sensation of being provoked into spending by the sweet friction of Alice's cunt against hers as something heavenly, so much so that the girls seldom did anything else but satisfy their lustful cravings and desires in this way. One evening, Alice apparently was very randy and insisted on frigging Fanny, first tying her down to the four bedposts, then making Fanny tie her down similarly and tickle her cunt with a feather till she spent three times. It was clear that the girls were devoted to each other. I asked Fanny what she thought would be the arrangement if we succeeded in converting Mrs. Blunt to their ways. She blushed and said she didn't think it would affect her and Alice's relations, and she hoped Connie would sometimes spend the night at Alice's and give her a chance!

Chapter 6

A few days later I received a note from Mrs. Blunt saying that Alice was staying with her and she would be delighted if I would dine there with them quite quietly. I naturally accepted the invitation.

I was somewhat of a stranger to Mrs. Blunt. I had met her more than once and admired her radiant beauty, but no more. Now that there was more than a possibility that she might have to submit herself to me, I studied her closely.

She was more voluptuously made than I had fancied and was a simply glorious specimen of a woman, but she was something of a doll, rather shallow and weak-willed, and I saw with satisfaction that I would not have much trouble in terrorizing her and forcing her to comply with my desires.

During the evening Alice brought up the subject of my rooms and their oddity and made Mrs. Blunt so interested that I was able naturally to suggest a visit and a lunch there—which was accepted for the following day, an arrangement that made Alice glance at me with secret exultation and delighted anticipation.

In due course my guests arrived, and after a dainty lunch which drew from Mrs. Blunt many compliments, we found ourselves in the Snuggery. The girls at once commenced to examine everything, Alice taking on herself the role of showman while I, in my capacity of host, did the honours. I could see that Fanny was at her post of observation—and now awaited, with some impatience, the critical moment.

In due course Mrs. Blunt and Alice finished their tour of inspection and made as if they would rest for a while.

"What comfortable chairs you men always manage to get about you," remarked Mrs. Blunt as she somewhat critically glanced at my furniture.

"You bachelors do study your creature comforts—and so remain bachelors!" she added somewhat significantly, as she was among our deluded friends who planned a match between Alice and me.

"Quite true!" I replied with a polite smile, "so long as I can by hook or by crook get in these rooms what I want, they will be good enough for me, especially when I am permitted to enjoy the visits of such angels!"

"That's a very pretty compliment, isn't it Alice?" exclaimed Mrs. Blunt as she moved towards the Chair of Treachery which stood invitingly close, then gracefully sank into it.

Click! The arms folded on her. "Oh!" she exclaimed as she endeavored to press them back.

"What's the matter, Connie?" asked Alice, quickly hurrying to her friend, but in a flash I was onto her and had tightly gripped her. "Oh!" she screamed in admirably feinted fright, struggling naturally. I picked her up and, carrying her to the pulleys, made them fast to her wrists and fixed her upright with hands drawn well over her head, to Mrs. Blunt's horror! As I approached her. she shrieked, "Help. . . help!" pressing desperately against the locked arms and striving to get loose.

"It's no use, Mrs. Blunt!" I said quietly as I commenced to wheel the chair towards the second pair of pulleys. "You're in my power! You'd better yield quietly!"

Seizing her wrists one at a time, I quickly made the ropes fast to them, set the machinery going and, just as she was being lifted off her seat, I released the arms and drew the chair away, forcing her to stand up. In a very few seconds she was drawn up to her full height, facing Alice, both girls panting and gasping after their struggle! "There, ladies," I exclaimed, as if well pleased with my performance, "now you'll appreciate the utility of this room!"

"Oh! Mr. Jack!" cried Mrs. Blunt in evident relief, "how you did frighten me. I was sure that something dreadful was going to happen!" With a poor attempt to be sprightly she continued, "I quite made up my mind that Alice and I were going to be. . ." she broke off with a silky, self-conscious giggle.

"I gladly accept the suggestion you have so kindly made, dear lady," I said with a smile of gratitude, "and I will do you and Alice presently!" She started, horrified, stared aghast at me as if she could not believe her ears. She seemed to be dumb with shocked surprise, and went deadly pale. I was afraid to glance at Alice lest I should catch her eye and betray her.

With an effort, Mrs. Blunt stammered brokenly, "Do you mean to say. . . that Alice and I. . . are going to be. . . to be. . ." She stopped abruptly, unable to express in words her awful apprehension.

"Fucked is the word you want, I think, dear Mrs. Blunt!" I said with a smile.

"Yes, dear ladies, as you are so very kind, I shall have much pleasure in fucking you both presently!"

She quivered as if she had been struck, then screamed hysterically, "No, no! I-I won't! Help! Help! . . . Help!"

I turned quietly to Alice (who I could see was keenly enjoying the trap into which Mrs. Blunt had fallen) and said to her, "Are you going to be foolish and resist, Alice?"

She paused for a long moment, then said in a voice that admirably counterfeited intense emotion, "I feel that resistance will be of no avail, but I'm not going to submit to you tamely. You will have to. . . force me!"

"Me also!" cried Mrs. Blunt, hysterically.

"As you please!" I said equably. "I've long wanted a good opportunity of testing the working of this machinery; I don't fancy I'll get a better one than you are now offering me, a nice long afternoon—two lovely rebellious girls! Now, Mrs. Blunt, as you are chaperoning Alice, I am bound to begin with you." And I commenced to unbutton her blouse.

"No, no, Mr. Jack!" she screamed in dismay as she felt my fingers unfastening her upper garments and unhooking her skirt—but I steadily went on with my task of undressing her, and soon had her standing in her stays with bare arms and legs—a lovely tall slender half-undressed figure, her bosom heaving and palpitating, the low-cut bodice allowing the upper half of her breasts to become visible. Her flushed face indicated intense shame at this indecent exposure of herself, and her eyes strained appealing towards Alice as if to assure herself of her sympathy.

"Now I will give you a few minutes to collect yourself while I attend to Alice!" I said as I went across to the latter, whose eyes were stealthily devouring Mrs. Blunt's provoking dishabille. "Now, for you, dear!" I said, as I quickly set to work to undress her.

She very wisely was adopting the policy of dogged defiance and maintained a sullen silence as one by one her clothes were taken off her till she also stood bare-armed and bare-legged in her stays. But instead of pausing, I went on, removed her corset, unfastened the shoulder straps of her chemise and vest and pushed them down to her feet, leaving her standing with only her drawers on, a sweet, blushing, dainty, nearly-naked girl on whose shrinking trembling figure Mrs. Blunt's eyes seemed to be riveted with what certainly looked like involuntary admiration!

But I myself was getting excited and inflamed by the sight of so much unclothed and lovely girl-flesh, so eagerly returning to Mrs. Blunt, I set to work to remove the little clothing that was left on her. "No, no, Mr. Jack!" she cried piteously as I took off her stays. "Oh!" she screamed in her distress when she felt her chemise and vest slip down to her feet, exposing her in her drawers only, which solitary garment, she evidently concluded from the sight of Alice, would be left on her. But when, after a few admiring glances, I went behind her and began to undo the waist-band and she realized she was to be exposed naked, Mrs. Blunt went into a paroxysm of impassioned cries and pitiful pleadings. In her desperation she threw the whole of her weight on her slender wrists and wildly twisted her legs together in the hope of preventing me from pulling her drawers off. But they only required a few sharp tugs—down to her ankles they came! A bitter cry broke from her, her head with its wealth of now disordered golden hair fell forward on her bosom in her agony of shame. Connie Blunt was stark naked.

I stepped back a couple of paces and exultingly gazed on the vision that met my eyes. Close in front of me was revealed the back of Mrs. Blunt's tall, slender, naked figure, uninterrupted from her heels to her up-drawn hands, her enforced attitude displaying to perfection the voluptuous curves of her hips, her luscious haunches, her gloriously rounded bottom, her shapely legs.

Facing her stood Alice, naked save for her drawers, her face suffused with blushes at the sight of Connie's nakedness, her bosom heaving excitement not unmixed with delight at witnessing the nudity of her friend and trepidation at the approaching similar exposure of herself. I saw from the stealthy gloating glances she shot at Connie that she was longing to have a good look at her but dared not do so, lest her eyes should betray her delight, so I decided to give her the opportunity. I went over to her, slipped behind her, passed my arms around her and drew her against me and, holding her thus in my embrace, I gazed at the marvelous sight Connie Blunt was affording to us as she stood naked!

She was simply exquisite! Her pearly dazzling skin, her lovely shape, her delicious little breasts standing saucily out with their coral nipples as they quivered on her heaving bosom, her voluptuous hips and round smooth belly, her pretty legs, her drooping head exhibited her glorious golden hair, while, as if to balance it, a close clustering mass of silky, curly, golden-brown hairs grew thickly over the region of her cunt, hiding it completely from my eager eyes! In silent admiration I gloated over the wonderful sight of Connie Blunt naked—till a movement of Alice recalled me to her interests. She was keeping her face steadily averted from Connie, her eyes on the floor, as if unwilling to distress her friend by looking at her in her terrible nudity.

"Well, how do you like Connie now?" I asked loud enough for Mrs. Blunt to hear. She shivered; Alice remained silent.

"Aren't you going to look at her?" Alice still remained silent.

"Come, Alice, you must have a good look at her. I want to discuss her with you, to have your opinions as a girl on certain points. Come, look!" I gently stroked her naked belly.

"Oh! Don't, Jack!" she cried, affecting a distress she was not feeling. Connie glanced hastily at us to see what I was doing to Alice, and blushed deeply as she noted my wandering hands, which now were creeping up to Alice's breasts.

I seized them and began to squeeze them. "Don't, Jack!" again she cried.

"Then obey me and look at Connie!" I said sternly.

Slowly Alice raised her head, as if most reluctantly, and looked at Connie, who colored hotly as her eyes met Alice's. "Forgive me, darling!" cried Alice tearfully, "I can't help doing it!" But her throbbing breasts and excitely agitated bottom told me how the little hypocrite was enjoying the sight of Connie's nakedness!

"Now, no nonsense, Alice!" I said sternly, and I gave her breasts a twist that made her squeal in earnest and immediately rivet her eyes on her friend lest she should get another twist. And so, for a few minutes, we silently contemplated Mrs. Blunt's shrinking form, our eager eyes greedily devouring the lovely naked charms that she was so unwillingly exhibiting to us! Presently I said to Alice, whose breasts were still captives in my hands, "Now, the plain truth, please—speaking as a girl, what bit of Mrs. Blunt do you consider her finest point?"

Alice blushed uncomfortably, pretended to hesitate, then said shamefacedly, "Her. . . her. . . private parts!"

Connie flushed furiously and pressed her thighs closely together as if to shield her cunt from the eager eyes which she knew were intently looking at it! I laughed amusedly at Alice's demure phraseology and said, "I think so too! But that's not what you girls call it when you talk together. Tell me the name you use, your pet name for it!"

Alice was silent. I think she was really unwilling to say the word before Mrs.

Blunt, but I mischievously proceeded to get it out of her. I gave her tender breasts a squeeze that made her cry, "Oh!" and said, "Come, Alice, out with it!"

Still she remained silent. I let go of one of her breasts and began to pinch her fat bottom, making her wriggle and squeal in grim reality, but she would not speak!

Seeing that Mrs. Blunt was watching closely, I moved my hand away from Alice's bottom and made as if I was going to pass it through the slit in her drawers.

"Won't you tell me?" I said, moving my hand ominously.

"Cunny!" whispered Mrs. Blunt in hot confusion.

"You obstinate little thing!" I said to Alice with a laugh that showed her that I was only playing with her. "Cunny!" I repeated significantly. "Well, Alice, let Mrs. Blunt and I see your cunny!"— and as I spoke, I slipped the knot off her drawers, and down they tumbled to her ankles before she could check them with her knees, exposing by their disappearance the lovely cunt I knew so well and loved so dearly, framed so to speak by her plump rounded thighs and her sweet belly.

I sank on my knees by Alice's side and eagerly and delightedly inspected her delicious cleft, the pouting lips of which, half-hidden in their mossy covering, betrayed her erotic excitement! She endured with simulated confusion and crimson cheeks my close examination of her 'private parts,' to use her own demure phrase! At last I exclaimed rapturously, "Oh! Alice, it is sweet!" As if overjoyed, I gripped her by her bottom and thighs and pressing my lips on her cunt, I kissed passionately! "Don't, Jack!" she cried, her voice half-choked by the lascivious sensations that were thrilling through her.

Seeing that Alice was perilously near to spending in her intense erotic excitement, I quitted her and went across to Mrs. Blunt, by whose side I knelt in order to study her cunt.

"Oh, Mr. Jack! Don't look, please don't look there!" she cried in agony of shame at the idea of her cunt being thus leisurely inspected by male eyes—and she attempted to thwart me by standing on one leg and throwing her other thigh across her groin.

"Put that leg down, Connie!" I said sternly.

"No, no," she shrieked, "I won't let you look at it!"

"Won't you?" said I, and drew out from the bases of the pillars between which she was standing two stout straps, which I fastened to her slim ankles in spite of her vigorous kicking. I set the mechanism working. A piercing scream broke from her as she felt her legs being pulled remorselessly apart, and soon, notwithstanding her desperate resistance and frantic struggles, she stood like an inverted Y with her cunt in full view!

"Won't you?" I repeated with a cruelly triumphant smile as I proceeded to blindfold her, she all the while pitifully protesting. I noiselessly set Alice loose and signaled to Fanny to join us, which she quickly did, stark naked as directed. The three of us knelt in front of Connie, I between the girls with an arm around each, and with heads close together delightedly examined her private parts, Alice and Fanny's eyes sparkling with undisguised enjoyment as we noted the delicate and close-fitting, shell-pink lips of her cunt, its luscious fleshiness, and its wonderful covering of brown-gold silky hairs! She quivered in her shame at being thus forced to exhibit the most secret part of herself to my male eyes.

I motioned to the girls to remain as they were, detached myself from them, leaned forward and gently deposited a kiss on Connie's cunt. Taken absolutely by surprise, Mrs. Blunt shrieked: "O-h-h!" and began to wriggle divinely, to the delight of the girls, who motioned to me to kiss Connie's cunt again, which I gladly did. Again she screamed, squirming deliciously in her fright. I gave her cunt a third kiss, which nearly sent her into convulsions, Alice and Fanny's eyes now sparkling with lust. Not daring to do it again I rose, slipped behind her noiselessly and took her in my arms, my hands on her belly!

"No, no, Mr. Jack!" she cried, struggling fiercely, "don't touch me! . . . Oh-h-h!" she screamed as my hands caught hold of her breasts and began to feel them! They were smaller than Alice's, but firmer, soft, elastic and strangely provoking—most delicious morsels of girl-flesh. I toyed and played with them, squeezing them lasciviously to the huge delight of the girls, till I felt it was time to feel her cunt. Releasing her sweet breasts, I slipped my hands over Mrs. Blunt's stomach and her cunt.

"Oh! My God!" she shrieked, her head tossing wildly in her shame and agony as she felt my fingers wander over her private parts so conveniently arranged for the purpose. Over her shoulder I could see Alice and Fanny's faces as they watched every movement of my fingers, their eyes humid, their cheeks flushed, their breasts dancing with sexual excitement! From the fingers' point of view, Alice's cunt was the more delicious of the two because of its superior plumpness and fleshiness, but there was a certain delicacy about Connie's cunt that made me revel in the sweet occupation of feeling it.

Presently I inserted my forefinger gently between the close-fitting lips. The girls' eyes glistened with eagerness and they bent forward to see if Fanny's information was true, and I smiled at the disappointment expressed in their faces when they saw my finger bury itself in Connie's cunt up to the knuckle! She was not a virgin! But she was terribly tight, much more so than Fanny was when I first felt her, and Mrs. Blunt's screams and agonized cries clearly indicated that, for want of use, her cunt had regained its virgin tightness.

Keeping my fingers inside her, I gently tickled her clitoris in order to test her sexual susceptibility. She gave a fearful shriek accompanied by an indescribable wriggle, then another—then bedewed my hand with her sweet love-juice, her head falling on her bosom as she spent, utterly unable to control herself. I kept my finger inside her till her ecstatic crisis was over and her spasmodic thrills had quieted down— then gently withdrew it as I lovingly kissed the back of her soft neck and left her to herself.

As I did so, Alice and Fanny rose, their eyes betraying their intense enjoyment of the scene. With an unmistakable gesture they indicated each other's cunts, as if seeking mutual relief—but I shook my head, for Alice had now to be tortured. Quickly I fastened her up again while Fanny noiselessly disappeared into my alcove. I removed the bandage from Connie's eyes. As she wearily raised her head, having scarcely recovered from the violence of her spending, I clasped her to me and passionately showered kisses on her flushed cheeks and trembling lips. I saw her eyes seek Alice's as if to learn her thoughts as to what she had witnessed. Both girls blushed vividly as if in symphony. I pushed a padded chair behind Connie, released her legs and lowered her till she could sit down in comfort and left her to recover herself while I went across to Alice, who was now to be the prey of my lustful hands.

But I was now in an almost uncontrollable state of lust! My erotic senses had been so irritated and inflamed by the sight of Mrs. Blunt's delicious person naked, her terrible struggles, her shame and distress during her ordeal, that my lascivious cravings and desires imperiously called for immediate satisfaction. And the circumstances that all this had taken place in the presence of Alice and Fanny, both stark naked, both in a state of intense sexual excitement and unconcealed delight at witnessing the torturing of Mrs. Blunt, only added further fuel to the flame of my lust. But to enjoy either Connie or Alice at the moment did not suit my program, and my thoughts flew to Fanny now sitting naked in my alcove and undoubtedly very excited sexually by Mrs. Blunt's struggles and cries!

Slipping behind Alice, I took her in my arms, seized her breasts, and said not unkindly while watching Mrs. Blunt keenly, "Now, Alice, it's your turn! You've seen all that has happened to Mrs. Blunt and how in spite of her desperate resistance she has been forced to do whatever I wanted—even to spend! Now I'm going to undress." Mrs. Blunt looked up in evident alarm.

"While I am away, let me suggest that you consult your chaperone as to whether you had not better yield yourself quietly to me!" I disappeared into my alcove, where Fanny, still naked, received me with conscious expectancy, having heard every word!

I tore off my clothing, seized her naked person and whispered excitedly as I pointed to my rampant prick, "Quick, Fanny!" She instantly understood. I threw myself into an easy chair. In a moment she was kneeling between my legs with my prick in her mouth, and she sucked me deliciously till I spent rapturously down her throat! Having thus delightfully relieved my feelings, I drew her onto my knees and whispered as I gratefully kissed her, "Now, dear, I'll repay you by frigging you, while we listen to what Alice and Connie are saying." Slipping my hand down to her pouting and still excited cunt, I gently commenced the sweet junction, she clasping silently but passionately as my active finger soothed her excited senses. From our chair we could clearly see Connie and Alice and hear every word they said.

Their embarrassed silence had just been broken by Alice, who whispered in admirably simulated distress: "Oh, Connie! What shall I do?"

Connie colored painfully. With downcast eyes as if fearing to meet her friend's agitated glances, she replied in an undertone, "Better yield, dear! Don't you think so?"

"Oh! No! I can't!" cried Alice despairingly, playing her part with a perfection that brought smiles from Fanny and me. With a change of voice she asked timidly, "Was it very dreadful Connie?"

Connie covered her face with her hands and replied in broken agitation. "I thought I should have died! The awful feeling of shame! The terrible helplessness! The dreadful position into which I was fastened! The agony of having a man's hand on my. . . cunny! Oh-h-hh!"

Fanny began to wriggle deliciously on my knees as she felt her pleasure approaching. Her eyes closed slowly; she strained me against her breasts.

Suddenly she agitated herself rapidly on my finger, plunging wildly with quick strokes of her buttocks. She caught her breath, murmured brokenly, "Oh-h-h!" and inundated my finger as she spent ecstatically! My mouth sought hers as, little by little, I slowed down the play of my finger in her cunt till she came to, deliciously satisfied!

"Now I'd better go to them," I whispered, and after a few more tender kisses I went out. My appearance, naked save for my shoes and socks, caused Mrs. Blunt to hurriedly cover her face with her hands as she hysterically cried, "Oh! . . . Oh! . . . Oh!"

I ignored her and took Alice into my arms as before and said to her encouragingly, "Well, dear, what is it to be?" whispering inaudibly in her ear, "You're to be tickled!"

Alice stood silent with downcast eyes. In her anxiety to hear Alice's decision, Mrs. Blunt uncovered her face and looked eagerly at us! At last it came! "No," spoken so low that we could just hear her.

"Oh, Alice! You are a silly girl!" exclaimed Mrs. Blunt, now afraid about herself. Alice cast a reproachful glance at Connie and said, almost in tears, the little humbug, "I can't! Oh, I can't!"

Without a word I fastened straps to Alice's pretty ankles and dragged her legs apart till she stood precisely as Mrs. Blunt had done. I carefully blindfolded her and seated myself just below her on the floor within easy reach of her, and began to amuse myself with her defenseless cunt, knowing that Mrs. Blunt could see over my shoulder all that passed.

With both hands I felt all of Alice's private parts, touching, pressing, stroking, parting her lips, even pulling her hairs every now and then, and peering into her interior—an act invariably followed by an ardent kiss as if in apology, she squirming deliciously. She submitted herself to the sweet torture in silence till I pretended to be trying to push my finger into her cunt, when she screamed in horror, "Don't, Jack, don't!" as if unable to endure it! "Hurts, does it, Alice!" I said smiling meanly. "Then I won't do it again! I'll try something softer than my finger!" After fetching a feather, I resumed my position on the carpet.

Alice's color now went and came and her bosom began to heave uneasily, for she guessed what was now going to be done to her, and although she rather liked having her cunt tickled, the existing conditions were not what she was accustomed to. She awaited her ordeal with a good deal of trepidation.

Quietly I applied the tip of the feather to her cunt's now slightly pouting lips with a delicate yet subtle touch. "O-h-h!" she exclaimed, quivering painfully. I gave her three or four more similar touches, after which she began to wriggle vigorously, crying: "Oh! . . . Oh! . . . Don't, Jack!" I was just beginning to tickle her cunt in real earnest when Connie, horrified at the sight, shrieked: "Stop! . . . stop! . . . oh, you awful brute! . . . you coward! . . . to torture a girl in that way! . . . oh! my God!" she moaned, quite overcome at the sight of Alice being tortured!

How thankful I was that I had blindfolded Alice! I am sure that she otherwise would have given the game away—she must have laughed! In fact, some of her convulsions were undoubtedly caused by suppressed laughter and not by her torture!

"There's no better way of curing a girl of obstinacy than by tickling her cunt, Connie," I said unconcernedly, and I again commenced to tickle Alice.

"No, no, stop!" Connie shrieked frantically. "Oh! You cruel brute! . . . you'll kill her!"

I laughed. "Oh, no, Connie, she's all right—only a little erotic excitement!" I explained equably as I resumed the tickling, this time making Alice wriggle and scream in real earnest. She had not been allowed to satisfy her lustful cravings, induced by the sight of Connie's agonies, and by now she was in a terrible condition of fierce concupiscence and unsatisfied desires, dying to spend, but so far unable to do so for want of the spark necessary to provoke the discharge! More and more hysterical became Connie's prayers and pleadings, shriller her cries of genuine horror at the sight of Alice's cunt being so cruelly tickled—wilder and wilder became Alice's struggles and screams, till suddenly she shrieked, "For God's sake, make me spend!" Immediately I thrust the feather well up her cunt and rapidly twiddled it, then tickled her clitoris! A tremendous spasm shook Alice, her head fell back, then dropped on her bosom as she exclaimed: "A-h-h. . . ah-h-h!" in a tone of blessed relief, quivering deliciously as the rapturous spasm of the ecstasy thrilled through as she spent madly!

As soon as she came to herself again, I said to her, "Well, will you now yield yourself to me, or do you want some more?"

"Oh, no! No!—my God, no!" she cried, feigning to be completely subdued.

"You'll then be a good girl?"

"Yes!" she gasped.

"You'll do whatever I tell you to do?"

"Yes! Yes!" she cried.

"You'll let me. . . fuck you?"

"Oh, my God! . . ." she moaned, remaining silent. I touched her cunt with the feather. "Yes! Yes!" she screamed. "Yes!"

"That's right, dear!" I said encouragingly. Quickly I released her and put her into a large and comfortable easy chair in which she promptly coiled herself up, as if utterly exhausted and ashamed of her absolute surrender, but really to escape the sympathetic and pitying glances from Connie. It was as clever a piece of acting as I had ever seen!

I went across to Mrs. Blunt and without a word, I touched the springs and set the machinery at work. "Oh! Oh!" she cried as she felt herself drawn up again and her legs being remorselessly dragged asunder till she had resumed her late position. When I had her properly fixed, I said to her, "Now, Connie, I am going to punish you for abusing me. You'll have something to scream about!" I applied the feather to her lovely, but defenseless, cunt!

"Don't, don't! . . . Oh, my God!" she screamed. I saw we were about to have a glorious spectacle, so I stopped, blindfolded her, and beckoned to Fanny, who promptly came up, Alice also. Handing a feather to each, I pointed to Connie's quivering cunt.

Delightedly both girls applied their feathers to Connie's tender slit, Alice directing hers against Connie's clitoris, while Fanny ran hers all along the lips and as far inside as she could, their eyes sparkling with cruel glee as they watched Connie wriggle and listened to her terrible shrieks and hysterical exclamations. It was a truly voluptuous sight! Connie naked, struggling frantically, while Alice and Fanny, also naked, were goading her into hysterics with their feathers! But soon I had to intervene. Connie by now was exhausted; she couldn't stand any more. Reluctantly, I stopped the girls, signaled to Fanny to disappear and Alice to return to her chair while I released Connie's bandage.

She looked at me seemingly, half-dazed, panting and gasping after her exertions.

"Now will you submit yourself to me, Connie?" I asked.

"Yes! Yes!" she gasped.

"Fucking and all!"

"Oh, my God! . . . Yes!"

I set her free. As she sank into her chair, Alice rushed to her as if impelled by irresistible sympathy. The two girls fell into each other's arms, kissing each other passionately, murmuring: "Oh, Connie! . . ."

"Oh, Alice!" The first part of the play was over!

Chapter 7

I produced a large bottle of champagne and, pretending that the opener was in my alcove, I went there, but my real objective was to satisfy in Fanny the raging concupiscence which my torturing of Alice and Connie had so fiercely aroused in me.

I found her shivering with unsatisfied hot lust. I threw myself into a chair, placed my bottom on the edge and pointed to my prick in glorious erection.

Instantly Fanny straddled across me, brought her excited cunt to bear on my tool and impaled herself on it with deliciously voluptuous movements, sinking down on it till she rested on my thighs, her arms 'round my neck, mine 'round her warm body, our lips against each other's. Working herself divinely up and down on my prick, she soon brought on the blessed relief we both were thirsting for, and in exquisite rapture we spent madly.

"Oh! Sir! Wasn't it lovely!" she whispered as soon as she could speak.

"Which, Fanny," I asked mischievously. "This!—or that!" pointing to the room.

She blushed prettily, then whispered saucily, "Both, Sir!" as she passionately kissed me.

I begged her to sponge me while I opened the champagne, which she did sweetly, kissing my flaccid prick lovingly, and soon she removed from it all traces of our bout of fucking. I poured out four large glasses and made her drink one, which she did with great enjoyment, and took the other three out with me to the girls.

I found them still in each other's arms and coiled together in the large armchair, Alice half-sitting on Connie's thighs and half resting on Connie's breasts—a lovely sight. I touched her; she started up while Connie slowly opened her eyes.

"Drink this, it will pull you together!" I said, handing each a tumbler. They did so, and the generous wine seemed to have an immediate good effect and to put new life into them. I eyed them with satisfaction. Raising my glass, I said, "To your good health, dears, and a delicious consummation of Connie's charming and most sporting suggestion!" then gravely emptied my tumbler.

Both girls turned scarlet, Connie almost angrily. They glanced tentatively at each other but neither spoke.

To terminate their embarrassment, I pointed to a settee close by, and soon we arranged ourselves in it, I in the center, Alice on my right and Connie on my left, their heads resting on my shoulders, their faces turned towards each other and within easy kissing distance, my arms clasping them to me, my hands being just able to command the outer breast of each! Both girls seemed ill at ease. I think Connie was really so, as she evidently dreaded having to be fucked by me, but with Alice it was only a pretense.

"A penny for your thoughts dear!" I said to her chafingly, curious to know what she would say.

"I was thinking how lovely Connie is. . . naked!" she murmured softly, blushing prettily. I felt a quiver run through Connie.

"Before today, how much of each other have you seen?" I asked interestedly.

Silently, both girls pointed to just above their breasts.

"Then stand up, Connie dear, and let us have a good look at you," I said, "and Alice shall afterwards return the compliment by showing you herself! Stand naturally, with your hands behind you."

With evident unwillingness she complied, and with pretty bashfulness she faced us, a naked blue-eyed daughter of the gods, tall, slender, goldenhaired, exquisite—blushing as she noted in our eyes the pleasure the contemplation of her naked charms was giving us! "Now in profile, dear!"

Obediently she turned. We delightedly noted her exquisite outline from chin to thigh, her proud little breasts, her gently curving belly, its wealth of golden-brown hair, standing out like a bush at its junction with her thighs, the sweep of her haunches and bottom, and her shapely legs!

"Thanks, darling," I said appreciatively. "Now Alice!" And drawing Connie onto my knees, I kissed her lovingly.

Blushingly Alice complied, and with hands clasped behind her back, she faced us, a piquant, provoking, demure, brown-eyed, dark-haired little English lassie, plump, juicy, appetizing. She smiled mischievously at me as she watched Connie's eyes wander approvingly over her delicious little figure! "Now in profile, please!"

She turned, and now we realized the subtle voluptuousness of Alice's naked figure, how her exquisitely full and luscious breasts were matched, in turn being balanced by her glorious fleshy bottom and her fat thighs, the comparative shortness of her legs only adding piquancy to the whole, while her unusually conspicuous Mount Venus, with its dark, clustering, silky hairs, proudly proclaimed itself as the delightful center of her attractions! "Thanks, darling!" we both exclaimed admiringly as we drew her to us and lovingly kissed her, to her evident delight and gratification.

"Now, Connie darling!" I said. "I want you to lie down on that couch!" I removed my arm from her waist to allow her to rise.

"No, Jack!" she begged piteously and imploringly, her lovely eyes not far from tears. "Please, Jack! Don't insist!"

"You must do it, darling!" I said kindly but firmly as I raised her to her feet.

"Come, dear!" and I led her to the couch and made her lie down.

"I must put the straps on you, Connie, dear," I said, "not that I doubt your promise, but because I am sure you won't be able to lie still. Don't be frightened, dear!" I added, as I saw a look of terror come over her face. "You are not going to be tortured, or tickled or hurt, but you will be treated most sweetly!"

Reluctantly Connie yielded. Quickly Alice attached the straps to her wrists, while I secured the other pair to her ankles. We set the machinery to work and soon she was lying flat on her back, her hands and feet secured to the four corners, the dark-brown upholstery throwing into high relief her lovely figure and dazzling fair hair and skin! I blindfolded her very carefully in such a way that she could not get rid of the bandage by rubbing her head against the couch. Now that Connie was at our mercy, I signaled to Fanny, who gleefully rushed to us noiselessly and hugged her mistress with silent delight.

"Now, Alice, dear!" I said, "make love to Connie!"

"Oh-h!" cried Connie in shocked surprise, blushing so hotly that even her bosom was suffused with color. But Alice was already on her knees by Connie's side and was passionately kissing her protesting mouth in the exuberance of her delight at the arrival at last of the much-desired opportunity to satisfy her lusts on Connie's lovely person, cunt against cunt.

I slipped into a chair and took Fanny on my knees, and in sweet companionship, we settled ourselves comfortably to watch Alice make love to Connie! My left arm was 'round Fanny's waist, the hand toying with the breasts which it could just command, while my right hand played lovingly with her cunt.

After Alice had relieved her excited feelings by showering her kisses on Connie's lips with whispered fond endearments, she raised her head and contemplated, with an expression of intense delight, the naked figure of her friend which I had placed at her disposal! She proceeded to pass her hands lightly over Connie's flesh. Shakespeare sings, substituting the feminine pronoun for the masculine one he uses: To win her heart she touched her here and there,—Touches so soft that conquer chastity! This is what Alice was doing! With lightly poised hands, she touched Connie on the most susceptible parts of herself: her armpits, navel, belly, and especially the soft tender insides of her thighs—evidently reserving her breasts and cunt for special attention. Soon the effect on Connie became apparent. Her bosom began to palpitate in sweet agitation, while significant tremors ran through her limbs. "Is it so nice then, darling?" cooed Alice, her eyes dancing with delight as she watched the effect of her operations on Connie's now quivering person. She rested her lips on Connie's and gently took hold of her breasts!

"Oh, Alice!" cried Connie, but Alice closed her lips with her own, half choking her friend with her passionate kisses. Raising her head again, she eagerly and delightedly inspected the delicious morsels of Connie's flesh that were imprisoned in her hands. "Oh, you darlings!" she exclaimed as she squeezed them. "You sweet things!" she said as she kissed them rapturously.

"Oh, what dear little nipples!" she cried, taking them in turn into her mouth, her hands all the while squeezing and caressing Connie's lovely breasts till that worthy woman faintly murmured, "Oh, stop, darling!"

"Oh, my love! Was I hurting you, darling?" cried Alice with gleaming eyes, as with a smile full of mischief towards us she reluctantly released Connie's breasts. For a moment she hesitated, as if uncertain what to do next. Her eyes rested on Connie's cunt, so sweetly defenseless. An idea seemed to seize her.

With a look of delicious anticipation, she slipped her left arm under Connie's shoulders so as to embrace her, placed her lips on Connie's mouth, extended her right arm and, without giving Connie the least hint as to her intentions, she placed her hand on Connie's cunt, her slender forefinger resting on the orifice itself! "Oh-h, Alice!" cried Connie, taken completely by surprise and wriggling voluptuously. "Oh-h-h, Connie!" rapturously murmured Alice between the hot kisses she was now raining on Connie's mouth, her forefinger beginning to agitate itself inquisitively but lovingly! "Oh darling! Your cunny is sweet!" she murmured as her hand wandered all over Connie's private parts, now stroking and pressing her delicate Mount Venus, now twisting and pulling her hairs, now gently compressing the soft, springy flesh between her thumb and forefinger, now passing along the delicate shell-pink lips, and finally gently inserting her finger between them into the pouting orifice! "I must! . . . I must look at it!" Quickly she withdrew her arm from under Connie's shoulders, gave her a long, clinging kiss, and shifted her position by Connie's side till her head commanded Connie's private parts. She squared her arms, rested herself on Connie's belly, and with both hands proceeded to examine and study Connie's cunt, her eyes sparkling with delight.

Again she submitted Connie's delicious organ of sex to a most searching and merciless examination, one hand on each side of the now slightly gaping slit, stroking, squeezing, pressing, touching! With fingers poised gently but firmly on each side of the slit, Alice gently drew the lips apart and peered curiously into the shell-pink cavity of Connie's cunt, and after a prolonged inspection, she shifted her finger rather higher, again parted the lips and with rapt attention gazed at Connie's clitoris which was now beginning to show signs of sexual excitement, Connie all this time quivering and wriggling under the touches of Alice's fingers.

Her curiosity apparently satisfied for the time, Alice raised her head and looked strangely and interrogatively at me. Comprehending her mute enquiry, I smiled and nodded. She smiled back, then dropping her head, she looked intently at Connie's cunt, and imprinted a long clinging kiss in its very center.

Connie squirmed violently. "Oh-h-h!" she exclaimed in a half-strangled voice. With a smile of intense delight, Alice repeated her kiss, then again and again, Connie at each repetition squirming and wriggling in the most delicious way, her vehement plunging telling Alice what flames her hot kisses had aroused in Connie.

Again she opened Connie's cunt, and keeping its tender lips wide apart, she deposited between them and right inside the orifice itself a long lingering kiss which seemed to set Connie's blood on fire, for she began to plunge wildly with furious upward jerks and jogs of her hips and bottom, nearly dislodging Alice. She glanced merrily at us, her eyes brimming with mischief and delight, then straddled across Connie and arranged herself on her so that her mouth commanded

Connie's cunt while her stomach rested on Connie's breasts and her cunt lay poised over Connie's mouth, but not touching it. Her legs now lay parallel to Connie's arms and outside them.

Utterly taken aback by Alice's tactics, and in her innocence not recognizing the significance of the position Alice assumed on her, she cried, "Oh, Alice! What are you doing?" Alice grinned delightedly at us and lowered her head, ran her tongue lightly half a dozen times along the lips of Connie's cunt and set to work to gamahuch her! "Oh-h-h!" shrieked Connie, her voice almost strangled by the violence of the wave of lust that swept over her at the first touch of Alice's tongue. "Oh-h-h! . . . Oh-h-h. . ." she exclaimed in her utter bewilderment and confusion as she abandoned herself to strangely intoxicating and thrilling sensations hitherto unknown to her, jerking herself upwards as if to meet Alice's tongue, her face in her agitated movements coming against Alice's cunt, before it dawned on her confused senses what the warm, moist, quivering hairy object could be! In wild excitement Alice thoroughly searched Connie's cunt with her active fingers, darting deeply into it, playing delicately on the quivering lips, sucking and tickling her clitoris, and sending Connie into such a state of lust that I thought it wise to intervene.

"Stop, dear!" I called out to Alice, who at once desisted, looking interrogatively at me. "You are trying her too much! Get off her now and let her recover herself a little or you'll finish her, which we don't want yet!" Quickly comprehending the danger, Alice rolled off Connie, turned 'round, contemplated for a moment Connie's naked wriggling figure, then got onto her again, only this time lips to lips, bubbies against bubbies, and cunt against cunt. She clasped Connie closely to her as she arranged herself, murmuring passionately, "Oh, Connie! . . . At last! . . . At last! . . ." then commenced to rub her cunt sweetly on Connie's.

"Oh-h-h, Alice!" breathed Connie rapturously as she responded to Alice's efforts by heaving and jogging herself upwards. "Oh-h-h. . . darling!" she panted brokenly, evidently feeling her ecstasy approaching by the voluptuous wriggles and agitated movements, as Alice now rubbed herself vigorously against her cunt with riotous down-strokes of her luscious bottom.

Quicker and quicker, faster and faster, wilder and wilder became the movements of both girls, Connie now plunging madly upwards, while Alice rammed herself down on her with fiercer and fiercer thrusts of her raging hips and buttocks till the delicious crisis arrived! "Connie! . . . Connie!" gasped Alice, as the indescribable spasm of spending thrilled voluptuously through her. "Ah-h-h. . . ah-h-h! . . . Aн-H-H! . . ." exclaimed Connie rapturously as she spent madly in exquisite convulsions, dead to everything but the delirious rapture that was thrilling through her as she lay tightly clasped in Alice's clinging arms!

The sight was too much for Fanny! With the most intense interest, she had watched the whole of this exciting scene, parting her legs the better to accommodate my hand, which now was actually grasping her cunt, my forefinger buried in her up to the knuckle, while my thumb rested on her clitoris, and she had already spent once deliciously. But the spectacle of the lascivious transports of her mistress on Connie set her blood on fire again. She recollected her similar experience in Alice's arms, the sensations that Alice's cunt had communicated to hers, the delicious ecstasy of her discharge, and, as the two girls neared their bliss, she began to agitate herself voluptuously on my knees, on my now active finger, keeping pace with them, till with an inarticulate murmur of, "Oh! . . . Oh-h, Sir-r," she inundated my hand with her love-juice, spending simultaneously with her mistress and her mistress's friend.

As soon as she emerged from her ecstatic trance, I whispered to her inaudibly, "Bring the sponge and towel, dear!"

Noiselessly she darted off, sponged herself, then returned with a bowl of water, a sponge, and a towel just as Alice slowly raised herself off Connie with eyes still humid with lust and her cunt bedewed with love-juice. I took her fondly in my arms and kissed her tenderly, while Fanny quickly removed all traces of her discharge from her hairs, then proceeded to pay the same delicate attention to Connie, whose cunt she now touched for the first time.

Presently we heard Connie murmur, "May I get up now, Jack!"

"Not yet, darling!" I replied lovingly as I stooped and kissed her. "You have to make me happy now!"

"No, Jack! Please," she whispered, but Alice intervened. "Yes, darling, you must let Jack have you! You must taste again the real article," she cooed. "Let me work you into condition again!" And she signaled to Fanny, who instantly knelt by Connie and began playing with her dainty little breasts and feeling her cunt, her eyes sparkling with delight at thus being permitted to handle Connie who, not noting the difference of touch as Fanny's ministrations to her cunt had accustomed Connie to her fingers, lay still in happy ignorance of the change of operator.

Soon Fanny's fingers began to bring about the desired recovery. Connie's breasts began to stiffen and grow tense, and her body began to tremble in gentle agitation. She was ready—and so was I!

Without a word I slipped onto her. "Oh, Jack!" she murmured as I took her into my arms, holding up her lips to be kissed—no reluctance now! My rampant prick found her sweet hole and gently made an entrance; she was terribly tight, but her discharge had well-lubricated the sweet passage into her interior, and inch by inch, I forced myself into her till my prick was buried in her cunt, she trembling and quivering in my clasp, her involuntary flinchings and sighs confessing the pain attending her penetration! But once she had admitted me all the way into her and I began the sweet up-and-down movement, she went into transports of delight, accommodating herself deliciously to me as, with lips closely against each other, we exchanged hot kisses! I set to work to fuck Connie in earnest. Straining her to me till her breasts were flattened against my chest and I could feel every flutter of her sweet body, I let myself go, ramming into her faster and faster, more and more wildly—till, unable any longer to restrain myself, I surrendered to love's delicious ecstasy and spent madly into Connie just as she flooded my prick in rapturous bliss, quivering under me in the most voluptuous way! We lay closely clasped together till our mutual ecstatic trance slowly died away. With a sign, I bade Fanny disappear. As soon as she had vanished, Alice removed the blindfold from Connie's eyes. As they met mine, bashfully and shamefacedly, blushing deeply at thus finding herself naked in my arms, Connie timidly held up her mouth to me. Instantly my lips were on hers and we exchanged long lingering kisses till we panted for breath. Gently I released her from my clasp and rose off her, and, with Alice's help, unfastened her. Alice gently led her to her alcove where she sedulously attended to her, while Fanny silently but delightedly did the same for me.

It was now only four o'clock. We had a good hour before us. There was now no possible doubt that Connie had surrendered herself to the pleasures of Tribadism and Lesbian love as far as Alice was concerned. So when the girls rejoined me, Connie with a tender look on her face, and we had refreshed ourselves and recovered our sexual appetites and powers, I said to Connie, "Now, dear, you are entitled to take your revenge on Alice—will you?"

She cast a look of love at Alice, who blushed sweetly, then turning to me she murmured, "Please, Jack!" at the same time giving me a delicious kiss.

"Come along, Alice!" I said as we all rose, and I led her to the couch— the veritable Altar of Venus. "How will you have her, Connie?" I asked as Alice stood nervously awaiting the disposal of her sweet person.

Connie blushed. With a glance at Alice, she replied, "Tie her down, Jack, just as you did me!"

Blushingly Alice lay down, and soon Connie and I had her fastened down in the desired position.

"Will you have her blindfolded, dear?" I enquired.

Connie hesitated, looking oddly at Alice, then replied, "No, Jack! I want to see her eyes!" so significantly that Alice involuntarily quivered as she colored hotly again.

"May I do just whatever I like to Alice, Jack?" asked Connie, almost hesitatingly with a fresh access of color.

"Anything within reason, dear!" I replied with a smile. "You mustn't bite her bubbies off, or stitch up her cunt, for instance." Alice quivered while Connie laughed. "And you must leave her alive, for I am to follow you!"

"Oh, Jack!" exclaimed Alice at this intimation, blushing prettily.

Connie turned eagerly to me. "Are you going to fuck her?" she asked with sparkling eyes. I nodded, smiling at her eagerness.

"And may I watch you?" she demanded.

"Why, certainly, dear—and perhaps help me! Now what are you going to do to Alice? See how impatiently she is waiting!"

Both girls laughed, Alice a trifle uneasily. Connie looked intently at her for a moment. Seating herself by Alice's side, she began playing with Alice's breasts, keeping her eyes steadily fixed on Alice's.

"Your bubbies are too big for my hands, darling!" she said presently as she stooped to kiss her. "But they are lovely!" She squeezed them tenderly for a while, then deserted them, shifting her position, and began to feel Alice's cunt, which she lovingly stroked and caressed.

"Your cunny is fat, darling!" she exclaimed presently with heightened color as she held Alice's cunt compressed between her finger and thumb and gently squeezed the soft springy flesh, while Alice squirmed involuntarily.

Suddenly Connie leaned forward, took Alice's face in her hands and whispered, "Darling, I'm going to fuck you twice, eh?" and lovingly kissed her while Alice's eyes sought mine shamefully.

Quickly Connie got onto Alice, took her into her arms and, keeping her head raised so as to look right into Alice's eyes, she began to rub her cunt against Alice's, gently and slowly at first with a circular grinding sort of movement. Presently her action quickened and became more and more irregular. Soon Connie was rubbing herself up and down Alice's cunt with quick agitated strokes of her bottom, all the while intently watching Alice's eyes as if to gauge her friend's sensations. Soon both girls began plunging and heaving riotously, Alice especially, as they both felt the crisis approaching.

Then came a veritable storm of confused heaving, thrusting and plunging.

"Kiss... me... darling!" exclaimed Alice, now on the verge of spending. But Connie only shook her head with a loving smile, rammed her cunt against Alice's fiercely, intent on Alice's now-humid eyes, and apparently restraining her own discharge! A frantic heave from Alice—"Ah-h-h, dar-rling" she gasped as her eyes half closed in ecstasy—then she spent with delicious quivering. Immediately Connie glued her lips to Alice's, agitated herself rapidly against Alice's cunt. "Alice!" she breathed in her delirious frenzy as a spasm thrilled through her, and Alice's cunt received her lovejuice as she spent ecstatically.

For some moments the girls lay silent, only half-conscious, motionless save for the involuntary thrills that shot through them. Then Connie raised her head and, with the smile of the victor, surveyed Alice, whose eyes now began to open languidly. She blushed deliciously as she met Connie's glances and raised her mouth as if inviting a kiss. Instantly Connie complied with passionate delight. "Wasn't it nice, darling?" I heard her whisper. "Oh, Connie, just heavenly!" murmured Alice tenderly and with loving kisses.

"Are you ready again, darling?" whispered Connie eagerly. "Yes! Yes!" replied Alice softly, beginning to agitate herself under Connie.

"Our mouths together this time, darling, eh!" whispered Connie with excitement. "Don't stop kissing me, darling!" she added tenderly as she responded to Alice's movements under her and set to work to rub her cunt against Alice's. Soon both girls were hard at work with their cunts squeezed against each other, slit to slit, clitoris against clitoris—Connie's bottom and hips swaying and oscillating voluptuously while Alice jerked herself up madly. With mouths glued to each other they plunged, curveted, wriggled, squirmed, till the blissful ecstasy overtook them both simultaneously, when madly they bedewed each other with their love-juice to the accompaniment of the most exquisite quivering, utterly absorbed in rapture! With a deep-drawn sigh of intense satisfaction, Connie presently rose slowly off Alice and tenderly contemplated her as she lay—still fastened by her widely extended limbs—to the four corners of the couch, her closed eyes and her involuntary tremors indicating that she was still tasting bliss. Connie turned to me and whispered rapturously, "Oh, Jack, she is sweet!" I kissed her lovingly and resting her on my knees, I sponged and dried her, then begged her to perform the same office to Alice, whose cunt was positively glistening with her own and Connie's spendings. As soon as Alice felt the sponge at work, she dreamily opened her eyes, and, on recognizing me, she made as if to rise; but when she found herself checked by her fastenings and realized that she was now to be fucked by me, she smiled somewhat uneasily as our eyes met, for as often as she had tasted love's ecstasy in my arms, she had invariably, after that first time, been free. Now she was tied down in such a way as to be absolutely helpless, and in this equivocal position, she had to accommodate herself to me and to satisfy my lustful passions and desires. But I smiled encouragingly back to her, seated myself by her side, and tenderly embracing her defenseless body, I whispered, "Darling, may I have you like this?"

Her eyes beamed gratefully on me, full of love; she was now perfectly happy because I had left it to her to say whether or not she would be fucked while tied down in the most shamelessly abandoned attitude in which any girl could be placed in. So with love's own light in her shining eyes and with pretty blushes on her cheeks, Alice whispered back tenderly, "Yes, darling, yes!"

Promptly I got on her, took her in my arms, and gently drove my prick home up her cunt. "Do you like it like this, darling?" I murmured softly. "Shall I go on?" She nodded sweetly, our lips met, and I began to fuck her.

Tied down as she was, she was simply delicious! I had had first Fanny and then Connie in precisely the same attitude, but voluptuous as was the act of fucking them so, the pleasure fell short of what I was now tasting! To a certain extent, both Fanny and Connie were unwilling recipients of my erotic favors.

Fanny was really ravished and Connie practically so, and their movements under me were the outcome of fright, shame, and even pain; but Alice was yielding herself sweetly to my caprices and was doing her best to accommodate her captive body to my movements. Perhaps her little plump rounded figure suited the attitude better than the taller and more slender forms of Fanny and Connie—but whatever may have been the reason, the result was undeniable, and Alice, fucked as a helpless captive, was simply delicious. Her double spend under Connie made her usual quick response to love's demands arrive more slowly than was customary with her, and as this was my fourth course that afternoon, our fucking was protracted to a delicious extent, and I adopted every method and variation known to me to intensify our exquisite pleasure.

Commencing slowly, I fucked Alice with long strokes, drawing my prick nearly out of her cunt and then shoving it well home again, a procedure which always delighted her and which she welcomed with appreciative and warm kisses. I agitated myself more rapidly on her, shoving, pressing, thrusting, ramming, now fast, now slow, holding her so tightly clasped that her breasts were flattened against my chest while she, panting and gasping, plunged, wriggled, and heaved herself wildly under me in her loyal endeavors to cooperate with me to bring about love's ecstasy. Presently she thrilled exquisitely under me! Fired by her delicious transports, I re-doubled my efforts, as did she also. I began to feel my seminal resources respond to my demand on them. Soon we both were overtaken by the tempestuous prelude to the blissful crisis, and then came the exquisite consummation of our wildly sexual desires! With a half-strangled, "Ah-h. . . Jack," Alice spent in rapturous convulsions just as I madly shot into her my boiling tribute!

Oblivious to absolutely everything except the delicious satisfaction of our overwrought feelings, we lay as if in a trance! We were roused by Connie's gentle warning voice, "Alice! . . . Alice! . . . Alice, dear!" as she set to work to undo Alice's fastenings. Taking the hint, I rose after giving Alice a long lingering parting kiss. We helped her to get up and Connie tenderly took her off at once to the girl's alcove, while I retired to mine, where Fanny deliciously attended to me, her eyes sparkling with gratified pleasure at the recollection of the voluptuous spectacle she had been permitted to witness through the peep-hole.

As it was getting late. We all dressed ourselves, and after a tender parting, I put Connie and Alice into a taxi and started them off home.

On returning to my room, I found Fanny ready to depart. She was full of delighted gratitude to me for having managed that she should see all that went on and also have a share in the afternoon's proceedings, and when I slipped a couple of sovereigns into her hand, I had the greatest difficulty making her accept them. Finally she did so, saying shyly and with pretty blushes, "You've only got to call me, Sir, and I will come." I kissed her tenderly, put her into a hansom and sent her home. I wended my way to my Club, where I drank to the three sweet cunts I, that afternoon, had enjoyed, and their delicious owners; Alice, Connie, and Fanny!

Chapter 8

I did not see anything of Alice for some little time after the conversion of Connie, but I did not distress myself, for I knew she would be in the first flush of her newly developed Tribadic ardor and newly born passion for her own sex and would be hard put to satisfy Connie and Fanny, and I felt sure that she would, of her own volition, come to me before long. Meanwhile, another matter began to occupy my serious attention.

A few months ago, I had made the acquaintance of Lady Betty Bashe at the house of a mutual friend. She was a consolable widow of something under forty and was busy introducing her daughter into Society, and for some perverse reason, she took it into her head that I would make an excellent son-in-law and proceeded to hunt me persistently, her daughter aiding and abetting her vigorously till they became a real nuisance.

I had taken a dislike to both mother and daughter from our first meeting, although they both were decidedly attractive. Lady Betty was a tall, robust, buxom woman of under forty, after the type of Ruben's fleshy females, but somewhat over-developed, and owed a good deal to her corseter. I guessed that without her stays she would be almost exuberant, but nevertheless a fine armful. Molly, her daughter, was a small and dainty edition of her mother, and with the added freshness and juiciness of her eighteen years, she was really a tidbit. But both mother and daughter were silly, affected, insincere, and unscrupulous, and Lady Betty's juvenile airs and youthful affectations only tended to confirm my distaste for her.

I had told Lady Betty plainly one day that I was not in the matrimonial market; but she nevertheless continued to pursue me pertinaciously till it became intolerable, and I determined I would stop her at any cost.

Matters culminated at a dinner given by the same hostess whose kindly suggestion brought about the reconciliation of Alice and myself, as already related in the first chapter. She, of course, again gave me Alice as my dinner partner, an arrangement that did not commend itself to Lady Betty. I think she must have taken a little too much of our hostess' champagne, but in the middle of dinner she called out in a tone that attracted everyone's attention and checked the conversation, "Jack, we're coming to lunch day after tomorrow; mind you're in!"

I was intensely annoyed, first by the use of my Christian name and then by the intolerable air of proprietorship she assumed, but the look of distress on my dear little hostess's face impelled me to face the music. I promptly responded with a smile, "That will be very nice of you, Lady Betty; you shall have some of my famous soufflé, and you will be the first to see my new curios!" The conversation turned on my curios and soon became general, much to my hostess's relief, and the rest of the dinner passed off pleasantly.

As I was driving Alice home, she said sympathetically, "Poor Jack, what a bad time you'll have day after tomorrow."

"Not at all, dear," I replied cheerily, "somebody else will have the bad time, for unless I am greatly mistaken, there will be a lot of squealing in the Snuggery on that afternoon. Her Ladyship will be made to remember the pleasures of married life, and there will be one virgin less in the world!"

Alice started in surprise. "You don't mean to say, Jack, that you mean to. . . to. . ."

"I do!" I said stoutly. "I'm sick of this annoyance and mean to stop it. Will you come and see the fun, dear?"

"I will, gladly," Alice replied energetically. "But, Jack, do ask Connie also, for we both have a certain bone to pick with her Ladyship."

"Why not include Fanny as well, dear?" I asked mischievously.

"Jack! That would be just lovely!" Alice exclaimed with sparkling eyes. "Yes, Jack! Please let Fanny come! We'll then be three couples, very convenient, Sir, and we'll be three couples in the undressing and the. . . the. . . sponging! Yes, Jack! Let's have Fanny also. We can have a regular orgy with Lady Betty and Molly as the main attraction!" she added, eagerly hugging me in her excitement while one hand wandered down to the fly of my trousers.

I was hugely taken by her idea luscious woman and a voluptuous maiden on whom to exercise our lustful ingenuity! "A most excellent idea, darling," I replied. "You bring Connie with you, let Fanny follow and hide in my alcove till she's wanted, as before, and we'll give Lady Betty and Molly an afternoon entertainment they won't easily forget, and also have a heavenly time ourselves!"

Alice smiled delightedly. Cuddling up to me she whispered, "Now, Jack, I'm going to ask a favor. I'm longing to be fucked in my own little room in the middle of my own familiar things on my own bed! Come in tonight, darling, and do me!"

"Yes! . . . Yes. . . Yes!" I whispered passionately, punctuating my reply with kisses and noting with delight how she thrilled with sweet anticipation. Soon we arrived at her flat. Fanny, with pretty lashes, ushered me into Alice's dainty bedroom and on her little bed in the quaint surroundings of her most intimate self, Alice, stark naked, received me in her arms and expired deliciously five times, while I twice madly spent into her. So excited was I by my voluptuous experience of fucking an unmarried girl in her bedroom, and on her own bed, that I began a third course, but Alice murmured, "No, Jack, darling! Not again! I've got to console Fanny presently, and she'll be very excited!" Whereupon I reluctantly rose off her, dressed, and after a hundred kisses (not confined to her mouth by any means) I went home, imagining on my way Fanny in her mistress's arms, the cunts of both in sweet conjunction.

The eventful afternoon came around. Lady Betty was disgusted at finding that she and Molly were not going to have me at their mercy by myself all the afternoon, and vented her spite on Alice and Connie more than once in her ill-bred way. But they knew their vengeance was at hand and they took her insulting impertinence with well-bred indifference. In due course we were all collected in the Snuggery, Fanny concealed in my alcove.

"Jack, why don't you have those nasty pulleys taken down; they are not pretty, they're useless, and they're horridly in the way!" exclaimed Lady Betty after she narrowly escaped coming up against one.

"Why, they form my gymnasium, your Ladyship!" I replied. "I couldn't do without them!"

Molly now joined in eagerly. "How do you work them, Jack?" she asked.

"What's the idea of the loops? I'm a dab at gymnastics but never saw this arrangement before."

"The loops are wristlets, Miss Molly," I replied. "You must fasten them 'round your wrists and then grasp the rope with your hand—thus you divide your weight between wrist and hand instead of it all coming on the fingers as in a trapeze."

Of course all this was nonsense and rubbish, yet this "dab in gymnastics" believed it all solemnly; it was a fair sample of her ways.

"Oh, how clever!" Molly exclaimed in her affected fulsome way. "Let me try, Jack! Alice, please fasten me!" Alice complied demurely with a sly glance at me.

"I used to be the best girl at gymnastics in school," said Lady Betty complacently. "Molly takes after me." By this time, Alice had fastened the ropes to Molly's wrists and the latter began to swing herself slowly and gently, backwards and forwards.

"Oh, Mother, it is jolly!" cried Molly. "Do try it!"

Ever anxious to show herself to be a juvenile, Lady Betty rose briskly. "Will you fasten me, Jack?" she said as she raised her arms for the purpose. "I'm afraid I'm too old and heavy for this sort of thing now! Will the ropes bear me, Jack?"

"They carry me, Lady Betty," I replied as I fastened the wristlets to her arms.

"Why malign yourself so cruelly?"

Lady Betty glanced at me approvingly for my pretty speech, little dreaming that she and Molly were now our prisoners by their own actions. Alice and I exchanged exulting looks; we had our victims safe!

Following Molly's lead, Lady Betty swung herself gently to and fro a few times, then stopped, remarking, "I can't say I like it, dear, but I'm not as young you are! Let me loose, Jack!"

Instead of doing so, I passed my arms 'round her buxom waist, and drew her to me as I replied, "Not yet, dear Lady Betty. We're going to have some fun with you and Miss Molly first!"

Something significant in my voice or in my eyes told her of what was in store for her and her daughter! She flushed nervously, then paled, while Molly, startled, stopped swinging herself as Alice and Connie quietly took up positions, one on each side of her.

For a moment there was dead silence, then Lady Betty said somewhat unsteadily, "I don't follow you at all Jack. Loose us both at once please. I don't mind a joke in the least, but you're going too far, Sir!"

"Will this help you to understand our ideas, dear Lady Betty?" I rejoined with a mischievous smile as I slipped my hand under her clothes and pulled them up till they rested on her fat thighs.

"Oh!" she screamed, utterly taken aback by the quickness of my action and its most unexpected nature. "How dare you, Sir!" she shrieked as she felt my hand forcing its way upwards and between her legs. "Stop! . . . Stop!" she yelled, now furious with rage at such an outrage, while Molly screamed sympathetically, horror-stricken!

I withdrew my hand. "You're awfully nice and plump dear Lady!" I remarked cruelly as I watched her flustered face and heaving bosom. "If the rest of you is like what I have just had the pleasure of feeling, you'll give us even a more delicious time than we expected! We really must undress you to see. You won't mind, will you?"

"WHAT!!" cried Lady Betty, staring wildly at me as if unable to believe her ears, while Molly shrieked hysterically, "No, no!"

"Make Molly comfortable in that easy chair, dears, till we want her," I said quietly to Alice and Connie, who instantly pushed the Chair of Treachery up to Molly and gently forced her into it till the arms firmly held her prisoner.

They took the ropes off her wrists, as she was sufficiently under control now, Molly, all the time struggling frantically, shrieking, "Oh, Mother! Help! Help!" But Lady Betty had her own troubles to attend to, for to her bewilderment, Fanny suddenly appeared before her in response to my signal, and the sight of this trim smart lady's maid ready to commence to undress her was evidently an awful proof that we intended to carry out our intentions as to her and her daughter.

"Undress Lady Betty, Fanny," I commanded quietly, and Fanny instantly began to do so!

"I won't have it! I won't have it! Stop her Jack," screamed Lady Betty, now purple with wrathful indignation and the sense of her powerlessness, for her frantic tugs at the ropes availed her nothing. "Mother! Oh mother dear!" yelled Molly in an agony of dismay as she saw Fanny deftly remove Lady Betty's hat and proceed to unfasten her dress. Intent on going to her mother's aid, she made desperate efforts to drag the heavy armchair after her, but Connie easily frustrated her attempts at rescue, and seeing that Molly was safe in Connie's hands, I signaled to Alice to assist Fanny, which she was delighted to do. Between the three of us, Lady Betty's clothes slipped off her in a way that must have been marvelous to her. By the time we had reduced her to her stays, bare-legged and bare armed, she evidently saw she was doomed, and in place of threats she began to plead for mercy. But we were deaf to her prayers and entreaties. Off came her stays, then her chemise and vest, leaving her standing with only her drawers on! "For God's sake, Jack, don't strip me naked!" she shrieked in terrible distress, her face crimson with shame. I simply nodded to Alice. A twitch at the tape and down came the drawers leaving Lady Betty standing naked from head to foot!

"Oh!" she wailed as her agonized eyes instinctively sought Molly's and read in her daughter's face her horrible anguish at the sight of her naked mother.

"Cover me up! For God's sake, cover me up, Jack!" she piteously pleaded as she involuntarily squeezed her legs together in a despairing attempt to shield her private parts from view. I touched the spring and made the ropes draw her off the ground, so that Alice and Fanny could remove the tumbled mass of her garments. "Oh-h-h!" she shrieked as she found herself dangling by her wrists, her struggles to touch the ground exposing her person deliciously.

Quickly Fanny cleared away Lady Betty's clothes. I let her down till she could stand erect comfortably, and joined Alice and Connie at Molly's side, my intention now being to compel Molly to inspect her naked mother and to harrow her already tortured feelings by criticizing Lady Betty's naked charms! She must have been a simply magnificent woman in her prime; even now, in spite of an exuberance of flesh, Lady Betty was enough to provoke any man into concupiscence with her massive, though shapely, arms and legs, her grand hips and round fat thighs, her full ample belly, and her enormous breasts, which though naturally pendulous, still maintained their upstanding sauciness to a marvelous degree. But what attracted all our eyes (even her daughter's) was the hair which grew over her cunt. I do not think I ever saw such an enormous tract. A dinner plate would not have covered it! It seemed to spring from somewhere between Lady Betty's legs; it clustered so thickly over the cunt itself that her crack was quite invisible. It extended all over her groin and abdomen and reached her navel, closely curling and silky and fully two inches deep all over her Mount Venus! A simply wonderful sight! In spite of the attraction of Lady Betty's naked figure, I closely watched Molly. She had been terribly distressed during the undressing of her mother, especially when the naked flesh began to be exposed, and she hysterically joined in her mother's futile prayers and piteous pleadings as she watched her quickly growing nudity with a fascination she could not resist; but when the terrible climax arrived and Lady Betty stood naked, the poor girl uttered a heart-broken shriek as buried her face in her hands. I could see that every now and then she glanced stealthily through her fingers at her mother's naked body as if unable to resist the fascinating temptation.

I turned to the three girls, who with gleaming eyes were devouring Lady Betty's naked charms, their arms around each other. Our eyes met. "Isn't she splendid, Jack!" cried Alice enthusiastically. "What a lovely time she'll give us all!" And they laughed delightedly as Lady Betty shivered.

"And you, my pet!" cooed Connie to Molly, "are you anything like Mummy?" And she began to pass her hands over Molly's corsage as if to sample her body. The girls' individual predilections were clear even at this early stage.

Alice was captivated by Lady Betty's fleshy amplitude, while Connie coveted Molly's still-budding charms.

"Oh, don't, Mrs. Blunt, please, don't!" cried Molly, flushing deeply as she endeavored to protect herself with her hands, thereby uncovering her face.

This was what I desired. I intended that Lady Betty should now be felt in front of her daughter, and that Molly should be forced to look at her mother and witness her shame and anguish and involuntary struggles while my hands wandered lasciviously over Lady Betty's naked body and invaded her most private parts.

"Sling Molly up again, girls," I said quietly. "No, no," screamed Molly in an agony of apprehension, but in a trice she was standing upright with her hands secured over her head, her eyes full of silent terror! "Do you think you could slip Molly's drawers off her without disturbing the rest of her garments?" I asked.

"Yes, of course!" replied Connie, and the three girls dropped on their knees 'round Molly. Their hands disappeared under her skirts, her wriggles and cries and agitated movements proclaiming how she was upset by their attacking hands. Then came a shriek of despair from her, and Connie rose with an air of triumph, waving Molly's drawers.

"Good!" I exclaimed, a smile of congratulation on my lips. "Now, Connie, take Molly in your arms and hold her steady. Alice and Fanny, slip your hands under Molly's clothes and behind her till you can each command a cheek of her bottom!" Merrily the girls carried out my commands, Molly crying, "Don't, don't!" as she felt the hands of Alice and Fanny on her bottom.

"Now, Molly, I'm going to amuse myself with your mother! You must watch her intently! If I see you avert your eyes from her, whatever may be the cause, I'll signal to Alice and Fanny, and they will give you such a pinching that you won't repeat the offence. Now be careful!" and I turned towards Lady Betty who, having heard every word, was now trembling with nervous apprehension as she brokenly exclaimed, "Don't touch me!" Ignoring her pleading, I passed behind her, slipped my arms 'round her and caught hold of her large, full breasts! "Oh-h-h!" shrieked Lady Betty.

"Oh, Mother!" screamed Molly, coloring painfully as she watched her mother writhing in my embrace with her breasts in my hands.

"Don't Jack," again shrieked Lady Betty as I proceeded to squeeze and mould and toy with her voluptuous semi-globes, reveling in their exquisite fleshiness, now pulling now stroking, now pressing them against each other, causing her intense distress but affording myself the most delicious pleasure! I glanced at the group of four girls facing Lady Betty. Alice, Connie, and Fanny were simply beaming with smiles and gloating at the sight of Lady Betty's sufferings, while poor Molly, with staring eyes and flushing face, gazed horror-stricken at her tortured and naked mother, not daring to avert her eyes! After a few more minutes of toying with Lady Betty's huge breasts, I suddenly slipped my hands downwards over her hairy, fat belly and attacked her cunt! "Mother! Oh, Mother!" shrieked Molly hysterically as she saw my eager fingers disappear in the luxuriant growth that so effectually covered her mother's cunt. Utterly unable any longer to endure the sight of her mother's shame and agony, she let her head drop on her heaving bosom.

"Oh, my God! Don't, Jack!" yelled Lady Betty, her face crimson with shame, her eyes half-closed, as she frantically attempted to defeat my hands by squeezing her plump thighs together. But it was useless! With both hands, I set to work to thoroughly explore the fattest and longest cunt I had ever touched, at the same time nodding meaningfully to Alice. Instantly came a series of ear-piercing shrieks from Molly, whose wiggles were almost more than Connie could subdue. She continued to keep her face averted for a few seconds, then the agony of the pinches became more than she could endure, and slowly and reluctantly she nerved to again contemplate her mother, who now was writhing and wriggling frenziedly while filling the room with her inarticulate cries as my fingers tortured her cunt with their subtle titillation, one indeed being lodged up to the knuckle! For a minute or so I continued to explore and feel Lady Betty's delicious private parts till it was evident I was testing both her and her daughter beyond their powers of endurance, for Lady Betty was now nearly in convulsions while her daughter was on the verge of hysterics. Unwillingly, I removed my hands from her cunt and left the tortured lady to recover herself, first gently placing her in the Chair of Treachery and releasing her arms.

"What does she feel like, Jack?" cried Alice and Connie excitedly as I joined them by Molly.

"Gloriously ripe flesh, dears," I replied, "and the biggest cunt I ever came across!" They looked joyously at each other, their eyes sparkling with pleasurable anticipation.

"And Molly?" I asked in my turn.

"Just delicious, Jack!" replied Alice delightedly. "Do let us undress her now!"

"Certainly!" I replied. Whereupon Molly screamed in terror. "No, no, no, oh, Mother, they're going to undress me!"

"Oh, no, Jack! For pity's sake, don't!" cried Lady Betty, now fully roused by the danger threatening her daughter. "Do anything you like to me, but spare my Molly, she's only a girl still."

But Connie, Alice, and Fanny were already hard at work on Molly's clothes, the stays of which were now visible in spite of her frantic exertions to thwart their active hands. As the girls did not require any help from me, I returned and stood beside Lady Betty, who with the intense anguish in her face, was distractedly watching the clothes being taken off her daughter. "For God's sake, Jack, stop them," she cried agonizingly, stretching her clasped hands towards me appealingly, as if unable to endure the sight.

"No, Lady Betty!" I replied with a cruel smile. "Molly must contribute her share to the afternoon's entertainment! We must have her naked!"

"Oh, my God!" she wailed, letting her head drop on her agitated bosom in her despair. Just then Molly screamed loudly. We looked up and saw her in her chemise struggling in Connie's grasp, while Alice and Fanny dragged off her shoes and stockings. Promptly, they proceeded to undo the shoulder fastenings of her two remaining garments and stepped quickly clear. Down these slid, and with a bitter cry of, "Oh-h-h, oh, Mother!" poor Molly stood naked.

"Oh, my God," Lady Betty shrieked again, frantically endeavoring, chair and all, to go to her daughter's rescue, but I quietly checked her efforts. "My darling! I can't help you," she wailed, hiding her face in her hands in her anguish at the sight of her daughter's helpless nakedness. My eyes met the girls'—they were gleaming with delight. They joined me behind Lady Betty and together we stood and critically inspected poor shrinking Molly's naked person! Alice had chosen the correct word—Molly naked was just delicious, so exquisitely shaped, so perfectly made, so lithe and yet so charmingly rounded and plump, so juicy and fresh, so virgin! She took after her mother in her large, firm, upstanding breasts with saucy little nipples, and few girls could have shown at eighteen the quantity of dark moss-like hair that clustered so prettily over her cunt, which, like her mother's, was peculiarly fat and prominent. I noticed with secret pleasure how Connie's eyes glistened as they dwelt rapturously on Molly's tender organ of sex.

For a minute or so we gazed admiringly at Molly's charming nudity. Then Alice whispered, "Jack, let us put them side by side and examine them."

"An excellent idea!" I replied, rewarding her with a kiss. We moved Molly's pulleys closer to the pillar on her left and wheeled Lady Betty across to Molly's right and quickly slung her up in spite of her stubborn resistance.

Mother and daughter stood naked side by side! They formed a most provoking, fascinating spectacle. It was delicious to trace how Molly's exquisite curves were echoed by her mother's exuberant fleshiness, how both the bodies were framed on similar lines, how the matron and the virgin were unmistakably related! Conscious that our eyes were devouring them greedily and traveling over their naked persons, both mother and daughter kept their faces down and stubbornly averted their eyes from us.

"Turn them so that they face each other," I said presently. Quickly Connie and Alice executed my order, Connie taking Molly. "Oh, how can you be so cruel?" moaned Lady Betty as Alice forced her 'round till she faced Molly.

There was just space to stand behind each of them while mother and daughter were about four feet apart. I saw their eyes meet for a moment, horrible dread visible in both.

Their profiles naked were an interesting study—Molly: lithe, graceful, with exquisite curves—Lady Betty: paunchy and protuberant, but most voluptuous. One striking feature both possessed: the hair on their cunts stood out conspicuously like bushes.

After we had to some extent satisfied our eyes, I said to the girls, "I've no doubt Lady Betty and Molly would like to be alone for a few minutes, so let us go off and undress." And we disappeared into the alcoves, Fanny coming into mine so as not to crowd her mistress and Connie.

We undressed quickly in silence, being desirous of hearing all that passed between our naked victims, and presently we heard Molly whisper agitatedly, "Oh, Mother, what are they going to do with us?"

"Darling, I can only guess!" replied Lady Betty faintly. "Their going off to undress makes me fear that you and I will have to satisfy their. . . lust! Darling, I'm very afraid that Jack will violate you and outrage me, and then hand us over to the girls—and girls can be very cruel to their own sex."

"Oh, Mother!" stammered Molly, horror-stricken. "What shall I do if Jack wants me?" And her voice shook with terror.

Before Lady Betty could reply, Connie appeared, naked save for shoes and stockings. She went straight up to Molly, threw her arms 'round the shrinking girl and passionately kissed her flushed face, gently rubbing her breasts against Molly's and murmuring, "Oh, you darling! Oh, you sweet thing!" She slipped behind Molly and gently seized her lovely breasts.

"Don't, Mrs. Blunt!" shrieked Molly, now turning and twisting herself agitatedly. Just then Alice emerged, and seeing how Connie was amusing herself, she quickly slipped behind Lady Betty and caught hold of her huge breasts and began to squeeze and handle them in a way that drew cries from Lady Betty. It was delicious to watch the mother and the daughter writhing and wriggling, but I did not want their cunts touched yet by the girls and so appeared on the scene with Fanny, whom I had refrained (with difficulty) from fucking when she exposed herself naked in my alcove.

"Stop, darlings!" I commanded, and reluctantly Connie and Alice obeyed.

Under my instructions they pushed the padded music-bench under the skylight. We released Lady Betty's wrists from the pulleys and forced her onto her back on the bench, where I held her down while Alice and Connie and Fanny fastened first her arms and then her legs to the longitudinal bars of the bench, in fact, trussed her like a fowl, her arms and legs being on each side of the bench, her knees being separated by the full width, thus exposing her cunt to our attack! Having thus fixed the mother, we turned our attention to her trembling daughter. We placed a chair in a position to command a view of Lady Betty. I seated myself on it, and the girls dragged Molly to me and forced her onto my knees with her back to me. While I held her firmly, they drew her arms backwards and made them fast to the sides of the chair. Seizing her delicate ankles, they forced her legs apart and tied them to the chair legs. In short, they tied Molly onto the chair as she sat in my lap, thereby placing her breasts and cunt at my disposal and in easy reach of my hands.

It is needless to say that this was not effected without the most desperate resistance from both Lady Betty and Molly. The former struggled like a tigress till we got her down on the bench, while Molly had really to be carried and placed on my knees. But now both were satisfactorily fixed and nervously awaited their fate, their bosoms panting and heaving with their desperate exertions.

"Now, my darlings, Lady Betty is at your disposal!" I said with a cruel smile.

"I'll take charge of Molly! My pet," I added, as the girls hastily arranged among themselves how to deal with Lady Betty, "I'll try and make you comprehend what your mother is feeling, from time to time!"

"Let me have charge of Lady Betty's breasts," cried Connie.

"Excellent!" said Alice. "Fanny and I want her cunt between us! Now, your Ladyship," she added as Fanny knelt between Lady Betty's legs and Connie stationed herself by her shoulders, greedily seizing Lady Betty's breasts in her little hands, "you're not to spend till we give you leave!" And kneeling down between Connie and Fanny and opposite the object of her admiration, she placed her hands on the forest of hair and while Fanny's fingers attacked Lady Betty's crack, Alice proceeded to play with Lady Betty's cunt.

"Oh, my God! Stop!" yelled the unhappy lady as her breasts and private parts thus became the prey of the excited girls. "Mother! Oh, Mother!" shrieked Molly at the sight of her naked mother being thus tortured. I seized Molly's breasts. "Don't, Jack!" she screamed, agitating herself on my lap, her plump bottom roving deliciously on my thighs and stimulating my prick to wild erection. Molly's breasts were simply luscious, and I handled them delightedly as I watched her mother's agonies and listened to her cries.

Steadily and remorselessly, Connie's hands worked Lady Betty's breasts, squeezing, kneading, stroking, pulling, and even pinching them. She simply reveled in the touch of Lady Betty's ripe flesh, and while she faithfully attended to the duties committed to her, she delightedly watched Alice and Fanny as they played with Lady Betty's cunt. Every now and then they would change positions, Alice devoting herself to the gaping orifice itself, while Fanny played with the hairs. It was while they were thus dividing the duty that Alice suddenly rose and fetched the box of feathers.

Connie's eyes glittered delightedly as Fanny lent herself to Alice's caprice by carefully parting the dense mass that clustered on Lady

Betty's cunt and thus cleared the way for the feather. With a finger on each side of the pouting slit, she kept the curling black hairs back. Then Alice, poising her hand daintily, brought the tip of the feather along the tender lips.

A fearful shriek burst from Lady Betty, followed by another and another, as Alice continued to tickle Lady Betty's cunt, now passing the feather along the slit itself, now inside, now gently touching the clitoris! Every muscle in Lady Betty's body seemed to be exerting itself to break her fastenings and escape from the terribly subtle torture that was being so skillfully administered. She wriggled her hips and bottom in the most extraordinary way, seeing how tightly we had fastened her. She would arch herself upwards, contorting herself frantically and disturbing Connie's grasp of her breasts, all the time shrieking almost inarticulate prayers for mercy. It was a wonderful sight—a fine voluptuous woman, naked, being tortured by three pretty girls, also naked—and my lust surged wildly in me.

So far, I had confined my attentions to Molly's delicious breasts so that she should not have her attention distracted too much from her mother by her own sensations. She was wild with grief and terror at the sight of the cruel indignities and tortures being inflicted on her naked and helpless mother, and with flushed face and horrified eye, she followed every movement. But when she saw the feather applied to her mother's cunt and heard her fearful shrieks and witnessed her desperate struggles, she completely lost her head.

"Mother, dear, dear! Oh! My darling! "Stop them, Jack! Stop, Alice, you're killing her! Oh, my God, stop!" she yelled as she desperately endeavored to get loose and go to her mother's aid. I really had to hold her tightly, lest she hurt herself in her frantic efforts. But it was now time for me to intervene, for Lady Betty was fast being driven into madness by the terrible tickling of so sensitive a part of herself; so I called out to Alice, who reluctantly stopped, Connie and Fanny at the same time ceasing their attention.

"Oh-h-h!" moaned Lady Betty with evident heartfelt relief as she turned her head unconsciously towards us, her eyes half-closed, her lips slightly parted.

The three girls gloatingly watched her in silence while I soothed poor Molly; and, before long, both Lady Betty and her daughter regained comparative command of themselves.

I intercepted an interrogating glance from Lady Betty to her daughter as if seeking to learn what had happened to the latter. I thought it as well to answer. "Molly is all right, Lady Betty. She was so interested in watching you that I haven't done more than play with her breasts; but now that you are going to have a rest and can watch her, we'll proceed!" I slid my hand down to Molly's virgin cunt!

"Oh!" the girl shrieked, utterly upset by the sensation of a male hand on her tender organ.

"No, Jack, don't!" cried Lady Betty, again horrified at the sight of Molly's distress. Promptly the three girls crowded 'round me to watch Molly, taking care not to interfere with Lady Betty's view of her daughter.

"Oh, don't Jack!" Molly again shrieked as she felt my fingers begin to wander inquisitively over her cunt, feeling, pressing, stroking, and caressing it tenderly but deliberately and rousing sensations in her that frightened her by their half-pleasant nature.

"Don't be afraid darling!" cooed Connie. "You'll like it presently!" I continued my sweet investigations and explorations, my fingers moving gently all over Molly's private parts, playing with her silky hairs, stroking her cunt's throbbing lips. As she became calmer and submitted herself more quietly to having her cunt felt, I tenderly tested her for virginity by slowly and gently pushing my finger into her. "Stop, Jack!" she cried agitatedly. "Oh, stop! You're hurting me!" her face crimson with shame, for it was evident to her what my object was! I smiled congratulatingly at Lady Betty, whose eyes never left Molly in her maternal anxiety and distress. "I congratulate you, your Ladyship," I said.

"Your daughter is a virgin, and as I haven't had a virgin for some time, I'm all the more obliged to you for allowing me this opportunity and the privilege of taking Molly's sweet maidenhead."

"No, no! Oh, Mother!" cried Molly in terrible distress, while her mother, now knowing that remonstrances would be to no avail, moaned heartbrokenly, "Oh, Jack! How can you be so cruel?"

Suddenly, Molly seemed to be seized with a fit of desperation. "You shan't have me! Oh, you brute! You coward! You shan't have me!" she shrieked as she frantically struggled to break loose. "Oh, oh, Molly," I said chidingly.

"What a naughty temper, darling."

"Let me loose, you beast!" she cried, making another furious struggle. "You shan't have me! I won't let you, you beast!" she hissed. "Leave me alone! Take your hand away, you cruel lustful brute! Oh! Oh!" she shrieked, as again I forced my finger into her cunt and began to agitate it gently. "Help, mother," she yelled, again struggling desperately. "Oh! Jack! Do stop! Oh, you're hurting me," she pleaded as she relapsed into her usual mood.

I nodded to Connie who at once came up. "Get a feather, dear, we must punish Molly. You can tickle her cunt; it will perhaps cure her temper."

Quickly and in huge delight, Alice handed Connie a sharp-pointed feather.

"No, no, Mrs. Blunt, don't tickle me!" she cried in terror as the recollection of her mother's agony flashed through her mind. But Connie was now on her knees before us, and with a smile of delight, she applied the feather to Molly's tender cunt! "Oh, my God!" shrieked Molly.

"Jack, don't!" cried Lady Betty, appreciating from her recent experience what her daughter must be feeling.

"Stop, Mrs. Blunt—Mrs. Blunt, do stop! Oh, my God, I can't stand it! Oh, Mrs.

Blunt! Dear Mrs. Blunt! Stop it. Stop! I'll be good. I'll do anything you like, Jack! You can have me, Jack! Oh, Mrs. Blunt! Mrs. Blunt!" shrieked Molly, mad with the awful tickling she was getting.

"Stop for a moment, Connie," I said. With a tender forefinger, I soothed and caressed Molly's tortured and irritated cunt till the girl was herself again.

"Now, Molly," I said gravely, "of your own free will, you've declared that you'll be good, that you'll do anything I want, and that you'll let me have you.

You were rather excited at the time; what do you say now?"

Molly shivered. "Oh, Jack," she stammered, "I'll be good—but. . . but. . . I can't do the rest!"

"Go on, Connie," I said briefly.

"No, no, Jack, not again!" cried Molly, but the feather was now being again applied to her cunt—only this time I pulled its lips apart so that Connie could tickle Molly's delicately sensitive interior, which she gleefully did.

Molly's screams and struggles now began to be something fearful, and poor Lady Betty, horror-stricken at the sight of her daughter's agony, cried, "Promise everything darling, you'll have to submit!"

"Yes, Jack! I'll submit! I'll do it all! Oh, stop, stop, Mrs. Blunt! I can't stand it any longer!" shrieked Molly.

Again I stopped Connie and soothed Molly's cunt with a loving finger, and when she had regained her self-control, I said, "Molly, there must be no mistake. You'll have to do whatever I tell you, whether it be to yourself, or to me, or to any of the girls, or even to your mother. Do you promise?"

"Yes, Jack, yes!" she gasped brokenly. Quickly the girls set her free and she fell half-fainting off my knees into Connie's arms, whose caresses and kisses soon restored her.

By now we all were in a terrible state of sexual excitement. Connie was absorbed with Molly, but Alice and Fanny were casting hungry glances towards Lady Betty as she lay on her back with widely parted legs, invitingly provocative. I could hardly contain my lust, but to fuck Lady Betty now would be to spoil her for the girls, so I decided to let them have her Ladyship first. Quickly I lengthened the bench on which she was fastened down by adding the other half. Bending over the agitated woman, I said with a cruel smile, "Now, Lady Betty, we're all going to have you in turn, Alice first!"

"Oh, my God, no! No!" she screamed, but Alice was already on her, and Lady Betty felt herself gripped by Alice's strong young arms as she arranged herself on her, so that her cunt pressed against Lady Betty's fat, hairy organ, and then slowly began the delirious rubbing process which she loved, but which was new to Lady Betty, for, woman of the world though she was, she had never been fucked by one of her own sex.

It was delicious to watch her in Alice's arms, utterly helpless, forced to lend her cunt to satisfy Alice's lust. Her color went and came, she began to catch her breath, her eyes shot wavering glances at us—especially at her daughter, who, seated on Connie's knees, was watching her mother with undisguised astonishment, blushing furiously as Connie in loving whispers and with busy fingers made her understand all that was happening. Soon she began to feel the approach of love's ecstasy as Alice agitated herself more and more quickly against Lady Betty's cunt. Soon Lady Betty surrendered herself to her sexual impulses, now fully aroused by the exciting friction communicated to her by Alice's cunt, and began to jerk herself upwards wildly as if to meet Alice's downward thrusting. Her eyes closed and her lips slightly parted as the spasm of ecstasy thrilled through her and Alice simultaneously. Alice quivered deliciously as she hugged Lady Betty to herself frantically, caught up in the raptures of spending! Presently the spasmodic thrills ceased. Slowly Alice rose, her eyes still humid with the pleasure she had tasted on Lady Betty, who lay motionless and only half-conscious, absorbed in her sensations. Mutely I invited Connie to take Alice's place, and before Lady Betty quite knew what was happening, she found herself in Connie's embrace.

"Oh, please don't, Mrs. Blunt!" she exclaimed, flushing hotly as she felt Connie's cunt against hers and the exciting friction again commencing.

Connie was evidently very much worked up, and she confessed afterwards that the consciousness that she was fucking Molly's mother in Molly's presence sent her into a feverish heat. She plunged furiously on Lady Betty as she frenziedly rubbed her cunt against hers, Lady Betty's hairy tract intensifying the delicious friction till both were overtaken by the ecstatic crisis, Connie spending with divine tremors and evident rapture.

As she rose, I nodded to Fanny, who by now was just mad with desire. Like a panther, she threw herself on Lady Betty, who had hardly recovered from the spend provoked by Connie. Fiercely she clasped Lady Betty to her and began to rub her cunt furiously against Lady Betty's now moist organ. "Don't, Fanny, don't!" cried Lady Betty, utterly helpless in Fanny's powerful grip and half alarmed by Fanny's delirious onslaught, but Fanny was now in the full tide of her sexual pleasure and reveling in the satisfaction of her imperious desire by means of Lady Betty's voluptuous body. With fast increasing impatience to taste the joys of the sweet consummation of her lustful passions, she agitated herself frenziedly on Lady Betty's responsive cunt until the rapturous moment arrived, then spent madly, showering hot kisses on Lady Betty's flushed cheeks as she felt her quiver under her in the involuntary thrills of her third spending! As Fanny rose, the girls looked significantly at me, evidently expecting to see me seize Lady Betty and fuck her, but I had something else in my mind.

"Sponge and freshen Lady Betty, Fanny," I said quietly, and quickly the traces of her three fuckings were removed, the operation affording Lady Betty a little time in which to recover herself.

"Now, Molly, fuck your mother, dear!" I said.

She looked at me as if she could not believe her ears, then turned to Connie as if seeking confirmation, noting as she did so the look of delightful anticipation on the faces of her companions.

Connie rose to the occasion. "Yes, darling," she said soothingly as she gently pushed Molly towards Lady Betty, "go and get your first taste of the pleasures of love from your mother's cunt!"

"Oh Mrs. Blunt, I couldn't! It's too horrible!" cried Molly aghast, while Lady Betty, utterly shocked at the idea of being submitted to her own daughter's embraces, frenziedly cried, "No, no!"

"Come along, Molly," I said as I pointed to her mother. "Come along—remember your promise!"

"Oh Jack, no, no, it's too horrible!" she cried as she buried her face in her hands, shuddering at the idea.

I took her gently but firmly by her shoulders and pushed her towards the bench on which her mother lay in terrible distress. "Now, Molly, please understand that you've got to have your mother," I said sternly. "If you won't live up to your promise, we'll tie you onto her and whip your bottom till your movements on and against her make her spend!"

"Oh, my God!" she moaned, then breaking from me, she threw herself on her knees by her mother and cried agitatedly as she kissed her. "Oh, Mother darling, what shall I do?"

Lady Betty's face became a lovely study of maternal love contending with personal predilections. For a moment she was silent, then she murmured faintly, "Come, darling."

Slowly poor Molly rose. Unwillingly she placed herself between Lady Betty's legs, then gently let herself down on her and took her helpless mother in her arms, then lay still as if reluctant to begin her repugnant task.

"Just see that Molly has placed herself properly, Connie!" I said, and delightedly Connie arranged Molly so that her cunt rested on her mother's, Fanny and Alice at the same time arranging Lady Betty's breasts so that her daughter should rest hers on them.

"Now she's fine, Jack," cried Connie excitedly. "Now, my pet, fuck Mummy!"

Unwillingly, Molly complied. Slowly and gently she agitated herself on her mother, cheek to cheek, breast to breast, cunt to cunt. Presently she began to move herself faster. Her sexual passions seemed to begin to dominate her. She clasped her mother closely to her as she strenuously worked her cunt against Lady Betty's, rubbing harder and harder, more and more wildly till the ecstatic climax arrived with an indescribable exclamation of "Oh-h-h, mother! Oh-h-h!!" She spent on her mother's cunt in delicious transports, Lady Betty's quivers under Molly showing that she too was spending! In admiring silence we watched the unusual spectacle of a mother and daughter spending in each other's arms till their thrillings and involuntary tremors died away. Then Molly seemed suddenly to remember where she was. Slowly she raised her face from against her mother's cheek where it had rested while she was absorbed in the bliss of her spending, and wailed, "Oh, Mother, forgive me! I couldn't help it! They made me do it!" And she passionately kissed her. Lady Betty, who had kept her eyes closed while her daughter was fucking her, now opened them and, with a look of infinite love, she put her lips up as if inviting a kiss. Passionately Molly pressed hers on them, and for a few moments, mother and daughter showered kisses on each other, a sight which drove my already over-excited self into an absolute fury of lust. Hardly knowing what I was doing, I seized Molly, pulled her off her mother, and pushed her into Connie's arms. I threw myself on Lady Betty, and with one excited stroke, I drove my prick right up her cunt as I madly gripped her luscious, voluptuous body in my arms and clasped her tightly to me.

"Oh-h-h!" she shrieked as she struggled wildly under me, her cunt smarting with the sudden distention caused by the violent entrance of my rampantly stiff organ into it. "No, no, Jack! Don't have me!" she cried as she felt herself being genuinely fucked. I heeded nothing but my imperious desires and rammed madly into her, reveling in the contact with her magnificent flesh and the delicious warmth of her excited cunt, inflamed as it was by the four girl-fuckings she had just received, which however, had not exhausted her love-juice, for I felt her spend as my prick raged wildly up and down her already well-lubricated cunt. Clenching my teeth in my desperate attempts to restrain the outpouring of my lust, and to prolong the heavenly pleasure I was tasting, I continued to fuck Lady Betty madly, her quivers and tremors and inarticulate exclamations along with her voluptuous movements under me, telling me that her animal passions now had control over her and that she had abandoned herself absolutely to the gratification of her aroused lust. But soon I could no longer control myself. I felt Lady Betty spend again with delicious thrills, inundating my excited prick with her hot love-juice. This broke down all my resistance. Wildly I rammed into her till our hairs intertwined. Clutching her against me in a frenzy of rapture, I spent madly into her, flooding her interior with my boiling essence, she exclaiming brokenly, "Ah! Ah! Ah!" as she felt the jets of my discharge shoot into her.

When she came to, she found herself still lying under me and clasped in my arms, my prick still lodged in her cunt, for I was loathe to leave such delicious armfuls. The storm of lust that overwhelmed her had died away with the last quivers of her ecstasy, and she was only conscious of the appalling fact that she had been forcibly outraged. In an agony of grief and shame she wailed, "Oh, Jack, what have you done?" her eyes full of anguish.

"I've only fucked you, dear Lady Betty!" I replied with a cruel smile. "And I found you so delicious, that after I've taken your daughter's maidenhead, I'll have you again!" I laughed delightedly at the look of horror that came into her eyes, then continued, "Molly must now amuse us while you rest and recover yourself sufficiently to allow you to endure the further tortures and outrages we've arranged for your amusement— and ours!" And with this appalling intimation, I rose off Lady Betty, unfastened her, and made her over to Alice and Fanny to be sponged and refreshed while I went off to my alcove for a similar purpose.

When I returned after a few minutes, I found Lady Betty in the fateful armchair with Molly's arms around her, the girls having allowed mother and daughter a little time to themselves. Connie eagerly advanced to meet me, asking excitedly, "What now, Jack?"

"Would you like to fuck Molly now, dear?" I asked with a smile.

"Oh, yes! Please let me, Jack! I'm dying to have her," she exclaimed, blushing slightly at her own vehemence.

"Very, well," I replied, "but don't take too much out of her just now. I'll violate her as soon as I'm myself again, and then we'll just work them both for all we can. Do you approve, dears?" I asked, turning to Alice and Fanny.

They both nodded delightedly. "Jack, please turn Lady Betty over to Fanny and me. Connie wants Molly left to her, and you can fuck them both whenever you wish. We want to do the torturing!" said Alice softly, looking coaxingly at me.

"Just as you please, dears," I said with a smile, distinctly pleased with the arrangements and delighted to find the girls so keen on exercising their refined cruelty on their own sex! Together we approached Lady Betty and Molly, who had not heard a word, being absorbed in the terrible fate indicated by me as awaiting them, regarding which they no doubt were whispering to each other softly.

"Molly, Mrs. Blunt wants to fuck you—come along!" I said quietly, as Connie advanced to take her.

"Mother! Oh, Mother!" cried Molly, clinging apprehensively to Lady Betty.

"Come, darling!" cooed Connie as she gently passed her arms 'round Molly's shrinking, trembling body and drew her away from her distressed mother who moaned in her anguish as she watched her daughter forced to lie down and separate her legs. Connie arranged herself on her, breasts to breasts, cunt to cunt. Shocked beyond endurance, Lady Betty covered her face with her hands, but Alice and Fanny (who had now assumed charge of her) promptly pulled them away and shackled her wrists together behind her back, thus compelling her to witness Molly's martyrdom under Connie, who now was showering hot and lustful kisses on Molly's trembling lips as she lasciviously agitated herself on her unwilling victim.

To the rest of us, it was a lovely spectacle. The two girls fitted each other perfectly—while the contrast between Connie's look of delighted satisfaction as she gratified her lust after Molly, and the forlorn, woebegone, distressed expression of the latter, as she passively let her cunt minister to Connie's concupiscence, was enough to rekindle my ardor and determined me to ravish Molly as soon as Connie had finished with her.

She did not keep me waiting unnecessarily. After testifying by her hot salacious kisses her satisfaction at holding Molly in her arms, cunt to cunt, she began to girl-fuck her ardently and with fast increasing erotic rage, rubbing herself raspingly against her victim's cunt till she felt Molly beginning to quiver under her. Redoubling her efforts, she went into a veritable paroxysm of thrusts and shoves and wild friction, which quickly brought on the delicious spasm of pleasure to both herself and Molly, whose unresisting lips she again seized with her own as she quivered and thrilled in the delicious consummation of her lust.

"There, Lady Betty, Molly has spent!" cried Alice gleefully as she gloated over the spectacle with eyes full of desire, which she turned hungrily on Lady Betty and then on me, as if begging leave to inflict some torture on her. But I shook my head. Lady Betty had now to witness her daughter's violation.

Presently Connie rose, after giving Molly a long clinging kiss expressive of the most intense satisfaction. Molly began to raise herself, but I quickly pushed her down again on her back and, lying down myself beside her, I slipped my arms 'round her so that we rested together, her back against my chest, her bottom against my prick, while my hands commanded her breasts and cunt.

"Let me go, Jack!" she cried in alarm, hardly understanding, however, the significance of my action, but it was quite patent to Lady Betty who screamed, "No, Jack, no!" while Alice and Fanny exchanged smiles of delight.

"Lie still, Molly dear!" I said soothingly, gently seizing one of her delicious breasts, while with my remaining hand, I played with her cunt.

"Oh, Jack, don't!" she cried, quivering exquisitely as she submitted reluctantly to my wishes and let my hands enjoy themselves, still not comprehending what was to follow! Presently I whispered loud enough for the others to hear, "Molly, you're quite ready now, let me have you, darling!"

She lay still for a moment. As her fate dawned on her, she made one desperate furious spring, slipped out of my hands, and rushed to Lady Betty.

She fell at her mother's knees and, clasping her convulsively, cried, "Don't let Jack have me, Mother! Oh, save me! Save me!" Alice and Fanny again exchanged delighted smiles with Connie, all three girls intently watching for the order to bring Molly back to me.

I rose from the couch and nodded to them. Like young tigresses, they threw themselves on Molly and dragged her away from her mother's knees in spite of her frantic resistance as she shrieked, "Mother, save me," while Lady Betty, frantic at her helplessness and distracted by her daughter's cries as she was being thus dragged to her violation, cried hysterically, "Jack! For God's sake, spare her!"

The girls had by now forced Molly on the couch again. I saw she would not yield herself quietly to me, so while they held her, I fastened the corner cords to her ankles and wrists and set the machinery to work. As soon as the girls saw the cords tightening, they let go of Molly, who immediately sprang up, only to be arrested and jerked onto her back on the couch. Inch by inch, she was extended flat with widely parted arms and legs as she shrieked with terror, while Lady Betty went into hysterics, which Alice and Fanny soon cured by twitching a few hairs off her cunt.

I seated myself by Molly, bent over her, and said gravely, "Now you've again broken your promise, Molly. I shall consequently amuse myself with you before I violate you!"

"No, no, Jack!" she shrieked as she again struggled to break loose. "Let me go! Don't. . . shame me! Oh! Don't. . . have me!"

I ignored her pleading and began to play with her breasts, which I caressed and squeezed to my heart's content, finally putting her little virgin nipples into my mouth and sucking them lovingly, at which the three girls laughed gleefully as they now knew that another part of Molly would also be sucked while virgin. Then I tickled her navel, a proceeding which made her squirm exquisitely. After that, I devoted myself to her cunt!

First I stroked and caressed it, she all the while frantically crying out and jerking herself about in vain endeavors to escape my hands. The girls now wheeled Lady Betty alongside the couch. Her hands were still tied behind her back so that she could not use them to shut out the dreadful sight of Molly spread-eagled naked, and was forced to look on and witness the violation of her daughter right in front of her eyes!

When Lady Betty had been properly placed so as to see all that went on, I leaned over Molly, seized one of her breasts with my left hand, and while squeezing it lovingly, I gently ran my right forefinger along the tender lips of her cunt, intently watching her telltale face as I did so.

A great wave of color surged furiously over her cheeks, even suffusing her heaving bosom as she screamed, "Don't, Jack, don't!" her eyes full of shame while her involuntary movements of hips and bottom betrayed her sexual agitation. It was simply delicious to have her thus at my absolute disposal, to know that the feeling of utter helplessness and the knowledge that her private parts were utterly defenseless was intensifying the mental and physical agony that my proceedings were making Molly suffer, and despite her prayers and her mother's imploring, I continued delightedly to tickle Molly's cunt with my finger till I considered she was sufficiently worked up to be sucked. I quietly rose, placed myself between her thighs and began to kiss her cunt, keeping my eyes on Lady Betty, so as to note the effect on her of this fresh torture to her daughter.

Lady Betty's eyes opened wide in shocked surprise and, as a half-strangled shriek broke from Molly, she screamed, "Oh, my God! Don't Jack! You'll drive Molly mad!" My tongue commenced to play on Molly's cunt, working along her lips, darting between them when they began to pout and every now and then caressing her clitoris, the subtle titillation sending Molly into shrieking convulsions as she felt she was being slowly driven against her wishes to the spending point! Again Lady Betty screamed, "Stop, Jack, for God's sake, stop!" as she saw her daughter squirming and quivering and heard her now half-inarticulate cries. I made a sign to the girls and promptly Alice and Fanny seized Lady Betty's breasts, while Connie forced her hand between Lady Betty's thighs and tickled her cunt! "Oh, my God! Leave me alone!" she shrieked, struggling frantically but unavailingly, her eyes remaining fixed on her daughter's now violently agitated body, for I had forced her to the verge of spending. A great convulsion shook Molly. "Oh-h-h," she exclaimed, then spent with exquisite tremors and thrills while an unmistakable shriek from Lady Betty proclaimed that Connie's fingers had brought about an unwilling but nevertheless delicious discharge.

Impatiently I waited till the thrills of pleasure had ceased. I sprang on her, seized her in my arms, brought my prick to bear on her cunt, and with a vigorous shove, I succeeded in forcing its head inside her maiden orifice in spite of her cries and frantic struggles. There her virgin barrier blocked the way. Gripping her tightly to me, I rammed fiercely into her, evidently hurting Molly dreadfully, for her shrieks rang through the room as I strove to get into her, Lady Betty, also terribly upset by the sight of her daughter's agonies and cries, frenziedly crying, "Stop, stop!" Molly was very tight, and in spite of her being tied down, she wriggled her strong young body so desperately that it was some little time before I could get a real good thrust, but presently I managed to pin her for a moment, then shoving furiously in her, I burst through her virgin defenses. A fearful shriek announced her violation, Lady Betty (whose breasts and cunt were still being handled and fingered by the girls) crying hysterically, "Oh, my darling! My darling!" as with eyes dilated with horror, she watched her daughter being ravished right in front of her and, indeed, recognized the very moment when Molly lost her maidenhead!

Now firmly lodged inside Molly, I drove my prick up to its roots in her smarting cunt and lay motionless on her for a moment till her cries ceased.

Then I set to work to fuck her in real earnest, first with long slow strokes, then with quicker and more excited ones, Molly submitting passively, as if recognizing that resistance now was useless. The deed had been done, her virginity had been snatched from her! Presently however, she began to agitate herself under me involuntarily as she succumbed to the imperious demands of her now fully aroused sexual emotions and erotic impulses. As my movements on her became more and more riotous and unrestrained, she responded half-unconsciously, half-mechanically, by jogging and heaving her bottom and hips upward as if to meet my vigorous down strokes. Soon our movements became a tempest of confused heaves, shoves, thrusts, and wiggles, then the heavenly climax overtook us! I felt a warm discharge from her as she quivered voluptuously in my arms. I spent madly, pouring my boiling essence into her virgin interior in rapturous ecstasy as I deliciously consummated Molly's violation, reveling in her exquisite thrills and tremors as she felt my hot discharge shoot into her, her movements being astonishingly like those of her mother when I spent into Lady Betty. But such was the violence of the sexual orgasm that shook Molly for the first time in her life that she went off into a semi-trance!

Chapter 9

As soon as I had recovered from the delirious ecstasy of my spending, I kissed Molly's still-unconscious lips, rose gently off her and cruelly displayed my blood-stained prick to Lady Betty and the excited girls. After exulting over Lady Betty's distress and the sight of this evidence of her daughter's violation, I said, "I fancy you would like to attend to Molly yourself, your Ladyship. If I let you both loose for that purpose, will you promise to allow yourselves to be fastened again in such a way as I may indicate?"

"Yes! Yes!" she cried feverishly in her maternal anxiety to attend to Molly.

Immediately we set them free. Hastily, Lady Betty caught up Molly in her arms and, after passionately kissing her, led her away to the girls' alcove, while they delightedly bathed and sponged away the marks of my victory from my rejoicing prick, kissing and caressing it as if in sweet congratulation.

"Now we'll wind up with a great orgy of cruelty, dears," I said. "You heard Lady Betty's promise?" They nodded excitedly. "It would hardly have been possible for us to have forced them into the soixante-neuf position; at any event it would have been very difficult. We'll now make them place themselves so, on the half-bench, then tie them down, Lady Betty on Molly.

We can command their cunts for feeling and fingering and tickling and frigging. By slightly moving Lady Betty backwards, we could suck them and I could fuck them standing upright, but you won't be able to do so. Do you want to do it?"

They glanced at each other for a moment, then shook their heads. "We shall be quite content to satisfy our desires when they get too imperious by fucking each other, Jack!" said Alice merrily. "Connie and Fanny haven't tried each other yet and will be delighted to do so presently." The two girls glanced tenderly at each other and blushed deliciously. "My God, Jack! What a doing the poor things will have had by the time we let them away. Do you think they can stand it?"

"Oh, yes, dear!" I replied with a smile. They are very strong. And it is about time we all had a little refreshment."

So I opened some champagne and poured out six tumblers, adding a little brandy to the two glasses meant for Lady Betty and Molly, who just then emerged from the alcove, Molly with both hands shielding her cunt. Lady Betty covered hers with one hand, while her other arm was passed 'round her daughter. Both looked terribly forlorn and disconsolate as they approached us, and when the girls crowded 'round Molly and congratulated her on having become a woman, poor Lady Betty's eyes sought mine with a look of shocked horror. I handed the champagne 'round and we all partook of it with relish, especially Lady Betty and Molly, who seemed to revive.

"Now let us resume," I cried cheerfully. "Come along, girls, come, Lady Betty, bring Molly with you." I moved towards the bench with the girls while our unhappy victims followed slowly and reluctantly.

"Now, Molly, you just lie down on your back on this bench, just as your mother was made to do. Open your legs, put one on each side." Reluctantly she obeyed, and soon she was lashed firmly to the bars by her wrists and ankles, a lovely sight.

"Now, Lady Betty, place yourself on your daughter reverse ways, your head between her thighs, her head between your legs. Lie on her, and when we have arranged you properly, we'll tie you down!"

Lady Betty flushed painfully, horror-stricken. "Oh, Jack, I can't! Really, I can't do it! It's too horrible!" she exclaimed, burying her face in her hands and shuddering at the idea.

"Now remember your promise, Lady Betty," I said somewhat sternly, as if I was annoyed. "Come, no nonsense—lie down on Molly."

"Oh, my God!" she wailed. With an effort, she slowly went up to the bench on which poor Molly was lying, bound down and helpless, and shivering with dread. She stood still for a moment as if struggling with repugnance, then stooping down, she kissed her daughter passionately, whispering, "My darling, I can't help it!" Reluctantly she passed one leg over Molly's face and laid herself down on her daughter as ordered. Promptly Alice and I adjusted her so that her cunt came within reach of Molly's lips while her mouth commanded Molly's cunt. We strapped her arms by the wrists and her legs by the ankles to the crossbar of the bench, one on each side of Molly, pulling the straps as tightly as we could, thereby further securing Molly, who now lay between her mother's arms and legs and was pinned down by her not inconsiderable weight.

The pair afforded a remarkable spectacle to us and for some little time we stood in gloating admiration. Neither could move in the slightest degree without the other being instantly conscious of it, and realizing its significance.

Lady Betty now had her daughter's freshly violated cunt right under her eyes and only a few inches off. Right above Molly's eyes, and also only a few inches off, hung her mother's cunt. Neither could avoid seeing what was being done to each other's private parts! Were ever a mother and a daughter so cruelly placed?

After a few moments of gloating, I said quietly, "Molly, dear, I'm going to see how your cunt has been altered by your having been deflowered!" I knelt down between her widely parted legs while the girls crowded 'round to watch, Molly crying imploringly, "Don't touch me there, Jack, it's so sore!" at which the girls laughed delightedly.

Critically, I examined Molly's delicious organ of sex. "I think it is swollen a bit, and that the slit is longer. Don't you believe so, Lady Betty?" I remarked.

She only moaned inarticulately, evidently feeling her position acutely. With a gentle forefinger I proceeded to touch and press Molly's soft, springy flesh, each touch producing a cry of pain from her and involuntary writhing which even her mother's weight could not subdue. I gently drew apart the tender lips and inspected with curiosity the gash-like opening into which I had, with so much difficulty, effected an entrance, poor Molly crying, "Oh, don't, Jack!" Her cunt was clearly inflamed and she must have suffered a good deal of pain while being ravished, and, as I closed the lips again, I gently deposited a loving kiss on them as if seeking their pardon, Molly exclaiming, "Oh!" and quivering deliciously as my caress tingled through her. Then I slowly and gently introduced my forefinger into her cunt!

"Oh!" shrieked Molly, writhing with pain. "Don't Jack!" cried Lady Betty, her eyes full of agony at the horrible sight she was being forced to witness.

Remorselessly I pushed my finger into Molly's cunt till it was buried up to the knuckle, and retained it there, gently feeling her interior and reveling in the warm, soft flesh, still moist with my spendings, and noting delightedly how her gentle muscles were involuntarily gripping my finger as I tenderly touched her clitoris with my free hand and generally excited her. She was still deliciously tight, and the corrugations of her tender flesh clasped my finger in a way that augured exquisite pleasure to my prick when next it was put into her cunt.

After a little while I withdrew my finger, to Molly's great relief, then said to Lady Betty, "Now I'll exhibit your cunt to your daughter, your Ladyship!" She moaned inarticulately, knowing that it was no use asking for mercy.

So 'round I went to Molly's side, the delighted girls following me. When there, I leaned over Lady Betty's bottom from one side of her, and as I looked down into Molly's flushed and pitiful face, I said quietly to her, "Now, Molly, remember the pinchings and keep your eyes on your mother's cunt!" Gently, with both hands, I drew its lips well apart and exhibited the large pink gap through which she had entered the world, saying, "Look, Molly, this is the first thing you came through!"

She was inexpressibly shocked at the sight of her mother's gaping cunt and exclaimed tremulously, "Oh, Jack! How can you be so cruel!" at which the girls laughed amusedly.

To her horror I pushed my finger in and began to feel her mother just as I had done to her. "Don't, Jack!" cried poor Lady Betty, agitating herself spasmodically on Molly as my curious finger explored her sensitive interior, reveling in her luscious flesh which throbbed in the most excited fashion. But after Molly's exquisite interior, her mother's seemed almost coarse, and very soon I drew my finger out of her and said softly to Alice, "Get a couple of feathers, dear, and we'll tickle them both at the same time!"

"No, Jack, no!" shrieked Molly in horrible distress at the approaching dreadful torture.

"What is it, darling?" cried Lady Betty, who had not heard what I said.

"They're going to tickle us together at the same time!" she cried agitatedly.

Immediately a shriek of terror came from Lady Betty. "My God! No, Jack! For pity's sake, don't!" Frantically both mother and daughter tugged at their fastenings in desperate but unavailing endeavors to get free, thereby affording us a delicious sample of the struggles we were about to witness when the feathers were applied to their tender cunts. Alice came back with half-a-dozen long feathers. She picked out one for herself and Connie selected another and, without any prompting from me, Alice placed herself by Lady Betty's cunt while Connie knelt between Molly's legs, then simultaneously applied the feathers to their respective victims' defenseless slits!

Two fearful shrieks filled the room. "Don't, Mrs. Blunt!" cried Molly, wriggling in a perfectly wonderful way, seeing how tightly she had been tied down and that she also had her mother's weight to contend against while Lady Betty writhed and contorted, twisted and squirmed as if she was in a fit, plunging so wildly on Molly as to make the poor girl gasp for breath. She seemed to feel the torture much more keenly than Molly did, possibly because of Alice's skill as torturer and her quickness in realizing the points where the touch of the feather had the cruelest effect. At any event, Lady Betty shrieked, yelled, curveted and wriggled till I thought it wise to stop the torture for a little while, and signaled to both girls to desist, which they unwillingly did, then rose and rushed excitedly to me with eyes glistening with lust and cruelty.

"Oh, Jack! Wasn't it lovely!" cried Alice rapturously. "Fanny, you take a turn now at Lady Betty; I'd like to watch her!" she continued, handing the feather to Fanny, whose eyes gleamed delightedly at the opportunity of torturing Lady Betty. She and Connie impatiently took their places by their trembling victims and awaited my signal.

A refinement of cruelty suddenly struck me. "Look here, dear," I said to Alice, "suppose you sit astride on Lady Betty's backside and looking down on Molly—you'll feel Lady Betty's struggles, you'll see the feather play on her cunt, and you'll be able to watch Molly's face at the same time!"

"Jack! You're a genius!" she cried delightedly. "Help me up, darling!" In a moment she was arranged astride Lady Betty, whose plump, fleshy buttocks she grasped firmly so as not to be dislodged by her Ladyship's struggles and plunges, her weight forcing Lady Betty's cunt almost onto Molly's face, so that Fanny had to poise her hand delicately so as not to bring the feather into play.

"Go ahead, dears!" Fanny cried, and immediately both feathers were applied to their respective cunts. Again Lady Betty and Molly shrieked frantically as their cunts were slowly and cruelly tickled and irritated and goaded almost into spending, but not allowed to taste the blessed relief! Lady Betty was going nearly mad, and, in spite of Alice's weight, plunging so wildly that Alice had some difficulty in sticking on, while poor Molly, whose chest had now to bear the weight of her mother as well as Alice, had scarcely enough breath to keep her going and so had to endure the terrible torture absolutely passively. Soon both of our victims had again been pushed to the extreme point of endurance, Molly being nearly in hysterics, while Lady Betty was fast going into convulsions—whereupon I stopped Connie and lifted Alice off.

"Hadn't we better soothe the poor things by stroking their cunts?" asked Alice as she watched our panting, quivering, trembling victims.

"I'm going to force them to suck each other now, dear," I whispered with a smile.

"Jack, how lovely!" she exclaimed in rapture, eagerly eyeing Lady Betty and Molly, who by now were getting more normal, though the involuntary heaves and tremors that ran through them showed significantly the nature of the relief they were craving.

I leaned over Lady Betty and whispered, "You can tell by your own feelings and by the sight of Molly's cunt what she wants! Suck her!"

"Oh," she exclaimed, shocked beyond expression.

"Suck her, Lady Betty!" I repeated. "Then she'll understand and she'll suck you!"

"Oh, I couldn't!" she cried. "Suck my own daughter?"

"Yes, suck your own daughter, Lady Betty, and she'll suck her own mother! You've got to do it, so you'd better do it quietly at once without further nonsense. Now suck Molly!"

"No, no!" she cried. "I can't! I can't!"

I turned to Alice. "Get me that cutting riding whip dear," I said quietly.

Quickly she brought it. I swished it through the air close to Lady Betty, who trembled with fright.

"Now, Lady Betty, please understand me clearly. You've got to do whatever I tell you. If you refuse, you'll be whipped into submission! Now suck your daughter's cunt!"

"Oh! Jack! I can't!" she wailed.

Down came the whip across her splendid bottom. She shrieked wildly as she writhed with the pain. I dealt her another cut—more shrieks; then a third—yet no compliance, but I could see that her obstinacy was giving way. I did not want to hurt her unnecessarily, so I aimed the fourth cut crossways, making the lash curl around her buttock and flick her cunt. A fearful yell of pain broke from Lady Betty. "Stop, Jack!" she screeched, then hurriedly she commenced to lick Molly's cunt!

"That's right!" I said encouragingly. "Keep on till I tell you to stop, Lady Betty!" Delightedly we all watched the piquant spectacle of a daughter being licked by her mother! Their faces were a study—Lady Betty's showing her disgust and repugnance at thus having to apply her tongue to her daughter's cunt, while Molly's was full of shame at being thus forced to spend by her mother. Heroically, she tried to retain herself—to refrain from spending—but in vain. Soon her control of herself broke down, and in sheer despair, she exclaimed brokenly, "Oh! I can't. . . help it! Ah! Ah!" as she spent frantically!

The sight was more than the girls could stand. Alice and Connie flew into each other's arms, too excited to rush to the couch. They fell on the soft thick carpet and madly cunt-fucked each other till their feelings were relieved.

Fanny, hardly knowing what she was doing, threw her arms 'round me and clinging closely to me whispered excitedly, "Oh, Mr. Jack, please frig me!" which I delightedly did. I would have gladly fucked her, but I had determined to have Lady Betty as she lay on Molly, making Molly lick my balls during the process, so I could spare nothing at the moment for Fanny.

Presently Alice and Connie rose, looking somewhat sheep-faced, but their countenances cleared when they saw that Fanny had been also obliged to relieve her excited feelings by means of my finger, and they exchanged sympathetic and congratulatory smiles as we again clustered 'round Lady Betty and Molly, whom we had left tied down and who began to tremble with dread as they saw that they were to be submitted to further indignities and tortures.

"Now, Molly, it's your turn, dear—suck your mother's cunt!" I said to her as I flicked her tender cunt sharply with the lash of my riding whip so as to stop the useless protest and pleadings I knew she was sure to make at receiving such a demand.

"Don't, Jack!" she screamed with pain. With loathing horror in her face, she placed her mouth on her mother's cunt and commenced to tongue its lips.

"Oh! Molly, don't!" cried Lady Betty, involuntarily wriggling her bottom and hips voluptuously as her daughter's tongue began to arouse her sexual appetites in spite of herself. Molly was too terrified by my whip to disobey me and so continued to tease and torture her mother's cunt with her tongue for some little time till I stopped her. Straddling over her head with my balls just touching her face, I shoved my rampant prick into Lady Betty's now gaping cunt till I had buried it inside her up to its root. As I did so, my balls traveled over Molly's face till they rested on her mouth, my thighs holding her head so firmly gripped between them that she could not avoid the shocking contact with my genital organs.

"Now, Molly, you're to lick my balls while I fuck your mother!" I said with a smile at the delighted girls, who in turn peeped between my thighs to view the extraordinary conjunction of Lady Betty's cunt, my prick and balls, and Molly's mouth. Lady Betty all the while inarticulately moaned in her distress at being thus fucked by me so unexpectedly and in such a position! I heard stifled cries come from Molly. I could feel her warm breath on my balls but not the velvet of her tongue, so I again sharply flicked her cunt. A smothered shriek of agony—then something exquisitely warm, soft, and moist began to caress my scrotum. It was Molly's tongue—the poor girl was licking my balls!

Oh! My delicious sensations at that moment as my prick luxuriated in the cunt of the mother while the mouth of the daughter reluctantly, but deliciously, was exciting me into spending! For some moments, I remained motionless save for thrills of exquisite pleasure, until I could no longer control my imperious desires. With piston-like strokes I began to work myself backwards and forwards in Lady Betty's cunt, moving faster and faster and getting more and more furious, till I spent rapturously into her, just as her quivering, wriggling backside proclaimed that she too was discharging, her head unconsciously resting on her daughter's cunt as the spasm of her pleasure vibrated through her!

When I had become myself again, I drew out my prick, and after gloating cruelly over the sight of poor Molly's flushed, shame-stricken, quivering, face and tearful, but tearless eyes, I pointed to her mother's cunt now visibly wet and bedewed from my discharge and said, "Now go on, again, Molly!"

She closed her horrified eyes with an expression of sickening, loathing and repugnance and moaned, "Oh, my God! Jack, I can't! I simply can't!"

"You can, and you shall, Molly!" I replied sternly as I sent the lash of my whip sharply across her tender cunt, drawing from her a terrible shriek which brought Lady Betty out of her semi-stupor.

"Go on, Molly!" I said, pointing to her mother's cunt as her eyes sought mine as if imploring mercy. Again she dumbly refused; again I caught her a sharp cut full on her cunt.

She yelled in agony, then slowly and with horrible repugnance, nerved herself to touch her mother's greasy and sticky cunt with her lips, nearly choking as her tongue slowly transferred the remains of my spend from her mother's gaping slit into her own mouth and down her throat! As soon as I saw she was fairly started, I put her in charge of

Connie with instructions to keep her at it, whatever happened. placing myself between Molly's legs, my prick all wet and semen-soiled close to Lady Betty's face. I touched the latter with my whip and said, "Now suck me clean, Lady Betty!"

"Oh!" she cried in horror, shuddering violently as she let her head again fall on her daughter's cunt. Raising the whip, I slashed her fiercely right down her left buttock, then along the other, my lash cutting well into her soft, plump flesh and evidently giving her intense pain from the lovely way in which she writhed and screamed. "Suck me clean, Lady Betty!" I sternly repeated as I sent cut after cut on her wriggling plunging backside till she could no longer endure the pain, and half-hysterically raised her head and opened her mouth. Instantly I ceased the flagellation and popped my humid prick between her unwilling lips, which closed softly but reluctantly on it as a look of intense repulsion passed over her agonized face!

For some time, Lady Betty simply held my prick in her mouth passively and in shamefaced confusion, for she had never before sucked a man and really did not know what to do! But I didn't mind! Her mouth was deliciously warm and moist, while the touch of her lips was voluptuousness itself, and as I watched her, gloating over her misery and shame, I could see her throat convulsively working, as from time to time she forced herself to swallow the accumulated saliva, now highly impregnated with our mingled spendings.

With the stimulus afforded by Lady Betty's mouth, my virility began quickly to revive. "Pass your tongue over and 'round my prick, Lady Betty," I recommended. "Lick and suck simultaneously!" Painfully, she complied. The action of her tongue was something exquisite, so much so that in a very short time my prick began to swell and stiffen (to her silent horror) till her mouth could just hold it! I was ready for action again. Should I spend in Lady Betty's mouth or fuck Molly again? Hurriedly, I decided in favor of Molly! Quickly, I pulled my prick out of Lady Betty's mouth. "Untie her," I cried to the girls as I pushed up the second half-bench and fastened it to the piece on which Molly was lying, still tied. Soon the girls freed Lady Betty and lifted her off her daughter, then guessing what was coming, they held her between them in such a way that she was compelled to see what happened to her. As soon as Molly caught sight of me with my prick in rampant erection, she instinctively divined that she was again to be ravished, and screamed for mercy. But I threw myself on her, took her in my arms, brought my prick to bear on the orifice of her cunt, and fiercely rammed it into her, forcing my way ruthlessly into her, while she shrieked with a pain hardly less keen than had accompanied her violation. Mad with lust and the exquisite pleasure of holding the voluptuous girl again in my close embrace, and stimulated by the spectacle of the lovely naked bodies of Alice, Connie, and Fanny. The three girls controlled Lady Betty's frantic struggles to go to her daughter's assistance while they made free with her breasts and her cunt. Watching the spectacle, I let myself go and, ramming myself furiously into the still shrieking Molly, I fucked her exquisite self rapturously, till love's ecstasy overtook me when I spent deliriously into her, flooding her smarting interior with the soothing balm of my boiling love-juice, which she received into her with the most voluptuous thrills and quivers, the sudden transition from the pains of penetration to the raptures of spending sending her into a semiswoon as she lay locked in my arms!

Reluctantly I quitted her, unfastened her, and made her over to her mother, who quickly took her off to the girls' alcove, while said girls crowded 'round me with delicious kisses as they congratulated me on my prowess in having fucked mother and daughter twice, each in each other's presence, and to the accompaniment of such exquisite licentiousness. Solicitously and tenderly, they bathed and sponged my prick and generally refreshed me.

"Now, what next?" I asked.

"I'm afraid we must be going, Jack," said Connie, "as we have to dine out!"

"And I think you've had enough, Sir," said Alice archly.

"Miss Molly looked quite played out, Mr. Jack," said Fanny, who had gone to offer her services but evidently had been brusquely refused.

"Well, perhaps we had better let the poor things off now!" I said musingly, "I don't think they will offend any of us again!" They laughed. "Well, dears, thank you all very much for your help today. We've had a lovely orgy, punished our enemies, and had a fine time ourselves. Now run away and dress. Perhaps you won't mind Fanny attending to Betty and Molly as they resume their clothing, Alice?"

Just then Lady Betty and Molly came out. They were evidently utterly exhausted. I hastily poured out some champagne for them, which greatly revived them. As they tremblingly awaited the resumption of their tortures, I said gently, "Now you can go, Lady Betty, with your daughter. Fanny will help you to dress yourselves. Now, if ever you breathe a single word as to what has happened here this afternoon, or if in word, or deed, or suggestion, you say or do anything to harm or wound these girls or myself, I'll get you both brought here again and what you've undergone today will be mild compared to what you'll then taste. Now each of you kneel in turn before Alice first, then Connie, then Fanny, and then me—kiss each cunt three times, also my prick three times, in token of apology and in promise of good behavior—then dress yourselves."

We arranged ourselves in the order indicated, standing in a line with our arms 'round each other. Shamefacedly, Lady Betty and Molly performed their penance, my prick quivering as their lips touched it. We all resumed our clothing; I put Lady Betty and Molly into a taxi, only breaking the contained silence with the remark, "Now don't forget!" then returned to the girls whom I found chatting eagerly and delightedly, all now daintily dressed.

"I'd like to fuck you all just as you are, dears!" I said as I eyed them lasciviously in their provoking daintiness.

"Think what our clothes would look like!" laughed Connie.

"Jack, we owe you a lot!" said Alice, more seriously. "Now Connie and Fanny, let's say good-bye in a new way. One by one, Jack, we'll let you suck us just as we are, through our drawers; then we'll make you lie down, take your prick out through your trousers, and suck you good-bye! I claim last turn so as to receive all that you've left in you!"

Delightedly, Connie and Fanny complied. One by one, they seated themselves in an easy-chair, while the other two pulled up the clothes and I, kneeling between their legs, sucked a tender farewell to each cunt through the opening of their dainty frilly drawers; then I lay down on my back on the couch. With a trembling hand, Connie excitedly opened my fly and gently pulled out my prick, kissed and sucked it lovingly. Fanny followed suit, her tongue provoking it into life again. Then Alice took charge and sucked and tongued me till she forced my seminal reserves to yield all they held, receiving in her sweet mouth my love-juice as I spent in quivering rapture.

We all four entered the waiting taxi and the girls drove me to my Club, where they left me with tender and insistent injunctions to "Do yourself well, darling!"

A Note About the Book

Written by an anonymous author, *The Way of a Man with a Maid* (1908) is a popular erotic novel published in England. Adapted for film several times, this story of sadomasochism continues to attract controversy for its portrayal of taboos such as incest, rape, and predatory behavior.

A Note from the Publisher

Spanning many genres, from non-fiction essays to literature classics to children's books and lyric poetry, Mint Edition books showcase the master works of our time in a modern new package. The text is freshly typeset, is clean and easy to read, and features a new note about the author in each volume. Many books also include exclusive new introductory material. Every book boasts a striking new cover, which makes it as appropriate for collecting as it is for gift giving. Mint Edition books are only printed when a reader orders them, so natural resources are not wasted. We're proud that our books are never manufactured in excess and exist only in the exact quantity they need to be read and enjoyed. To learn more and view our library, go to minteditionbooks.com

bookfinity & MINT EDITIONS

Enjoy more of your favorite classics with Bookfinity,
a new search and discovery experience for readers.
With Bookfinity, you can discover more vintage
literature for your collection, find your Reader Type,
track books you've read or want to read,
and add reviews to your favorite books.
Visit www.bookfinity.com, and click on
Take the Quiz to get started.

Don't forget to follow us
@bookfinityofficial and @mint_editions

CPSIA information can be obtained
at www.ICGtesting.com
Printed in the USA
JSHW030229170822
29311JS00006B/3